911
THE SHOCK-
SUPERTH
OF NEW YORK'S #
BY THOMAS CHASTAIN
BESTSELLING AUTHOR OF
PANDORA'S BOX

"A New York City maniac who explodes napalm-like bombs over Macy's Thanksgiving parade, ties bombs to the Rockefeller Center's Christmas tree, tears policemen in half and plants bombs all over the place while being tracked down by the wily police inspector, Max Kauffman, who is trying to stop this madman before it's too late . . . too late comes the minute this book is opened."

—*Chicago Sun-Times*

"This tight, expertly plotted and thoroughly well-researched novel . . . takes on a terrifying immediacy and realism."

—*Publishers Weekly*

"TENSION MOUNTS QUICKLY."
—*Ellery Queen's Mystery Magazine*

"Doing for the NYPD what Joseph Wambaugh has done for Los Angeles cops in *The New Centurions* . . . Gripping plot and action."

—*Charlotte, N.C. Observer*

HOW DO YOU FIND
A MAD BOMBER
AMONG EIGHT MILLION
VICTIMS OF TERROR?

911

THIS NUMBER COULD
SAVE YOUR LIFE

In New York City, 911 gets you police or
an ambulance in an emergency.

It connects you directly with the police department's new emergency center. New
York is the first major city to get this uni-
versal emergency number. Your city gov-
ernment, working with New York Telephone, set it up. Remember . . . 911.

—from a notice sent by the New York Telephone Company to its Manhattan subscrib-
ers, July 1, 1968.

911

Thomas Chastain

BANTAM BOOKS · LONDON · TORONTO · NEW YORK

*This low-priced Bantam Book
has been completely reset in a type face
designed for easy reading, and was printed
from new plates. It contains the complete
text of the original hard-cover edition.*
NOT ONE WORD HAS BEEN OMITTED.

911
*A Bantam Book | published by arrangement with
Mason/Charter Publishers, Inc.*

PRINTING HISTORY
*Mason/Charter edition published March 1976
2nd printing .... May 1976
Mystery Guild edition published March 1976
Bantam edition | September 1977
2nd printing*

ISBN 0–553–02889–8

Published simultaneously in the United States and Canada

PRINTED IN THE UNITED STATES OF AMERICA

To
Katherine, my sister
and
Ross, my brother-in-law
with an overdue acknowledgment
of love and affection

CHAPTER ONE

The room was in a rundown building on West Forty-third Street near Ninth Avenue, in New York City. It was the kind of building that had no name, only a sign out front which read: HOTEL.

The room was small, gloomy, and chill. It contained a bed, a dresser, and a wooden table and chair. Threadbare carpeting covered part of the floor and the wallpaper, a floral design of leaves and roses, was stained and aged so that both the green of the leaves and the red of the roses had faded yellow. The only natural light came from a single window looking out on an airshaft and the blind side of the building next door. Rain beat against the window pane and the loose frame rattled in the November wind, creating a draft in the room. Despite the draft, the room had a stuffy, capryllic smell, as if its countless occupants over the years had exhausted most of the oxygen in the air.

The man sat at the table, his coat draped over the back of the chair. His face was in shadow since the gooseneck lamp cast its concentrated cone of light on the table top and the various articles arrayed there: a mound of black gunpowder—the man's own mixture, a concoction of charcoal, sulfur, and potassium perchlorate—a hair tonic bottle containing a pint of raw gasoline, a small alarm clock, a roll of black electrician's tape, a length of copper wire, a 1.5-volt transistor radio battery, and an empty talcum powder can.

Hunched over the table, the man removed the top of the talcum powder can and, using a blank sheet of paper which he took from his coat pocket, scooped up the mound of gunpowder and let it trickle into the can. When the can was full, he replaced its top, wiped the surface of the table clean of the few remaining traces of black powder, and sat back in the chair, lighting a cigarette.

He hadn't known Adrienne was in the room behind him and he was momentarily startled when she called to him asking him not to be much longer, and to hurry *please*.

"I'm almost finished," he said. He turned in the chair and looked at her. Enough of the light from the lamp spilled over into the room so he could see her lying on the bed against the fluffed-up pillows, nude except for the thin gold chain and locket around her neck. She lay with her head back, her tawny blond hair framing her face, her lips moist. The length of her body was bronzed golden by the sun except for the two thin, bikini-shaped strips of white skin across her full breasts and the downy v between her legs. He felt a catch in his throat as she shifted her body slightly, opening her legs provocatively, one leg stretched out in front of her, the other, bent at the knee, upraised.

"I'll be right there," he said, his voice husky. "Just in a minute."

He turned back in the chair, his attention centered once more on the articles on the table. He began to imagine how it would be, when the time came, to assemble the various pieces, taping together the can of gunpowder, the gasoline-filled bottle, the clock, and the battery, then wiring the battery to the gunpowder through the clock, which would serve as the triggering mechanism. The result would be a compact incendiary device with low explosive power—the ignition of the gunpowder would blow apart the bottle of gasoline and set it afire—but sufficiently lethal to do the job for which it was designed.

He ran his hands almost lovingly over the various components of the unassembled bomb. The excitement he felt when he thought of the moment-to-come of the explosion, days from now, worked like a

2

massive stimulant on his nervous system. His heart began to palpitate rapidly, his eyes glazed over, he began to perspire, his throat was dry; inexorably the sensation built to a near-erotic intensity.

"Adrienne!" he called hoarsely, now wanting her, stumbling up from the chair. He took a couple of steps toward the bed and stopped. She was nowhere in sight. He looked around the room, looked in the bathroom and closet. He was momentarily bewildered. Then he shook his head and crossed to the bed. She was gone but the gold chain and locket were lying on the pillow. He picked them up and turned the locket over in his fingers. It was small, heart-shaped. Carved into half of the outside shell was her initial and into the other, his. He snapped the locket open with the tip of a fingernail. Inside were tiny portraits of her and him. He closed the locket after a moment and stuffed locket and chain into his pants pocket.

He went back to the chair, removed a small notebook from the pocket of his coat, and put the coat on. He needed a woman. One page of the notebook was filled with names, Honey, Dixie, Bambi, Felice, Chrissy, Carla, and a list of phone numbers. He'd have to call and find out which one was free. He'd use the phone in the hotel lobby.

Before he left, he took the precaution of removing the gasoline-filled hair tonic bottle and talcum can of gunpowder to a shelf in the bathroom. Then he replaced the battery in a small transistor radio sitting on the table and put the roll of tape and the length of copper wire in a drawer. He was reasonably sure no one would come into the room during his absence. The room was visited only once a week by a hotel cleaning woman and she'd been there the day before. But now even if anyone did come snooping around, it wouldn't be likely they'd examine all the various disconnected items and be able to figure out that these would, one day soon, become a bomb.

He took a black raincoat from the closet, switched off the lamp, and hurried out of the room, locking the door behind him.

3

Thanksgiving Day dawned clear and bitterly cold in Manhattan that year. The sky was cloudless and had a hard, shiny look to it the color of blue reflected in a stainless steel surface. There was a bright sun but the wind from the north had needles of ice in it and there was no warmth in the sun's light when it filtered to the asphalt pavements between the towering canyons of the city's skyscrapers.

Deputy Chief Inspector Max Kauffman, N.Y.P.D., had no real reason that day to report to the station house—the 16th Precinct, Patrol Borough Manhattan Central—which he commanded. He had previously made arrangements for one of his subordinates, Detective Captain George Heaton, to assume command for the holiday. But Max Kauffman's wife, Belle, was having a late-afternoon Thanksgiving dinner for his parents and his two sisters and brothers-in-law, and the stir and fuss of the preparations began to get on the Inspector's nerves soon after he had risen at 9 A.M.

The Kauffman apartment, on Sutton Place South overlooking the East River, had fourteen rooms and his wife had the help of two servants, a Swedish couple who had worked for them for almost eleven years but, even so, Max Kauffman couldn't escape the sounds of the activity and the cooking smells in the apartment. In midmorning he phoned the Precinct and asked that a car be sent to pick him up.

Belle Kauffman appeared surprised when a short time later he emerged from his bedroom wearing his overcoat and carrying his hat and gloves.

"I thought you had the day off," she said. "You aren't going out in this cold, are you?"

He nodded. "I'm just going to take a quick look in at the Precinct."

She was busy removing plastic slipcovers from the furniture in the living room. She was dressed in a beige turtleneck sweater and a brown checkered pantsuit.

He glanced at her as she bent over one of the chairs, thinking as he always did that pantsuits made her rump appear elephantine. They had had words

4

on the subject of pantsuits before. Now he fought down the impulse to make a derogatory comment when he remembered that the last time they'd argued about her wearing pantsuits their words had grown bitter. She had surprised him then by charging that the reason he didn't like them was because they posed a threat to his masculinity. He had quickly replied that, to the contrary, he considered them a threat to her femininity. And then, as he was to reflect later, he had gone too far, fuming that he suspected the whole concept of pantsuits was a devious plot on the part of the fags in the fashion industry to eliminate sexual competition by turning women into half-assed male impersonators. She had turned her head away and made no reply. He had instantly regretted his words on that occasion.

For years now he and she had maintained a precariously balanced asexual marriage—they had not been intimate since after the birth of their daughter, Deborah, now thirteen years old—and Max Kauffman was aware that in the remarks of each of them that day was a veiled sexual accusation aimed at the other. He knew how fatal this could be to their platonic relationship, a relationship which rested primarily on mutual respect; indeed, he was certain there were many marriages which survived without sex, that there could even be love, but that it was not possible for a relationship to exist between a man and a woman without respect, each for the other.

Besides, he felt his words, spoken in haste, had hurt her unnecessarily even if they were, as he believed, true. In addition, he had no desire to belittle her appearance. The fact was he could not help but be appreciative of the excellent care she had taken of her looks and her body over the years: there was still a womanly prettiness in her face and her figure remained good. He had suspected more than once that if he possessed the power to see her through a stranger's eyes he would be as strongly attracted to her as he had been when they first met. And he did, after all, truly care for her despite the long lack of any passion in their marriage.

5

So on this Thanksgiving Day he said nothing about the way she was dressed.

"You'll try to be back early?" she asked. "I'm planning dinner at five and they'll all be here around four so I'd like you to help with the drinks."

"Oh, yes, I'll be here in plenty of time," he said and then was grateful when he heard the sound of the house phone in the foyer and the doorman told him his car was waiting. He gave his wife a quick kiss on the cheek and escaped.

Once out in front of his apartment building, Max Kauffman turned up the collar of his overcoat against the cutting edge of the frigid wind gusting in off the East River a few yards away. The deep, penetrating cold had suffused the day with a kind of crystalline brilliance in which nearby objects on Sutton Place, a leafless tree, the corner of a building, a parked car, stood out like dark etchings traced on a giant sheet of glass. There was a faint sulphurous smell in the air and the surface of the concrete sidewalk had the feel of hard-packed, frozen snow underfoot.

Max Kauffman recognized the driver of the official limousine waiting at the curb as one of the new men at the 16th Precinct, but couldn't think of his name. The Inspector's regular driver, Detective Henry Lukin, had the holiday off. The new man was dressed in a brown tweed suit, matching topcoat, and was bare-headed. He had thick brown hair, hazel eyes, and a face on which all the features stuck out prominently: a large nose, big ears, and a wide mouth with a jutting chin. Big as the man was, well over six feet tall and over two hundred fifty pounds in weight, the Inspector made a mental note never to use him in decoy work unless the assignment called for a bouncer or strong-arm type.

Max Kauffman didn't like the idea of treating police officers as flunkies and he tried to get to the rear door of the car before the new man saw him but he wasn't quick enough.

Oh Jesus! Max Kauffman almost groaned aloud when the driver not only sprang out to the sidewalk and opened the rear door with a flourish but also

6

snapped him a salute, saying, "Detective Frank Kinnard, sir." Max Kauffman returned the salute stiffly and as soon as he was in the car, lit one of his cigars.

Detective Kinnard slid into the front seat behind the steering wheel and took an appraising look at his Precinct commander in the rearview mirror. He saw that behind the wreath of cigar smoke Max Kauffman was a stocky, broad-shouldered man, just under six feet in height, with black wavy hair graying at the temples and a face that looked like it had been sculptured out of some dark-toned substance while its subject had posed with expression impassive so no emotion showed.

The Inspector had removed his gray Homburg and he smoothed his hair with a hand before replacing the hat on his head. He wore a dark Chesterfield overcoat and his suit was a charcoal gray with a pinstripe; both pieces of clothing obviously of expensive cut, and tailor-made, Detective Kinnard decided.

Max Kauffman puffed on his cigar and waved a hand impatiently in the air. "Let's go, let's get going," he urged.

"Yes, sir," the detective said and as soon as they were underway, added, "Sir, I thought I'd take us across Forty-seventh Street, if it's all right with you? I mean I could go farther uptown or down to get across. But what I thought was the men from the Precinct are on traffic control in the area of Forty-seventh and Broadway so we shouldn't have any trouble."

Max Kauffman could see that the driver was watching him in the rearview mirror and waiting for an answer. He didn't know what the hell the man was talking about.

After a pause, Kinnard said, "You know, sir, on account of the Macy's Thanksgiving Day parade."

"Oh," Max Kauffman said, "yeah, sure." He understood now; the 16th Precinct was located on the opposite side of town, in the West Forties, and the Macy's parade would have all crosstown traffic tied up from Seventy-seventh Street along Central Park West, then down Broadway to Herald Square and on to below Thirty-third Street. He had forgotten all about the annual parade.

The limousine police-band radio was on, tuned to the 16th Precinct frequency. The calls were constant back and forth between the dispatcher and the squad cars patrolling the streets; a virtually unbroken series of 10–1s, 10–4s, 10–3s, 10–2s, which corresponded to: call the station house, acknowledge, call the dispatcher by direct line, and report to the station house.

Max Kauffman heard the radio exchanges without really listening to them. The calls were all reassuringly routine. The city was quiet, few people were out, and the blustery wind gave the deserted streets a fresh-swept look. Traffic around them was light until they were on Forty-seventh Street approaching Broadway. In the distance Max Kauffman could hear the brassy sound of band music.

While they were still half a block away from the intersection, Kinnard had to use the siren to clear the way. Then when they had finally reached Broadway, the patrolman on duty on the corner was forced to wave them to a stop even though he recognized the Inspector's car. With a helpless shake of his head the patrolman indicated the section of parade passing: endless rows of a marching band with short-skirted majorettes leading it.

"Sorry, sir," Kinnard said, turning in the front seat; "I guess we're stuck till they pass."

Max Kauffman grunted and then said, "Pull over to the curb. I might as well see what kind of job the men are doing with the crowds."

The Inspector got out of the car and maneuvered his way through the throng of spectators on the sidewalk until he had a clear view of Broadway and the parade.

The crowd lined the sidewalks on both sides of the street from the fronts of the buildings out to the edges of the curbs, where the police had set up wooden barricades as far as the eye could see up and down Broadway.

Despite the freezing cold there were as many

8

small children and infants in the crowd as there were adults. Most of the smaller children were being held aloft by their parents so they could see the parade as it passed.

The buildings along both sides of the street were of varying heights so the pavement was latticed with alternating stripes of sunlight and shadow. Periodic gusts of wind buffeted the crowd. Some of the people stamped their feet to keep warm. Others held their gloved hands up covering their ears. Max Kauffman turned up his coat collar again.

Out in the street beyond the barricades was a line of foot patrolmen and a small contingent of mounted police. In the frigid air vapors of steam issued from the flared nostrils of the sleek, well-groomed horses and their ironshod hooves struck fiery sparks from the pavement as the uniformed riders wheeled them around on the street. In addition, several squad cars cruised slowly up and down Broadway on either side of the parade. The Inspector noted with satisfaction that the police, on foot, horseback, and in the squad cars, displayed an easy good humor as they went about the job of keeping the crowd from spilling out into the street and in maintaining order.

He couldn't help but reflect briefly that the spot where he now stood in the Times Square area, along with the crowd of mothers, fathers, and children, was within a stone's throw of the city's raunchiest pornographic district. On the side streets all around them were the hotels which served as hangouts for Manhattan's thriving pimps, madams, and prostitutes, along with a varied assortment of pornographic movie houses, bookshops, peepshows, massage parlors, and bars and theatres featuring "live all-nude entertainment." From where he stood he could see the lurid marquee of at least one of the pornographic movie houses and the window fronts of a couple of dirty-book stores right on Broadway, juxtaposed with legitimate Broadway theatres and movies and shops lining the thoroughfare. The Hebrew word *l'havdil* came to mind; meaning to differentiate; to point out a contrast, as when, he thought, for this moment, a part of the tawdry underside of the city was obscured by the innocent, eye-catching spectacle of the parade.

Now out in the center of Broadway, the passing marching band, spread out almost from curb to curb, was playing "When The Saints Come Marching In." The group of majorettes, mixed in with the marching band, performed endless cartwheels on the street. Upended, their young flesh, bare from boot tops to skimpy panties, was enough to create goose pimples in the warmly clad but still shivering onlookers.

As the band passed by, Max Kauffman started to turn away to return to the car when he heard loud whistles and cheers from the crowd. He looked back and saw that next in line in the parade was an enormous helium-filled balloon in the shape of what looked like a giant teddy bear. The balloon, which floated high over the street, was five or six stories tall so it dwarfed the people below, and was controlled by guy ropes which were manned by fifty men who marched in the street beneath it.

The appearance of the balloon figure suddenly reminded the Inspector of a time, years past, when his two children, Lawrence and Deborah, were young. The family had lived on Central Park West then, the parade passed right in front of their building, and every year he and the children would put on warm clothing, go outside and stand in the cold and watch the parade. He even remembered that the children's two favorite balloon characters in those days were Snoopy and Mighty Mouse.

Now, watching the gigantic balloon teddy bear as it approached the street corner, Max Kauffman could tell from the excited reactions of the crowd around him that the bear was a current favorite. There was loud applause, more whistles, and happy shouts from the spectators as the balloon moved closer to the intersection.

The Inspector had forgotten how huge the parade balloons were until this one was almost directly over them, tossing at the ends of its ropes, literally blocking out the sky above. The Inspector, along with the rest of the crowd nearby, was leaning backward, looking straight up at the balloon drifting high overhead when the explosion came. At first there was just a burst of orange-colored flame from somewhere high in the guy ropes where they connected with the bottom of the balloon. There was a delay of a second or two before the sound accompanying the explosion, a sudden, sharp blast surprising as a clap of thunder on this cloudless day, carried to the street below. Max Kauffman, staring up, was momentarily transfixed, his brain instinctively registering: *a bomb!* as in the next moment the burst of orange flame expanded outward and upward, engulfing the balloon.

CHAPTER TWO

For seconds Max Kauffman stood frozen in place on the street as the sound of the explosion's blast went reverberating down the length of Broadway. In its wake an eerie silence settled over the block. A few faint notes of music from the marching band which had passed on down the street drifted back, sounding tinny and discordant in the midst of the absolute silence of the area where he stood.

For yet another brief instant, the giant teddy bear overhead, no longer a balloon, remained recognizable; a shape created by the flames consuming it. Then the mass fell apart, a rain of liquid fire showering down on the street and the people below, along with pieces of mortar and chunks of concrete knocked loose from the cornice of the nearest building by the force of the explosion. The happy exuberance of the spectators just moments before turned now into terrified screams and wailing moans as, panicked with fear, men and women, dragging or carrying the children, fled blindly back toward the fronts of the buildings to escape the flames and debris falling into the street.

Max Kauffman himself moved swiftly, bulling his way out into the street before he could get trapped and swept along in the mass of milling bodies. Out of habit he removed his shield from his wallet and pinned it to the front of his overcoat. Thus identified he was able to make his way out beyond the wooden barricades and the line of police. Bits of mortar and concrete pelted down on him, harmlessly, and he had to brush away some smoldering sparks which landed on his hat and overcoat. He quickly calculated that the real danger was not from the flames and falling debris but from the possibility of a full-scale riot brought on by the panic of the crowd.

At the same time so much was happening all at once on the street that Max Kauffman felt, briefly, totally disoriented, the scene around him fragmenting into little more than disjointed, blurred impressions.

Clusters of flame were spiraling down out of the sky out in the middle of the street. The fifty men who had been handling the guy ropes to the balloon pushed and shoved one another as they scrambled to escape the falling flames. One man's hair caught fire and he ran around and around in a circle, which only fanned the flames. Another was beating frantically with his bare hands at his burning jacket and pants. Several fell and were trampled in the rush.

On the sidewalk the still-terrified spectators were pressing as close as they could get to the fronts of the buildings. At least four of the crowd, two women, an elderly man, and a small girl, had been injured; they were lying on the sidewalk near the curb.

The horses of the mounted patrol in the center of the street shied violently away from the falling flames. The riders struggled to retain control, whip-sawing the reins, trying to ride out into the clear.

One beautiful chestnut horse was struck on the neck and rump by a shower of white-hot sparks. Max Kauffman saw the horse rear up, whimpering with fright, forelegs pawing the air. The rider was jolted backward in the saddle and lost the reins. The horse, head tossing frantically from side to side, came down on its forelegs and bucked, body arcing high in the air. The mounted patrolman was thrown. His blue helmet, jarred loose by the force of the fall, went spinning down the street while he landed hard on his back, his unprotected head striking the pavement. The man lay unmoving.

The riderless horse bolted, galloping straight toward the crowd on the sidewalk.

Max Kauffman ran forward, arms flailing the air,

and shouted to the police nearest the crowd: "Stop that horse! Head him off! Turn him!"

A couple of policemen raced forward, stationing themselves between the oncoming horse and the spectators, and waving their arms and shouting. When the horse continued to bear down on them, one of the policemen drew his revolver and fired a shot in the air.

The horse veered away. Max Kauffman could see that the animal, crazed with fear, was galloping blindly straight toward a spiked iron rail fence surrounding a concrete island in the center of Broadway. At the last moment, too late, the horse tried to hurdle the fence and, instead, impaled itself on one of the upthrust spikes. There was a horrified gasp from the spectators as the horse hung there briefly, then fell back into the street. Blood ran from a gaping hole in its belly. The animal tried to get to its feet and failed and collapsed in the street, able only to lift its head again and again and whinny.

Everything on the street had happened within a matter of seconds. Half a block up Broadway the rest of the Thanksgiving Day parade had come to an uncertain halt. There was still an eerie, unnatural silence where Max Kauffman stood though he could still hear the sound of festive band music coming from farther up Broadway and below Forty-sixth Street.

The police stationed along the parade route between Forty-seventh and Forty-eighth Streets were as stunned as the spectators. Max Kauffman strode quickly to one of the patrolmen and borrowed his walkie-talkie which the man carried as did all the officers on the scene.

"This is Inspector Kauffman!" he said in a clipped voice into the transmitter. "Let's move, you men! I want order maintained among those people on the sidewalk. Tell them there's no danger. Some of you see to the injured. You men up at Forty-eighth Street —attention: The parade is to be delayed until I give further orders. The rest of you are to secure the street

15

in and around the site of the explosion. Nothing's to be moved or touched on the street until we have a chance to examine the area. All right, let's move!"

They went into action. Some of the police crossed to calm the crowd of onlookers, others hurried to the assistance of the injured lying on the sidewalk and the street. More police fanned out, closing off Broadway at Forty-eighth Street ahead of the next section of parade, while another group of patrolmen quickly began setting up wooden sawhorses around the spot where the balloon had exploded. A nearby squad car supplied the patrolmen with square cardboard signs which they attached to the barriers. The signs read:

CRIME
SCENE
SEARCH AREA
STOP
NO ADMITTANCE BEYOND THIS POINT
UNTIL SEARCH IS COMPLETED
By order of Police Commissioner
POLICE DEPARTMENT

Max Kauffman, satisfied that the area was effectively sealed off, went to check on the mounted patrolman who was still lying in the street after being thrown from his horse. The Inspector recognized the injured man as Officer Ralph Yost.

Yost lay on his back with his eyes closed. A puddle of dark blood seeped out onto the pavement beneath his head. His breathing was shallow. A couple of patrolmen hurried over to where the injured man lay.

"Better not touch him," Max Kauffman said. "We'll get some ambulances here as quickly as possible."

The Inspector removed his own overcoat, unpinned his shield, and spread the coat over the unconscious figure. When he straightened up, he felt a

16

tap on his shoulder and he turned. His driver, Detective Kinnard, was standing there.

"Sir, are you all right?" Kinnard asked anxiously.

Max Kauffman nodded. "I'm okay. What I want you to do is get back to the car. Radio the station house. Tell them we need at least six ambulances. Also, every available man in the Precinct is to report over here on the double. Tell them I want the Bomb Investigative Unit—and fast—and they're to bring the Big Bertha bomb wagon."

"Yes sir," Kinnard said, and then he asked doubtfully, "you think it was a bomb, sir?"

The Inspector's face was grim. "I know it was a bomb."

As Detective Kinnard turned to go, Max Kauffman saw out of the corner of his eye one of the mounted patrolmen examining the horse that had thrown its rider. The patrolman had gotten down off his own horse and was kneeling beside the disabled horse in the street.

"Kinnard," Max Kauffman called, "you'd better tell the Precinct to contact the Sanitation Department. Advise them we need some equipment to haul away a horse. Let them know the horse is in bad shape, maybe dying."

Kinnard started away and then came back. He quickly took off his tweed topcoat and draped it around the Inspector's shoulders. "I'll be warm enough in the car," Kinnard said and left hurriedly.

Max Kauffman was grateful for the coat even though it flapped around him long and loose and he knew it looked ludicrous on him. The cold was deepening and there was a new, abrasive chill in the air. He pinned his badge to the front of the coat.

The Inspector heard his name being called and saw one of the policemen approaching with a civilian, a man wearing a bulky storm coat with a fur collar and a Persian lamb cossack hat. The man's eyes were watery and his nose was red and he kept blowing his nose into a damp handkerchief.

"Sir," the policeman said, "this fellow says he's

17

one of the parade supervisors and he wants to talk to whoever's in charge."

Max Kauffman nodded to the man. "I'm Inspector Kauffman. What's your problem?"

The man in the cossack hat blew his nose and said: "Ernest Guthridge is my name. I'm chief accountant at Macy's. Today it's my responsibility to keep the parade moving. Mind telling me what's going on here? All I've been able to pick up is some crazy rumor about one of the balloons exploding."

Max Kauffman already knew that most of the people involved in the Thanksgiving Day parade were year-round Macy's employees. However, instead of answering Guthridge directly, the Inspector asked: "Why would it seem crazy to you that one of the balloons might explode?"

Guthridge looked around at the chaos and the casualties in the street, then shook his head. "There's no way it could have happened. Not like this. No, sir."

"Why's that?" Max Kauffman asked.

Guthridge, still shaking his head, said: "Because of the way the balloons are constructed. You have to understand: inside each balloon are several individual compartments and it's these compartments which are filled with helium. The compartments are carefully balanced so if, by chance, one should be punctured the helium in the other compartments would still keep the balloon afloat." He paused, then added: "Now, you mind telling me what's going on here? And when we can get the parade moving again?"

Max Kauffman had taken a cigar from his pocket. He delayed speaking until he had lit it.

"Yeah," he said finally, "I'll answer your questions. In a minute. But first, tell me a little bit about what happens before the parade starts. I mean, where are the balloons kept? Where are they inflated? Who's around at the time? That sort of thing."

Ernest Guthridge blew his nose, sniffled noisily, and explained slowly. "The balloons are manufactured by the Goodyear Company out in Akron, Ohio. Then they're shipped to a warehouse over in Jersey.

18

Last night they were trucked into the city to the place where the parade starts. That's Seventy-seventh Street and Central Park West."

"Had the balloons already been inflated?" Max Kauffman interrupted to ask.

"Oh, no," Guthridge said quickly. "That was done last night, starting about eleven, up at Seventy-seventh Street and Central Park West by men sent in by Goodyear. There's a regular procedure they follow: spreading canvas over the street to provide a protective surface, then spreading netting over each balloon, to which the guy ropes are attached. When all that's done, they inflate the balloon. The larger ones —like this one they say exploded, the Huggy Bear character—often take more than three hours to inflate."

"What did you call this balloon?" Max Kauffman asked, curious.

"Huggy Bear," Ernest Guthridge smiled. "You must not have any young children around, Inspector. Huggy Bear's a very famous character with the little folks; a children's book, a comic strip, a TV cartoon."

Max Kauffman nodded. He thought for a moment, then said, "Tell me this: when these balloons were being inflated last night, were there many people around? What's it like up there?"

Guthridge made a vague gesture in the air with his hand. "Oh, you know, this is a city of gawkers. Every year on the night before the parade we draw our share of the curious up at Seventy-seventh Street and Central Park West. They come and stand around for a while watching the preparations and then leave and others come and take their places. It goes on all night long; there's always an audience in this town for a free show."

"So almost anyone around there last night could have gotten close to the balloons if he wanted?" Max Kauffman asked.

Guthridge nodded. "Yes, sure, I suppose so."

Max Kauffman took the parade supervisor by the arm and began to walk him up the block. "Look, you've been a big help. About all I can tell you now

19

is that this explosion appears suspicious. I want some of our specialists to take a look at things. Also, we have to clear out the injured. After that we'll try to get the parade moving again. We'd appreciate it if you'd all be patient until then."

The Inspector made a signal to the waiting policeman to escort the man away.

The first of the police reinforcements from the 16th Precinct had begun to arrive on the scene along with a police emergency van and in the distance Max Kauffman could hear the wail of approaching ambulance sirens. Down the street a couple of blocks, the huge beetle-shaped bomb wagon, known as Big Bertha, had just turned the corner and was now trundling up Broadway. The officer from the mounted patrol was still kneeling beside the horse bleeding in the street. Max Kauffman went over to the officer and leaned down.

"How bad is the horse's injury?"

"He's dying. And suffering." The mounted patrolman shook his head. "He ought to be put out of his misery."

"Do it," Max Kauffman ordered.

The Inspector rounded up some of the police reinforcements who had just arrived and instructed them to form a circle around the animal to shield what was about to happen from the eyes of the spectators. Max Kauffman, the mounted patrolman, and the horse were in the center of the circle. The horse was whinnying piteously. Max Kauffman nodded. The patrolman drew his .38 revolver, leaned in close, one foot on the horse's neck, and fired a shot into the animal's skull just behind the right ear. Two other policemen stepped in immediately and covered the carcass with a sheet of tarpaulin they'd gotten from the police emergency van. The circle broke up.

By then the bomb wagon, followed by a couple of squad cars, had pulled up and parked in the street a few yards away from Max Kauffman. The custom-built bomb wagon was an ugly, unwieldy vehicle with an enclosed cab compartment in front and in the rear an armored cage reinforced by sixteen layers of steel mesh designed to contain the blast of the most powerful explosives.

The first man to step out of the bomb wagon was Lieutenant John Tynan, who headed up the 16th Precinct's Bomb Investigative Unit. Tynan was five feet, eleven inches tall and looked slim because his average weight of 170 pounds was firm and well distributed over his frame. He had sandy hair and gray eyes. There was a sturdy formation to his face that came from strong cheekbones and a square chin over which the skin was stretched smooth, making him appear younger than his actual forty-two years. He was wearing a knitted stocking cap, black turtleneck sweater, dark slacks, and a flak vest to which his badge was pinned. The other men in the Bomb Investigative Unit—eight of them—were similarly dressed.

Max Kauffman had personally chosen John Tynan to command the 16th Precinct Bomb Investigative Unit a year earlier. The Inspector considered Tynan to be a true professional, the kind of man who was so confident of himself and so knowledgeable about his work that he could be casual, almost offhand, about any situation and yet you knew that he would do the job better than almost anyone else. In addition, Max Kauffman had the feeling that Tynan genuinely liked him whereas most of the other men under the Inspector's command were so intimidated by his official persona that there was seldom any real warmth in the relationships.

There was also the fact that the Inspector believed he recognized in Tynan a quality they both shared: an acceptance of separateness, that ability to distance oneself from others without arousing resentment, which was a prerequisite of command. Although he had never mentioned it to anyone, Max Kauffman fully expected that John Tynan would be the man chosen to head up the 16th Precinct when he, the Inspector, retired.

Now approaching Max Kauffman, Tynan asked, "What kind of a fuck-up have we got here, Inspector?"

"It looked like some kind of a bomb to me," Max

21

Kauffman said and began describing what he'd observed as he walked Tynan over to the spot where the balloon had exploded.

Tynan nodded. "Yeah, sounds like you had a live one, all right. We'll sweep up the crap, sift it down, and see what we come out with."

"There's another thing, Jack," Max Kauffman added. "Just as soon as we get the injured loaded up and out of here, I want us to make a check of all the other balloon floats up the street before the parade continues."

"It can't hurt," Tynan agreed and moved off with the men in his unit to gather up the debris in the street so it could be analyzed.

Meanwhile, ambulances from the nearest hospitals—the New York Infirmary, Beth Israel, French, Bellevue, St. Vincent's, and University—had pulled into the block. Police were helping the ambulance attendants load the injured into the vehicles. Two attendants from French Hospital were examining Patrolman Yost, who was still unconscious. Max Kauffman went over, identified himself and inquired about Yost's condition. One of the attendants told him the injuries appeared to be serious. They wrapped Yost in blankets, lifted him onto a stretcher, and placed him in the ambulance. Max Kauffman took back his own coat, which was now spotted with blood, and slung it over his shoulder. He then picked out another mounted patrolman, Sergeant Steve Wendler, and sent him along on the ride to the hospital, saying, "Check in with me at the Precinct as soon as you know something about his condition."

The Inspector ordered one of the radio car patrolmen to call the Precinct and tell the desk sergeant to notify Patrolman Ralph Yost's family of the officer's injuries and, if needed, to provide a squad car for any of the immediate family who wanted to go to French Hospital.

NBC Television had been covering the Thanksgiving Day parade, as the network did each year, with live cameras set up in front of Macy's. Now the Inspector saw that several of the cameras, along with

22

their crews, had moved into the block and were televising the happenings on the street. One of the television men, who had discovered that Max Kauffman was the ranking police officer present, tried to get the Inspector to make a statement about what was going on. Max Kauffman brushed the man off, trying to cover his impatience by apologizing that the investigation was still continuing and promising that there would be a full report from the Police Commissioner's office later.

To prevent any further conversation, Max Kauffman excused himself and hurried away when he spotted a huge Sanitation Department Auxiliary Field Force emergency truck pull into the block and back up near the dead horse. At the same time there was a shriek of sirens all along Broadway as, one by one, the ambulances carrying the casualties sped away.

Hands clasped behind his back, the Inspector stood near the A.F.F. truck and watched while the rear door opened, a ramp swung down from the truck, and a man inside operated a hoist which lowered an enormous chain to the pavement. Other sanitation men, joined by some of the police, looped the chain around the horse's neck and locked it. There was a noisy creaking of machinery and the chain rose, dragging the carcass into the truck. The ramp was pulled up and the doors closed. Then this vehicle, too, sped away.

Lieutenant John Tynan came back to join the Inspector, saying, "There's a definite stink of gasoline in the area of the explosion. It looks like you were right and it was a bomb."

Max Kauffman nodded.

The two of them set out on foot up Broadway to examine the rest of the balloons in the parade to make sure no additional explosives had been planted in the balloons' riggings. As a precaution, in case any such bombs were found and had to be removed, the bomb wagon followed behind them.

"I think we've got just about all the residue from the explosion," Tynan said when they passed the spot where the men in his unit were stuffing debris they'd cleaned up from the street into plastic bags they carried. Some of the men had put on black vinyl, zip-up jumpsuits on the backs of which were printed in capital gold letters the words: "BOMB SECTION."

"There's plenty there for the lab to analyze," Tynan added. He grimaced, paused, and scraped the sole of his right shoe against the edge of the curb. "Including the dog droppings I stepped into."

CHAPTER THREE

The air in Max Kauffman's office at the 16th Precinct was hazy with smoke, the smoke of cigarettes, pipes, cigars, and the glowing logs in the stone fireplace set in one wall of the office. It was 4:30 P.M., still Thanksgiving Day. A three-hour meeting presided over by the Inspector had just ended. Except for John Tynan, the thirteen men from the Precinct whom Max Kauffman had called together to work on the investigation of the parade bombing had left.

Max Kauffman sat in a high-backed, leather-covered swivel chair behind his desk, chewing on a dead cigar while he talked to the Police Commissioner on the phone. Tynan, in a chair on the opposite side of the desk, was thumbing through police department records of previous bombing cases in the city, hoping to spot a modus operandi similar to the parade explosion.

Earlier, the two men had conducted a thorough search of all the other balloon floats in the parade but had turned up no evidence of additional bombs. Max Kauffman had then given permission for the parade to continue. Soon after the parade had concluded without further incident, the Inspector and Tynan had proceeded to the station house. There the two of them had picked a dozen men from the 16th Precinct Bomb Investigative Unit—some of whom were off duty for the holiday and had to be called in from their homes—and detailed them full time to the case.

Half of the men—Detectives Stempler, Walsh, Doheny, Cortez, Riggins, Beelin—would work on the physical evidence picked up from the street at the

25

site of the explosion. As soon as the police laboratory had completed its analysis, the bits and pieces of the bomb would be turned over to these men and they would begin the painstaking task of attempting to trace the pieces to their source of purchase.

The other six men picked from the Bomb Investigative Unit—Detectives Braxley, Cohen, Pennell, Raucher, Manders, Gribaldi—would concentrate on trying to track down any persons, either ex-employees or customers of Macy's, who might have had a grudge against the department store. These six detectives would also round up and bring in for questioning any likely suspects and known participants in previous bombing cases who were listed in the police records now being examined by John Tynan. Tynan would be in charge of the entire operation, under Max Kauffman's command.

The Inspector finished his conversation with the Commissioner, hung up the phone, and swung around in his chair, facing the desk.

Tynan glanced up from the files he was reading and raised his eyebrows questioningly.

"He says," Max Kauffman said drily, "he has every confidence we'll get a quick make on the case. He says the Mayor says he has every confidence, too."

"Uh huh," Tynan said.

"He thinks it was a bad break for us that the TV guys got there and televised the scene. The media are already playing it big all across the country. It's going to increase the pressure on us, to say nothing of the fact that now the Department's going to be swamped with bomb scare calls from every nut in the city."

"At least double the number," Tynan agreed, knowing that bomb calls to the police averaged twenty-five to thirty on a normal day in Manhattan. "It always happens."

Max Kauffman leaned over and deposited his chewed-up cigar stub in the wastebasket. Then he took out a fresh cigar and lit it. "Come across any possible M.O.s in there?"

Tynan shrugged. "I did a count through the files

and came out with over a hundred investigations by the P.D. of bombing cases in the city so far this year. Almost all are the usual chickenshit variety."

Tynan began flipping through the files, reading aloud at random, his voice a flat monotone, musing to himself as much as talking to Max Kauffman: "Item: so-called 'Ping-Pong' bombs. Most times an empty cigarette pack was used, filled with highly flammable fluid and a Ping-Pong ball injected with acid. Strictly chickenshit stuff. Item: a suitcase with a pressure cooker inside it: inside pressure cooker were several pounds of gunpowder which was set off by a timing device. Item: a timing device explodes a cylinder containing propane gas. Item: a stick of dynamite stuffed inside an iron pipe along with gunpowder, and a solution of sulfuric acid in a glass vial with a cork stopper, triggered by a timer." Tynan closed the files and shook his head.

"With a whimper or a big bang," Max Kauffman said softly, "the paranoids *will* be heard, huh?"

"The paranoids *will* be heard," Tynan said. "Which is why you'd have to be a zonked-out freak yourself to be able to match up any of the cases in the files with today's episode." He began stacking the records together on the desk. "Still, I picked out a few candidates we'd better run in over the next few days for questioning."

The phone rang. Max Kauffman answered it. The call was from Sergeant Wendler, the officer Max Kauffman had sent along to French Hospital with the injured mounted patrolman.

"Sir," Wendler said, "they've still got Yost up in surgery and I can't find out anything."

"All right," Max Kauffman said. "Would you like to be relieved and I'll send another man over?"

"No, no, sir. I'd rather stay on here till we get some word. Some of the other men in the patrol who worked with Yost have been coming over as soon as they got off duty."

"Keep me informed," Max Kauffman said. "I may stop by myself when I finish up here."

The Inspector hung up the phone and looked at

Tynan. "Yost is still in surgery." He took a couple of puffs on his cigar, ran his hand over his face, and blinked his eyes. He suddenly felt very tired. There was a dull ache in the lower part of his back and the muscles in both his legs, just below and behind his knees, were quivering as if he had walked up too many flights of stairs.

"You know," Tynan said, "maybe we'll luck out this time and our bomber—having shot his wad—will crawl back into the woodwork. At least it doesn't appear to be any radical or militant group. A balloon, for God's sake!"

"We can hope."

Tynan pushed himself up from the chair and gathered up the files from the desk. "Meanwhile, I'll goose the lab for a quick report and bear down hard on the men. Anything else?"

Max Kauffman shook his head.

"Then," Tynan said, crossing to the door, "I bid you a happy Thanksgiving Day, Inspector Kauffman."

"Yeah, you too, Jack," Max Kauffman called out as Tynan left the office, closing the door behind him.

The fact that it was Thanksgiving Day had completely slipped the Inspector's mind until Tynan mentioned it, and now he reached for the phone and called his wife. She had already heard about the bombing on the news and had guessed that he was busy on the case.

"Do you know when you might be home?" she asked. It was a perfunctory question. He could tell from the sound of her voice that even as she spoke her attention was centered elsewhere. There had been a time, years ago, when she would be hurt or angry if she expected him and he didn't appear or phone promptly, but they had passed that point long since; she had learned to accept the situation and he never wasted time explaining or apologizing. In the brief silence over the telephone line he could hear the murmur of voices and the clatter of dishes in the background.

"No," he said, and then: "Did they all get there?"

"Yes, we're just getting ready to eat." She must

28

have put her hand over the mouthpiece briefly because there was dead air before she came back on the line to say, "Hold on a minute, Max. Your father wants to speak to you."

"Belle . . . Belle . . . Belle!" he said but apparently she had gone away from the phone. He waited, tapping the ash of his cigar against the edge of the ash tray.

"Hello, Max?"

"Hello, Papa."

"Max, we've been waiting dinner for you and now Belle says you don't know when you'll be here."

"That's right, Papa," Max Kauffman said. "You know about the bombing today? It's my case. I don't know how long it will be before I get home."

"I wanted to have a talk with you." The old man's voice was querulous and his next words came in a whisper: *You know, about that matter we discussed the other day. I need to talk to you.*"

Max Kauffman had already suspected what his father wanted to say to him and had hoped to avoid talking with him on the phone. Three months earlier his father, Aaron Kauffman, had had a severe myocardial infarction, had almost died, had been in the cardiac intensive care unit in Mount Sinai Hospital for fourteen days, had spent another three weeks in the hospital, and was still recuperating. It was the first serious illness Aaron Kauffman had suffered in his seventy-seven years of life. The heart attack had left him not only weak and shaky—the flesh of his big body now hanging loose and flabby from the elongated structure of his frame, face, hands, and feet as if his skin had suddenly become several sizes too large for his bones—but also worried and uncertain of himself.

Aaron Kauffman had not of course been able to run the family garment business, manufacturers of lower-priced clothing for women, during the past three months. Max Kauffman knew that "the matter" his father mentioned on the phone was the old man's worry about his two sons-in-law who had had to take charge of the business. Aaron Kauffman had already told the Inspector that one of the sons-in-law, Marvin Katz, was drinking too much and gambling, and the other, Seymour Greene, had suddenly become a woman-chaser. According to the old man the family business could be ruined if something wasn't done about the conduct of the two.

Max Kauffman, for his part, did not want to get involved. He had tried to keep his nose out of the family business ever since the time years earlier when his grandfather, Asa Kauffman, who had founded the company, left Max Kauffman a full one-third of the firm in his will before he died. Max Kauffman had sold the shares back to his father. The money he received, which he invested wisely, had allowed him to live a life of affluence far beyond the salary he earned as a N.Y.P.D. Deputy Chief Inspector.

Now all Max Kauffman said was: "Papa, I'll try to get by to have a long talk with you tomorrow or the next day. This week for sure."

"You won't forget now?" There was an unmistakable, pleading urgency in the old man's voice. "Always you were a good boy, Max." He added affectionately: "A gutte neshumah," the Yiddish phrase for "A good soul."

The Inspector paused to clear his throat before he said: "Try not to worry, Papa. Rest easy in your mind. Everything's going to be all right."

"Yes, yes," his father said. "I mustn't keep you. Goodbye, Max."

"Papa—"

The old man had hung up. Max Kauffman replaced the phone in its cradle and leaned back in his chair. The brief conversation with his father had disturbed him but he didn't want to think about it now. It was very quiet in the room. His office was in a corner of the station house building on the third floor, the top floor. Sounds from the street almost never carried to the room nor did the noises from the lower floors inside the building. And yet as he sat there in the stillness, he was so closely attuned to the ambience of the Precinct that he could sense a kind of restless vibration throughout the structure; it was always that way when one of the men had been injured or killed. He guessed that the station house was already beginning to fill with men who were off duty, had heard about Yost, and had come in as a way of paying their respects to their fellow officer.

The Inspector got up from his desk and went over to the fireplace and stood there, letting the warmth soothe the ache in his back. Usually he enjoyed the times when he was alone in his office. Years ago when he had been given command of the 16th Precinct he had asked for, and received, permission to decorate the office to his own personal taste and at his own expense. The result had been that now the enormous room had walls paneled in oak and exposed oak beams across the ceiling, louvered shutters covering the windows, indirect lighting recessed in the ceiling and the tops of the windows; an air-conditioning unit set into one wall and a stone fireplace in another.

Normally the room was also furnished with rich drapes across the windows, matching deep pile wall-to-wall carpeting, oil paintings on the walls and pieces of sculpture on low pedestals around the room. There was also his massive mahogany desk with its chairs, his leather-covered swivel chair behind the desk, and at the opposite end of the room a long, leather-covered sofa and several more chairs arranged around a gleaming mahogany table on which usually sat a silver coffee service and a crystal vase filled with fresh-cut flowers.

Tonight, however, the room was like a ghost of itself. The walls and floors were bare, the sculpture and paintings were stacked together in a corner and covered by a painter's drop cloth, as was all the other furniture in the room except for the desk and the three chairs belonging to it. The walls were streaked with replastered spots and there was a film of plaster over the bare floors and, despite the fire in the fireplace, the room felt chilly. A month earlier, the Inspector had decided to have the office redecorated. The work was supposed to take only a week to complete. But, as seemed to be the case with so many things these days, there had been delays and the one week of

31

work had stretched into four and there was still no end in sight. The Inspector was a man who sought to maintain a sense of order, of tidiness, in his immediate environment, in his personal affairs, his office, his home—it helped him keep his perspective in the midst of the chaos of crime with which he dealt each day—and now this room which usually comforted and pleased him only alternately irritated and depressed him.

When he had arrived at the Precinct that afternoon he had hung his soiled Chesterfield coat in the closet in his office. He now went to the closet, left that coat hanging there to be sent to the cleaners, took out a spare storm coat and put it on. He phoned to tell his driver that he was on his way down and to have his car ready out front.

Then he rode the creaking elevator to the first floor and before he left the Precinct checked with the sergeant on duty at the booking desk to make sure there were no special cases that required his attention. The sergeant had received a full report on the people who had been hurt in the parade bombing. None of them, fortunately, had been seriously injured.

As he had already guessed, the station house was full of policemen who had come in on their own time to stand around in the corridors and the squad rooms and discuss the injured mounted patrolman. The men nodded to him respectfully as he passed and he tried to give each of them a word or two or a brief handshake on his way out. He felt that both he and the men were performing a bit of meaningless, ritualistic bullshit, but then, he supposed, there were times when a little ritualistic bullshit didn't hurt.

Detective Kinnard was still on duty as driver and when Max Kauffman got into the limousine he instructed Kinnard to drive him to French Hospital on West Thirtieth Street. Once there the Inspector dismissed Kinnard for the night and went inside.

French Hospital was one of New York's older medical institutions. The lobby felt drafty and damp and seemed a cheerless place on this holiday night. And there was that hospital smell of strong disinfectant and what the Inspector always thought was ether and probably wasn't and what he thought couldn't be formaldehyde from the basement morgue and probably was.

The woman at the information desk in the lobby directed him up to the eleventh floor where he found Sergeant Wendler and four other policemen from the Precinct, in plainclothes, sitting in a waiting room, smoking and drinking coffee out of Styrofoam cups. The men all got to their feet when he entered and he waved them back to their seats.

Sergeant Wendler informed him that one of the nurses had been in to tell them that Patrolman Yost was out of the operating room, was in the recovery room, and that a doctor would be in to talk to them soon.

The sergeant pointed to the end of the hall where Max Kauffman could see three figures pacing back and forth, a man and two women. "That's Ralph Yost's wife and Pete Geary and his wife," Wendler said. "Pete works on patrol duty with Ralph. They're good buddies. Him and his wife picked up Annette Yost soon as they heard the news and brought her to the hospital. They all live near each other over in Staten Island."

Max Kauffman accepted a cup of coffee and walked over to the window. The window faced south. In the near distance was a large housing development, the windows glowing warm yellow as if the building were lit from within by thousands of candles, while in the far distance the twin towers of the World Trade Center blazed with white light like an electric wall against the dark, starless backdrop of winter sky.

The Inspector drank the lukewarm coffee and smoked a cigar. He could tell the other men were ill at ease at his presence, and so was he, and such talk as the men exchanged among themselves was strained and artificial. A couple of the men were discussing the horse that had been killed. Max Kauffman learned for the first time that the horse had been called Jigger. In addition to its name, each N.Y.P.D. horse was identified by numerals—similar to a patrolman

33

and his badge number—and the six-year-old chestnut gelding had been Number 77. Like all mounted patrol horses, Number 77 had gone through the Police Department's intensive training program to prepare it for the noise, confusion, and rigors of duty in the sometimes chaotic streets of Manhattan. The men agreed, though, that it was probably impossible to control the fear of a horse that was badly burned in the middle of a bizarre and terrifying bombing, as had happened to Number 77 that day.

To Max Kauffman the thirty-minute wait seemed endless. Finally a doctor came in, still wearing his surgical gown and with his gauze mask dangling from his neck. Yost's wife and the other couple came in from the hall and they all stood listening impassively while the doctor explained that Yost had a fractured skull—"gross involvement of the parietal lobe," he said—and they had had to operate to remove bone splinters from the brain. The doctor merely added that the patrolman's condition was serious.

Afterward, Max Kauffman assured Annette Yost that the Department would see that everything possible was done to provide her husband with the best care. He pressed her hand. "Try to get as much rest as you can, either here or at home. The hospital will keep us informed. If you're not here, we'll see that you get immediate transportation if there's any change in his condition."

She nodded her head and said, "Yes, yes," through bloodless lips, and thanked him.

The Inspector tried to say a few encouraging words to Sergeant Wendler and the other men and then left, anxious to be gone before, as he knew would happen, the Mayor and the Commissioner arrived to make statements for the television, radio, and newspaper reporters who would follow. More ritualistic bullshit.

CHAPTER FOUR

Outside the hospital, on West Thirtieth Street, Max Kauffman saw there were no taxicabs in sight, the street was deserted, and the neighborhood was dark and silent, with only a light here and there in the windows of the old buildings, most of them tenements, in the block. In the middle of the street clouds of steam from manhole covers drifted silent and ghostlike above the pavement before dissolving in the wind. It was one of the infrequent moments when the Inspector was conscious of the comforting weight of the .38 revolver in the shoulder holster under his coat. He walked briskly toward the corner and Eighth Avenue. Halfway there he began to feel the cold through his clothes and, walking into the wind as he was, he had to lower his head to keep his eyes from tearing and hold onto his hat so it wouldn't blow away.

He had another long wait at the corner, made more uncomfortable for him because the wind was too strong for him to light his cigar, before he finally spotted an empty cab heading up Eighth Avenue and signaled to it. When he climbed into the cab he was surprised to find himself giving the driver Catherine Devereaux's address on Beekman Place, instead of the address of his own apartment. He hadn't consciously planned to go to her apartment—she was out of town, in Delaware with her family for the holiday—but as soon as he had instructed the driver, he knew that that was where he wanted to go.

On the ride uptown he thought of the day's events. Bomb cases always bothered him. Unlike most other crimes, the motives were nearly always elusive.

35

Frequently they were nothing more than an individual acting out some private frustration in public. The perpetrator often acted alone, was seldom observed, was usually far from the scene when the actual crime (the explosion) occurred, and the crime itself (again, the explosion) more often than not destroyed whatever clues the bomber might have carelessly left behind. All of these things helped negate the normal investigative techniques of the police. In short, there were seldom any links leading backward, one by one, from the deed to the instigator for the police to uncover and follow, which was really how most crimes were solved.

The Inspector could only hope Tynan was right and that whichever psycho had set off the bomb had crawled back into the woodwork again. But he *knew* that if it turned out they had another crazy bomber on their hands, acting out of some hidden paranoia, chances were only dumb luck would solve the case. If, indeed, it was ever solved. Meantime, God, he hoped Yost didn't die and he felt so sorry for the wife.

He was so deep in thought that he didn't for a moment recognize where he was when the taxi stopped in front of Catherine Devereaux's apartment. Here, too, there was no one on the street because of the cold. But the difference between here and the area downtown around the hospital was that along Beekman Place, which was only two blocks long, there were cheery lights in most of the apartment windows and doormen to be seen in the bright-lit lobbies of the larger buildings. The street was like a self-contained community in the center of Manhattan, the city on one side, the East River on the other.

Max Kauffman paid the taxi driver and used his own key to let himself into the apartment. Catherine Devereaux lived in one of the smaller buildings on Beekman Place which he and she had chosen partly because there was no doorman to note his visits.

Out of habit, the Inspector went through checking the rooms. He always did this when he entered an empty house or apartment. On the first floor was a large living room which was an inverted L-shape with windows in front facing Beekman Place. Beyond the living room was a raised dining room with floor-to-ceiling windows that looked out on the East River. Between the living room and dining room was a door opening into a hallway that led to the bath and bedroom on the opposite side of the building. The bedroom windows also had a view of the river. At the back of the hall was another door behind which there were stairs to the second floor. On the second floor were the kitchen and separate living quarters for the Irish housekeeper who was always in attendance when Catherine Devereaux was in the apartment. To-night the housekeeper was also away for the holiday so the door to the stairs was locked.

Max Kauffman returned to the living room, took off his hat and coat, and loosened his tie. He went to the bar he'd had installed in a corner of the living room, complete with its own ice-making machine, and fixed himself a glass of Chivas Regal on the rocks. For the first time that day he felt, briefly, a sense of contentment.

He knew that, even in Catherine Devereaux's absence, the apartment soothed him because her essence—what he thought of as a quiet self-awareness of her femininity, unconsciously expressed with a kind of tantalizing sensuality—was everywhere evident.

The furniture was in the Hepplewhite style but of satinwood, that soft-toned, silky sheened wood, the drapes of heavy brocade in a soft pink tone with ivory embroidery around the edges, the carpet thick, cushiony, and pale avocado in color. There was a large mirror above the sofa on the wall opposite the windows. On the other walls were paintings, light pastel watercolors, originals that he and she had found and liked and purchased at various art galleries. There was also a large portrait of her done in charcoal. The sketch was a striking likeness of her, the hair—which was ash-blond, although, of course, it didn't show that way in charcoal—was pulled back from her face the way he preferred it, the artist accurately catching the look of her cool, lean beauty.

37

Carrying his drink, the Inspector went through the dining room, and down the hall to the bedroom. He had no feeling of intruding upon her privacy because he felt she would approve of what he was doing: trying, in her absence, to be as near to her as he could get.

Her special scent, the scent of Madame Rochas perfume, was in the room. It was there, lightly but unmistakably, when he opened the mirrored doors to her closet where her dresses hung, creations by Halston, Trigere, Simpson, Givenchy, Gres, and de la Renta.

He closed the closet door and sat on the side of the bed sipping his drink and staring at a photograph of himself in a silver Tiffany frame on the dresser top. He didn't think it was a very good photograph. It had been taken soon after they had begun their affair, nine years earlier, but the sight of it here in her bedroom gave him a sense of shared intimacy with her. Over the years that they had loved one another, holidays, like today, were always the worst times. They could almost never be together; he usually had to be with his family and so she usually went home to Delaware.

Still, most of the tension of the day had left him. He realized now that the reason he hadn't wanted to talk to his father on the phone, the reason he hadn't wanted to go home earlier, the reason he had, instinctively, wanted to come to her apartment, was because there were times—and this was one of them—that he had to keep something of himself for himself. The visit had accomplished that.

He finished his drink and went back through the rooms, turning out lights. He put on his hat and coat, then locked the apartment door behind him. He walked over to First Avenue, caught a cab, and rode the six blocks to his place.

There was a light on in the foyer when he let himself into his apartment but the rest of the rooms that he could see were dark and it was quiet even though it was only 9:20. He started toward his bedroom and saw a light shining from under the door of

38

his wife's room. He tapped on the door, said, "It's Max," and when she answered, went in.

Belle Kauffman was lying in bed watching television. She was wearing a gown and bed jacket. She'd removed her makeup and her face looked pale.

"How was the dinner?" he asked.

She turned down the sound on the television set. "Everybody seemed to enjoy it. They all left as soon as we finished eating. Your father seemed tired. Seymour and Bernice drove him and Mama home."

"Did you hear from the kids?"

Their children were away from home for the holiday. Lawrence, who was at Harvard, had stayed in Cambridge to study, and Deborah had gone to visit her best friend, Shirley Michaels, and her family, in Larchmont, New York.

"Debbie called while we were having dinner," Belle Kauffman said. "Lawrence phoned just a few minutes ago. They're both fine. They sent you their love. Deb'll be back Sunday night and Lawrence said he'll try to come home weekend after next if he gets his studies done."

Max Kauffman nodded. He'd removed his hat and storm coat. He took off his suit coat and started untying his tie.

She glanced at him. "Are you all right? They said on the news that a mounted policeman was injured in that bombing."

"He's in the hospital. And of course I'm all right."

"There's a plate of food for you in the kitchen," Belle Kauffman said. "I saved you a turkey leg and there's plenty of white meat left. I told Anna to put a half bottle of that chablis you like in the refrigerator. Do you want me to fix it for you? Or I could get Anna to do it."

"No, no," Max Kauffman said. "You both must be tired. I'll fix for myself."

She offered again to get up or get Anna up, but he shook his head. "I'll be all right. If you're still awake before I go to bed I'll look in on you."

He went across the hall to his own bedroom, and took off his shirt. The shirt and tie were new. He'd

39

worn them for the first time that day. Whenever he went to London for his Savile Row suits, as he had done a month earlier, he always bought a dozen shirts and ties from Turnbull and Asser of Jermyn Street, where the shirts were custom-made and the ties matched to exactly the width for each shirt. He examined the shirt and tie carefully and was relieved when he found no bloodstains on them.

He hung up his clothes and went into the connecting bath and washed his hands and face. He put on his robe before going to the kitchen where he heated up the food in the oven. He made a fresh pot of coffee and sat on a stool at the kitchen counter to eat his dinner and sip his wine.

He decided that he'd have a cigar with his coffee later. Afterward, he would take a steaming hot shower to get rid of the aches in his body and then go to bed early. The aches reminded him of the bombing case. He wondered if John Tynan had come up with any leads. As soon as he had the thought he dismissed it from his mind; of course Tynan didn't have any real information yet or he'd have phoned.

John Tynan had stayed on late at the station house preparing for the next day's all-out investigation of the parade bombing. Most of his time had been spent drawing up assignment lists for the twelve men he would direct. He wanted them out on the street and moving first thing in the morning.

He'd also made a final phone call for the night to the police lab. One of the lab men, Milt Nevers, told him they were beginning to assemble the pieces collected at the scene of the explosion. So far it looked like a small clock had been used and some kind of plastic container. The lab detector had also picked up the presence of hydrocarbon vapors among the debris, which indicated that an inflammable liquid, probably gasoline, had been used. The lab men would be working through the night. Tynan decided the information wasn't significant enough to phone the Inspector.

Tynan still hoped the bombing would turn out to be a one-shot fluke. But he remembered another bombing case in the city some years back when the perpetrator had gone on setting off bombs for sixteen years before he was finally caught. Tynan knew he couldn't count on any swift solution this time; nevertheless, he felt better knowing the machinery of investigation was already in motion.

He was still wearing his dark turtleneck sweater and slacks and before he signed out from the precinct he put on an overcoat and scarf from his locker. The garage where he kept his car in the city was a four-block walk from the station house. Once he was in the car, a red Porsche, he drove fast across town, trying to catch all the green lights, and down the F.D.R. Drive toward the Brooklyn Bridge. The lights of Manhattan were on both sides of him as he sped along the Drive, the actual lights of the buildings standing at the eastern edge of the city up above the Drive, to his right and, to his left, the reflections of those lights shimmering on the dark surface of the East River. Just beyond the reflection of lights on the water, out in the middle of the river, was a lone tugboat towing a barge. Beyond the tug and the barge the night-shrouded shoreline of the far side of the river was defined by the curving tracery of lights in Queens and Brooklyn. The only other southbound traffic was two *Daily News* trucks which he passed and left behind.

At the approach to the turnoff from the Drive leading to the Brooklyn Bridge, he spotted a prowl car ahead of him just in time and slowed his speed. He stayed behind the police car crossing the bridge, opened the window next to him a couple of inches, letting in the strong, dank smell of river, and lit a cigarette. Leaning forward, he turned on the car radio which was tuned to Station WTFM in Lake Success. Soft music filled the car.

He thought about Max Kauffman. He'd liked the Inspector ever since the first case they'd worked on together. At that time Tynan had been a member of the Department's Bomb Squad which had its headquarters at the Police Academy on East Twentieth Street. The Bomb Squad, an elite unit within the

41

N.Y.P.D., investigated cases citywide, and the two men met when Tynan was assigned to an investigation that fell within the jurisdiction of the 16th Precinct.

The case involved the bombing of an automobile in which the young wife of the owner of a West Side bar and grill had been killed. The husband, who was of Polish extraction, was named Teodor Demowski. He was thirty-five years old, his wife nine years younger. They had been married for only ten days. They lived in an apartment above the bar. The bombing took place on a spring night at around eleven. The car was parked in the back alley in preparation for a delayed honeymoon they planned to take to Florida the next day. Parts of suitcases and pieces of the wife's dresses, shoes, and other clothing were found along with her mangled body in the wreckage. Police determined that the bomb had been triggered by a timing device. Demowski, who had been working in the bar at the time of the explosion, speculated that his wife must have come down to put her suitcases in the car at precisely the moment the bomb went off.

Demowski blamed the bombing on members of a neighborhood Puerto Rican gang called "The Silver Sharks." He claimed the gang had been harassing him ever since he refused to serve them in the bar after an incident in which they'd disturbed other customers. Max Kauffman was deeply troubled by the case because he was afraid it might touch off a racial war in the area of the 16th Precinct where a mixed group of the city's poorer minorities lived.

As a matter of routine, the police still considered the husband a possible suspect, but they could turn up no motive, no evidence, pointing to his guilt. There was no insurance on the wife, all information indicated that the two had been devoted to each other and in love, and the husband was inconsolable and distraught—in the police's opinion, beyond any ability to pretend—at his wife's death.

The police lab determined that the bomb was constructed from an explosive substance called Iremite. Police were familiar with it since it had been used by a Puerto Rican terrorist group operating in Manhattan. Based on information in the files, police knew that the terrorist group—which claimed it was seeking independence for the island of Puerto Rico—was based in uptown Spanish Harlem, a vaguely defined area of the city just south and east of Black Harlem's 110th Street.

During the investigation, two Puerto Rican detectives from one of the Harlem precincts brought in an informer planted by police inside the terrorist group who testified he had been present when one of the terrorists passed a quantity of Iremite to a member of "The Silver Sharks." The member was identified as sixteen-year-old Carlos Escabar. The terrorist—who had since fled the city after an unrelated bombing—and Escabar were, according to the informer, cousins.

It looked like an open-and-shut case at that point, but Tynan had continued to dig into Demowski's background. He'd picked up a new lead from an offhand remark made by a mechanic at a neighborhood service station who said he frequently worked on Demowski's car. The mechanic thought Demowski was crazy to have been planning a trip to Florida in the old car he owned. Demowski would, the mechanic said, have been lucky to have made it as far as the Lincoln Tunnel and he sure must have known it.

Tynan was puzzled by this. The inconsistency of it bothered him: Why would Demowski be planning to take his new bride on a vacation in a car he knew couldn't possibly have made the trip? And then the car blows up just before they leave. The coincidence alerted Tynan for the first time to Demowski's possible complicity in the crime despite the fact that there as yet appeared to be no motive for such complicity.

Instinct led Tynan to probe more deeply into all Demowski's affairs and it didn't take him long to find out that Demowski carried an unusually large insurance policy on his bar and grill. Records showed that he had scrupulously made the stiff payments on the insurance even when, as police discovered, busi-

43

ness had been bad recently and Demowski had kept his creditors waiting. There was no crime in that, but suppose, Tynan had speculated, the bombing of the car was only meant to be a red herring? Insignificant in itself—if the wife hadn't died—but an opportunity for Demowski to implicate the Puerto Rican gang and set them up as the logical suspects in the later destruction of the bar and grill, *for which Demowski would collect handsomely, meanwhile throwing suspicion off himself.*

As it turned out, when confronted by Max Kauffman and Tynan with the evidence, and the testimony by the Harlem police informer, Escabar immediately broke down. He swore that Teodor Demowski had paid him fifty dollars to get the explosive, Iremite, for him from his cousin. There'd be no trouble, Demowski had told him and Escabar had believed him because he had once worked for Demowski and thought the man was his friend. After the wife had been killed in the explosion, Escabar had been terrified and afraid to talk because he thought the police wouldn't believe him.

Teodor Demowski also broke down easily and confessed freely that everything Escabar had said was true. Yes, he, Demowski, had planted the bomb in the car in order to set up the bombing of his own bar and grill to collect the insurance. From the beginning, Demowski confessed, he had planned to blame the bombing of the bar and grill on the gang, knowing that after the bombing of the car the police would suspect the gang. When his wife was killed, he couldn't think of any other story to tell except the one he'd originally planned. Weeping and almost incoherent, Demowski said he'd never considered the possibility that his wife would come downstairs that night to put her suitcases in the car, and that she'd be there at the exact moment he had set the timing mechanism to go off. It was God's joke on him. Lapsing into Polish, he repeated, *Boq zart.*

A royal fuck-up, Tynan had concluded disgustedly.

Demowski was never brought to trial. Long before that time Demowski, overwhelmed by grief, remorse, and guilt, had suffered a complete mental collapse and a judge had committed him to the Matteawan State Hospital for the Criminally Insane.

Max Kauffman, impressed by Tynan's work, had offered him command of the 16th Precinct Bomb Investigative Unit. Tynan agreed if the Inspector could arrange the transfer. A few weeks later Tynan received orders assigning him to the 16th Precinct where he was promoted to lieutenant and put in charge of the bomb squad.

As Tynan, in the red Porsche, turned off the Brooklyn Bridge and headed for Brooklyn Heights, the nine o'clock news was coming on. The lead story was on the day's parade bombing, but it was just a rehash of what he already knew. A couple of blocks beyond the bridge he lost the prowl car up ahead and took the chance that it was safe to pick up speed again. He drove fast until he was on his own street and could see his house at the end of the block. The lights were on, and Barbara Costa's car was in the driveway. He hadn't been sure until then that she'd still be there waiting for him.

CHAPTER FIVE

Tynan's house was a two-story brownstone, its stone facade freshly-sandblasted, standing above the Brooklyn Heights promenade that paralleled the river, and had a sweeping view of the Manhattan skyline. As soon as he pulled into the drive next to the parked Mach 1 Mustang, the front door to the house opened and Barbara Costa stood framed in the lights from the room behind her.

She was wearing a dark emerald wool dress that came to just below her knees, matching high-heeled suede pumps, a delicate jade necklace, and jade earrings. The color of the dress nicely set off her jet black hair which was styled in a short fringe and had a soft, lustrous texture. Her figure—the firm taut breasts, flat stomach, well-shaped legs—was what most men noticed first. But she had a pretty face with good bones and a smile which, when it came suddenly, startlingly transformed her prettiness into a kind of breathtaking beauty.

She smiled now as Tynan came into the house and closed the door behind him. She was a head shorter in height than he and as she moved to him, she went up on tiptoe, her arms going around him with the palms of her hands flat against his back. She kissed him hard on the mouth and clung to him for a time before she lowered her head and pressed it against his chest. He knew she'd never mention it but he guessed she'd heard the news about the bombing and had been worried about him. He lifted her head so she was looking up at him.

"Hey," he said smiling, "you know you never did

47

explain to me how you learned to kiss like that at that fancy all-girls school you went to."

"That came later," she said softly. "*You* ought to know that."

She helped him take off his overcoat and he said, "I'm sorry I'm so late. I hope I haven't screwed up dinner."

"It's all right," she said. "I planned the bird and all the trimmings so there'd still be time once you were here. If I know you you'll want to wash off all that awful trinitrotoluene before dinner." "Trinitrotoluene" had become a joke word between them ever since he'd taught her the full name for TNT.

She hung his coat and scarf in the hall closet while he went into the living room and stood in front of the fireplace where a stack of wood logs was blazing. The room was two stories high and ran from the front to the back of the house. Most of the furniture in the living room was massive, several large sofas and armchairs of leather, other chairs upholstered in dark-toned fabrics, two coffee tables fashioned from butcher's blocks, another constructed from a slab of marble fitted into a supporting iron frame with iron legs. Much of the furniture had been built or reconstructed by Tynan himself.

A couple of sturdy desks stood against either wall of the room, along with, on one side, a glass-front cherrywood cabinet and a large wooden gunrack, also with a glass front. On the other side was a mahogany sea chest and an upright grandfather clock that chimed on the hour and half hour. On the walls were reproductions of paintings and prints by Andrew Wyeth, Frederic Remington, Winslow Homer, and George Bellows.

In back of the living room was a dining area furnished in Early American. Tall, narrow windows in the rear faced the river. The dining room had originally been on the opposite side of the house in the front but Tynan had turned that room into a study and made a quarter of the living room into a dining area overlooking the river. He had also opened up the front hall so there was no partition between it and

48

the living room. Now the gracefully curving staircase, leading to the second-floor bedrooms and baths, could be seen from almost any spot in the living room. He had his workshop in the basement and a game room where he played poker with old friends every Friday night that he didn't have to work.

Tynan crossed back to the hall and gave Barbara a kiss on the cheek. "I'm going to go scrub," he said and went up the staircase.

He undressed in his bedroom and went into the adjoining bath where he ran water into the oversized tub. He got into the tub, soaped himself, then lay submerged up to his chin in the hot water. He had just settled himself when Barbara knocked on the door and came in carrying a martini on a tray.

"Good Lord," he said, "I don't know what I did to deserve this." He shook his head and smiled. "Or is it that you're setting me up for something you want me to do?"

Early in their relationship, which had begun a year previously, she had informed him she tried to live her life as a liberated person. Before he could be put off by the remark, she explained that, according to her definition, a truly liberated woman—any liberated person—is one who's willing to do whatever's necessary to get what she wants. As a confirmed bachelor, which he had informed her he was—also early in their relationship—he thought he could live with those ground rules if he understood them, which he wasn't sure he did. Sometimes, playing the man-woman game, he would deliberately pretend to misunderstand her words.

She smiled now and said, "No strings attached. It's Thanksgiving. Just give thanks."

"I do," he said. "I thank you." She blew him a kiss and left.

The martini was chilled and very dry, and the glass was frosty—just the way he liked it. He sipped the drink and shook his head again; she was *some* woman. He had dated many other girls in his life but she was a new experience.

He had met her when he was working on the

Demowski bombing case. She was a vice-president and manager of the claims department of the insurance company that had carried the policy on Demowski's bar and grill. Tynan saw her four or five times while he was putting together the insurance part of the evidence in the case. He liked her and sensed she might go out with him if he asked her. Because she would be called as a witness, he had to stay away from her until the case was resolved. When he did call, she surprised him by saying, quite matter-of-factly, that she had been waiting to hear from him. They began dating the next night.

Tynan had always had faulty perception when it came to judging the age of women—it sometimes seemed to him that every woman over twenty-one was more mature than any man at any age—and he was surprised to find that, despite her considerable achievements in the business world, she was still only twenty-nine years old.

She had been born and raised in Greenwich, Connecticut, had gone to an exclusive finishing school, graduated from Vassar, and had a master's degree in mathematics from Princeton. Her father was Italian and had his own importing company in Manhattan; her mother, Irish, and her parents still lived in Greenwich. She had her own apartment on Gramercy Park in New York and her mother and father also had an apartment in the same building for use when they were in the city.

On the night Tynan brought her to see his house in Brooklyn Heights, they had made love for the first time. That night he had been amused by her reactions to the house, her exclamations of pleasure, and her mock accusation that he must be on the take to be able to own the house and drive a Porsche. He told her the story of his own life and of the house and car which were a part of the story.

He had been born and grew up in a small house on Avenue A in Flatbush, Brooklyn during the time his father was a patrolman walking a beat in Canarsie. His father had died the year Tynan graduated from

Erasmus High School and his mother had gone to work in a small real estate office in Brooklyn.

Tynan had gone straight from high school into the army—he'd have been drafted anyway since there was a war in Korea—and had served as a demolitioneer with the Corps of Engineers in Korea. It was his first experience working with explosives and, because of the natural skills he showed in the work, he was recommended by his commanding officer to the army's Explosive Ordinance Disposal School at Indian Head, Maryland.

When he returned to the States he re-enlisted, was accepted at the school, and underwent rigorous training in recognizing, examining, and dismantling every conceivable type of explosive device from a letter bomb to a wired ton of TNT. When his training was completed, he was offered an instructorship at the school and stayed on, intending to make a career in the army. During his years as an instructor at the EOD School, he was frequently sent to work with police bomb squads throughout the United States. These assignments frequently took him to New York City, San Francisco, and Washington, D.C., in the 1960s when radical and revolutionary groups were conducting campaigns of bombing terror across the country. While he was serving at the EOD School, he also took accelerated courses at the University of Maryland and received his bachelor of science degree.

He had known, meanwhile, that his mother was prospering in the real estate office—modestly, he thought—and that she had taken over the business when the original owner died. However, he wasn't prepared to discover, at the time of her death of a lung embolism when he was thirty-five years old, how well she had done financially. In her will she had left him the house in Brooklyn Heights, which he had not known she'd acquired, the small place in Flatbush, and $50,000 in stocks and bonds. Because of the house in Brooklyn Heights, which he wanted to renovate and furnish the way he saw it in his mind's eye, and the inherited money, modest though it was, he resigned from the army and returned to New York to live. He had no intention of just loafing even if he could afford it, nor did he think seriously about looking for any other job except with the Police Department, and specifically the bomb squad. It was the work he did best. He passed the city police exam, trained at the Police Academy, and, as he had hoped, because of his experience and background in explosives, had been assigned to the bomb squad. By the time he met Barbara Costa and they started dating, he was generally satisfied with the way his life was shaping up.

Stretched out in the tub, Tynan drank the last of the martini and opened the drain to let the water out. He stepped out of the tub and dried himself off, then knotted a fresh towel around his waist. While he was soaking he had kept refilling the tub with hot water, and the bathroom was full of steam. The humid condensation had clouded over the mirror above the sink. He opened the bathroom door to let fresh air in and Barbara was standing there. The steam drifting out through the doorway slowly enveloped her nude figure, lubricating her bare flesh from head to toe with tiny, glistening beads of moisture. Her body was slick under his hands, like the feel of raw silk, as he pulled her to him, neither of them speaking.

They kissed. She caressed the back of his neck with her hand. In the heat the swirling mist was full of the perfumed scent of her hair, her flesh. Slowly— the sensation was of opening her body to him—her lips parted. He unknotted the towel around his waist. It fell away. Their bodies sought each other through the haze of steam, and touched. She arched her head. Her eyes were closed. He kissed her throat where a tiny pulse fluttered under the pale skin. Then his lips moved down the velvet smoothness of her body until she, grasping both sides of his head with trembling hands, lifted his face.

Her eyes were very wide now and soft. She took a step toward him and reached up. Her arms encircled his neck. Feet off the floor, she fitted herself to him, locking her legs around his hips. As Tynan, holding her to him, started toward the bedroom, he had the fleeting thought that this was probably as good a way as any to distract his mind from the nagging, worrisome memory of the day's bombing.

The man in the black raincoat had been sitting in the dingy West Side bar for the past several hours. He kept sipping beer but it was really the TV set that kept him there. Over and over again through the late afternoon and early evening, news broadcasts had repeated television film of the Thanksgiving Day parade bombing. Each time he saw pictures of the scene —the confusion, the police, the ambulances, the bomb wagon, the terrified crowd—he thought he would explode with excitement. Jesus! To think he was the one—the only one—who was responsible for the bomb. He'd showed the bastards. And this was only the beginning. Before he was finished with this city, he'd bring the whole population to its knees with fear. He'd make *them* pay for what *they* had done to him.

Again and again throughout the afternoon and evening he kept finding himself wishing Adrienne would show up so he could share his excitement with her, he knew how pleased she'd be at what he'd done for her, and they could go to bed and talk about it. Stimulated the way he was now, he knew he could keep screwing her all night. Once or twice he thought he saw her through the window of the bar, but each time it turned out to be another girl who walked on by. Maybe she'd still show up, though.

It was all he could do to keep his excitement bottled up inside him. Several times he had been tempted, if he couldn't have Adrienne, to call up one of the girls listed in his notebook. He'd barely managed to keep himself in check. The night wasn't over yet, the best was yet to come, and then, and then— God, how he was going to let himself go.

There'd been only a handful of customers in the bar during the time he'd been there, two sailors and three obvious hookers at one table, a man and woman at another table, a middle-aged woman and another man, sitting separately, at the bar, and the bartender, a sourfaced, balding man wearing a soiled apron. All of them had paid attention when films of the bomb came on TV, and the man in the black raincoat thought if he just stood up and told them who he was it would blow their minds.

For the past half hour he had kept glancing at his watch every ten or fifteen minutes. At exactly 9:45 he got up from the bar stool and headed for the phone booth in the rear of the room. He went into the booth and closed the door behind him. The TV set at the front of the bar was still on, but with the phone booth door closed the sound was just an indistinguishable blur. The program was some kind of Thanksgiving Day variety show—not that it mattered a damn anyway. He looked around the bar to see that no one there was observing him—not that that mattered a damn, either—but he was naturally nervous and trying to be cautious. Then he dropped a dime in the slot and dialed 911.

Max Kauffman had just finished taking his shower and had put on his pajama pants when the phone on the table beside his bed started ringing. The phone was a direct line to the 16th Precinct. His hair was still wet from the shower and he tried to dry it with a towel held in one hand while with the other hand he picked up the phone.

"Inspector Kauffman," he said.

He listened briefly to the staccato voice of the 16th Precinct dispatcher, then said quickly: "Tell them to clear out the place at once! Call in all emergency equipment! Have a squad car pick me up. Contact Jack Tynan. I want a squad car sent for him."

Max Kauffman hung up the phone and hurried to dress.

John Tynan and Barbara Costa were lying in bed with a sheet pulled up over them. They had been quiet for a while and then he had kissed her again, gently, on the lips and breasts. She had sighed contentedly, and he had smiled at her, saying softly, "I love you," and she had whispered, "Oh, how I love you."

He reached over, got a cigarette, and lit it. She said, "I heard a funny joke today, Jack."

"H'mmm?"

"Do you know," she asked, "how you can tell the bride at an Italian wedding? She's the one wearing something old, something new, something borrowed, something blue, green, orange, lavender, pink, purple—" she laughed. "Don't you think that's funny?"

"It's funny," he said.

She shook her head. "But you didn't really laugh. Just mention marriage and you get uptight, is that it?" she said, keeping her voice light. "You know, you really are a stupid *bastardo*. I love you, you love me. I could make you happy. We're good together, I know you know that. So what's this big hangup you've got about marriage?"

"I—" he paused, searching for words, and not knowing he was going to say it, said, "Marriage fucks up fucking."

They both laughed but she suspected he meant it. She looked at him. "You really believe that, don't you?"

He shrugged. "Partly. All I know is that even when two people have a lot going for them in a marriage, if the sex turns bad, the marriage does, too. It appears to be a matter of how to keep sex interesting. I guess I think it takes more work, more thought, more imagination, more time than most people ever give to it once they're married. *Maybe* you can, *maybe* I can. It's still one hell of a big risk."

Before either of them could say anything else, the phone rang. Tynan picked it up on the second ring.

"Hello," he said, "yeah, this is Tynan. I understand. Right away." He hung up the phone and moved swiftly, getting out of bed.

Barbara was up on her knees, watching him. "What is it, Jack? What's happening?"

He was at the closet, putting on the same clothes

he had taken off a short while earlier. "More madness," he said, his voice tight. "The police just got an anonymous phone call that there's a bomb planted in Radio City Music Hall. And the place is packed for the holiday show."

CHAPTER SIX

The squad car that had picked up Inspector Max Kauffman in front of his apartment building exactly eleven minutes earlier braked to a stop with a shriek of tires in front of Radio City Music Hall, Fiftieth Street and Sixth Avenue, at 10:17 P.M. Lines of uniformed patrolmen, hastily erected wooden barriers, and police cars parked slantwise across the intersections had already blocked off the streets and avenues—Fiftieth and Fifty-first Streets, Fifth and Sixth Avenues—on all four sides around the theatre. Several fire engines, an ambulance from Roosevelt Hospital, a dozen squad cars, a police van, the bomb wagon, and two bomb squad station wagons had already arrived and were parked on both side streets and along Sixth Avenue. An emergency service flatbed truck was parked in the middle of Sixth. Its powerful searchlight swept the street in front of the theatre, turning night into day.

To Max Kauffman, as he stepped out of the squad car, the scene was almost a duplicate of the one earlier in the day after the bomb exploded during the parade except that now the men manning the emergency equipment could only stand by and wait.

Police and Radio City Music Hall employees were still evacuating people from the theatre. The evacuation proceeded in orderly fashion and most of the people, once they were outside, seemed reluctant to leave the vicinity where they had a chance to view a real-life drama. Cold as it was in the night air, the Inspector calculated it must be down around 5 degrees above zero as he crossed the sidewalk, the

57

crowd continued to linger. Police herded the people behind wooden barricades set up on the sidewalk across the street.

Max Kauffman hurried into the building where he was recognized and passed on by the policemen stationed in the lobby. He joined a group of six men standing at the entrance to one of the center aisles. He already knew five of them—Kelleher and Jacobi of the 16th Precinct's bomb squad, working the four-to-midnight shift, Detective Sergeant Tolkin of the 16th Precinct, and Locklin and Bradlee, of the Police Academy bomb squad. Sergeant Tolkin introduced the sixth man as an assistant manager of the theatre. The assistant manager was explaining that in just another half hour the theatre would have been empty since after the stage show at 8:20 the last showing of the film went on at 9:18 and would have ended at 11:06.

Locklin had brought along two dogs, a German shepherd and a collie, which had been trained to sniff out hidden explosives. Max Kauffman had seen the dogs in action on other occasions and had been impressed at how swiftly they were led by their highly selective sense of smell to almost any explosive device that used chemical powder. The dogs were never overfed and as soon as they picked up a scent would follow it to the exact spot where the explosive was hidden and would sit and wait to be given a dog biscuit. Max Kauffman noticed now that both dogs were straining at their leashes.

Police and ushers were leading the last of the people who had been in the theatre out through the lobby. Locklin said, "I guess we're just about ready to let the dogs go."

"Hold it a minute," Max Kauffman said. Looking around the lobby, he spotted John Tynan coming in through a side door carrying a black bag which contained the tools he'd need if they found a bomb. Max Kauffman nodded to Locklin. "It's all right, go ahead."

Tynan joined the group as Locklin bent and unsnapped the leashes. Both dogs bounded through the doors and down the aisle of the empty auditorium, the men following. The house lights were turned up and the stage curtains were still open, revealing the blank movie screen.

The dogs went down the aisle to about halfway in the orchestra section, then darted between the rows of seats and ran across to the next aisle. When the men caught up with them, both dogs were sitting expectantly in the aisle next to an end seat under which a brown paper shopping bag lay on its side.

"There's your package," Locklin said. He fed each of the dogs a biscuit and led them away.

Tynan crouched on his haunches and placed his black tool bag on the floor beside him. "I'll take it from here," he said softly. "Jacobi, you want to give me a hand? The rest of you clear out."

Harry Jacobi was a heavyset man in his midforties with bushy gray hair, thick beetle eyebrows, and a swarthy complexion. He had already begun to sweat lightly, but his manner was calm and his hands steady. He and Tynan were wearing their flak vests. When handling explosives members of the bomb squad frequently put on so-called "shrapnel shields," which were steel-and-fiberglass-plated overcoats. These outfits provided more protection but constricted the wearer's body movement to little more than a few stiff-jointed gestures. For this reason Tynan and the men in his unit preferred flak vests. Each man also put on a pair of surgical gloves before he began handling the shopping bag so he wouldn't smudge any prints that might have been left by the bomber.

Max Kauffman followed the other men back out to the lobby and stood watching at the entrance to the aisle.

Tynan gave Jacobi a wink. "What do you say we see if this baby's pregnant?" He took a doctor's stethoscope from the black bag and fitted the earpieces to his head. "Just hold her nice and steady now," Tynan said. Jacobi took a firm grip on the handles of the shopping bag while Tynan listened intently, running the stethoscope's diaphragm carefully around the outside of the bag. He checked and rechecked for any ominous ticking before taking off the stethoscope. He nodded his head. "Beautiful," he murmured. "All is quiet." Now he knew that at least the package didn't contain a timing device. But it could still be booby-trapped.

"Gently, gently," he said to Jacobi. "We move the bag out and stand it up."

Both men were sweating profusely as they slid the shopping bag out from under the seat and set it upright on the floor of the aisle. They could see into it now. It contained a white cardboard cake box with "Coleman's Bakery" printed on top of it, and was tied around with twine.

Tynan took a single-edge razor blade from his black bag. Jacobi held the shopping bag at the top while Tynan split the bag open down both sides. They peeled down the two halves of the bag and flattened them around the cake box.

Tynan put the razor blade away and took out a knife with a long, sharp blade. Working cautiously, he cut a large round hole in the top of the box, carefully keeping the blade from touching the twine, and removed the cut-off section of cardboard with the tip of the knife. Through this hole they could see four large sticks of dynamite nestled side by side at the bottom of the box.

The dynamite was wrapped with strands of wire which were attached at one end to blasting caps embedded in the heads of the dynamite sticks and at the other end to two small metal clips which were, in turn, connected to two flashlight batteries. If the metal clips touched, current would flow through the wires to the blasting caps and explode the dynamite. The reason this hadn't happened yet was that one of the metal clips was pulled back and held in tension by a needle-thin wire. By lifting the cake box, Tynan could see a tiny hole in its bottom where the wire was hooked to the twine tied around the package. If the twine were untied or loosened, it would release the tension on the wire and the two metal clips would spring together and set off the dynamite.

Jacobi expelled his breath with a mournful sigh.

Tynan gave no sign he had heard the sound. He was concentrated totally on defusing the dynamite. He had reflected in the past that he seemed to function on two levels of awareness at times of stress like this. The sensation, he thought, was similar to his understanding of déjà vu—that curious sense of coming upon a person or a place or a scene for the first time which appears so intensely, yet elusively, familiar that one feels the experience must have been lived through before. He had once read a theory which set forth the hypothesis that this phenomenon was caused by a momentary lapse of memory; for a split second the brain lags while the eye is recording what it sees, then—an instant later—when the brain catches up again, the person or place or scene seems familiar because the eye has already taken it in.

In much the same way, Tynan felt during the times he was in danger while dismantling explosive devices that what he was doing was being done by a nerveless, competent stranger while he himself—the fear very real inside him—was distanced from the proceedings, observing what the stranger was doing and, a split second later, recognizing himself as the stranger.

He was working now with a pair of pliers which he carefully inserted into the cake box. He gripped the metal clip held in tension by the wire in the jaws of the pliers and snapped it off. There was no possibility now that the two metal clips could make contact and activate the current.

Before he could draw a breath of relief he had detected an equal danger: There was an unpleasant smell of mold emanating from the box. The sticks of dynamite were coated with beads of sweat, which meant that they were old and therefore unstable and could blow up at any time even without a detonator.

Tynan flicked the sweat from his forehead and said to Jacobi: "Get the carrier. Hurry!"

Jacobi left in a rush. Tynan remained settled on his haunches, staring hypnotically at the evil-looking TNT. It was, he thought, like staring at a rattlesnake coiled to strike—the dynamite could explode at any

61

moment—which could be provoked by any movement on his part.

It seemed a long time to him before Jacobi returned with Kelleher, the two of them carrying a large steel box between them. The bottom and sides of the box were thickly cushioned and padded with soft foam rubber. Working together, the three men lifted the cake box containing the dynamite and lowered it gently into the steel container.

Jacobi went ahead up the aisle, clearing people out of the way in the lobby of the theatre and on the sidewalk outside, while Tynan and Kelleher followed behind, lugging the steel box. By the time they reached the street, the bomb wagon had swung around and backed up to the curb and they deposited the box in the reinforced armored cage in the back of the vehicle. Tynan went around in front and got in the cab next to the driver. There was a wail of sirens as they pulled away, red warning lights flashing and, proceeded and followed by police cars, also flashing red lights, set out on the run to the Police Department's bomb disposal plant at Rodman's Neck in the Bronx where the dynamite would be safely detonated.

Max Kauffman had come out of the theatre to watch the bomb wagon leave. He knew that no one had yet been able to determine precisely just how powerful an explosion could be contained by the wagon's steel-layered cage. As the tail-lights of the vehicle disappeared up the street, all he could do was silently wish them a safe journey, to which he added, in Hebrew, *Alevai,*—I hope, I wish. . . .

Once the bomb wagon had gone, the searchlight on the emergency service truck was turned off, leaving the street in shadows. The crowd that had been watching from behind the barriers across the street began to drift away. The fire engines, the ambulance, and most of the police cars left, and the marquee lights on the front of the theatre went dark.

The squad car that had brought Max Kauffman was still waiting at the curb. As he crossed the sidewalk the chill wind stung his face and he was sure he could detect tiny ice crystals in the wind. It was probably snowing somewhere high up in the atmosphere, he thought, although the street pavements were dry.

If nothing else, the Inspector reflected wryly climbing into the back seat of the car, the Department sure knew how to put on one hell of a pony-and-dog show. He was pleased with the aptness of the phrase. Yet with all their trained horses and dogs and machines and manpower and scientific equipment, all they'd been able to do was haul the lousy bomb away and blow it up. And all that time, the madman behind it all freely roamed the streets of the city.

On the ride back to his apartment, he wanted a smoke but in his weariness the simple act of taking a cigar from his pocket and lighting it didn't seem worth the effort.

CHAPTER SEVEN

The note lying on Max Kauffman's desk at the 16th Precinct was crudely composed of cut-out printed letters:

The note, in an envelope addressed with the same kind of cut-out letters, had been dumped into a mail slot in the lobby of the *Daily News* sometime during the previous night, Thanksgiving night. The editors of the newspaper had contacted the police and turned the note and envelope over to them after reproducing the note on the front page of Friday morning's edition of the *Daily News*. The lead story in the paper was an account of the two Thanksgiving Day bomb incidents. The *Daily News* had also already coined a name, "The Christmas Bomber," for the anonymous writer of the note. Max Kauffman had found the note, the envelope, and a copy of the newspaper on his desk—where the night desk sergeant had placed them—when he arrived at the station house at 8 A.M.

Before he left his apartment that morning he had checked with the precinct and received a report that the bomb removed from Radio City Music Hall had been safely detonated at the Bronx bomb disposal plant shortly after midnight. The first thing he did when he reached his office was call down and ask John Tynan to come up. Then he sat at his desk, scanned the *Daily News* story of the two bombs, and read the note. While he was reading, he called French Hospital and was told Patrolman Yost's condition was unchanged. He was rereading the bomber's note when there was a knock on the door and John Tynan came into the office. Tynan was fresh-shaven and wore a change of clothes from the night before, but there were dark shadows of fatigue under his eyes.

"Have some coffee," Max Kauffman said. "How'd it go with the bomb last night?"

Tynan poured himself a cup of coffee from the silver pot sitting on a corner of the desk. "I had my gut sucked in the whole time. That dynamite was so rotten it reeked like Roquefort cheese. Whoever the creep is, he's living dangerously. We should be so lucky he'll blow his own head off. I'm thankful that last night it held until we blew it."

"Did everything go?" Max Kauffman asked.

"There was no way we could touch the wires and junk he had hooked up to it. But we saved the cake box and shopping bag. They're in the lab. There may be a lead there. And I've got a man checking the bakery, Coleman's, where the box came from." He nodded at the note and the copy of the *Daily News* lying on the Inspector's desk. "I saw the paper earlier. You think the note's authentic?"

"Yeah, I think so," Max Kauffman said. He lit a cigar. " 'This is only the second day of Christmas,' " he quoted from the note. "What do you suppose the son of a bitch means by that? The Twelve Days of Christ-

66

mas? And we're in for ten more days? Or ten more bombings?"

"Or he's trying to make us think so."

Max Kauffman glanced at the newspaper. "'The Christmas Bomber.' I guess it's as good a name as any to call him." He drummed his fingers on the desk. Thinking aloud, he said, "Why the parade and Radio City Music Hall? What's the connection? Simply because he knew they were sure to get him attention— or is there more to it? It's pretty far-fetched to think that it's because both of them are part of the holiday season scene in the city. And yet that *could* tie in with the Christmas mumbo jumbo he mentioned in his note." He grunted. "There's nothing for it except to wait and see if a pattern emerges."

"If you agree," Tynan said, "I'm going to call off any investigation of ex-employees or customers of Macy's. The Music Hall thing seems to eliminate any leads we might get on people with grudges against the store. This case looks different and bigger than that."

"I agree," Max Kauffman said. "Let's concentrate on previous bomb-case suspects and participants who can't account for their time night before last, yesterday, and last night."

Tynan nodded. "I've already got the men out making the rounds. They have orders to bring in anybody on the list who doesn't have an alibi."

"Good, good." Max Kauffman leaned forward in his chair. "Look, I had a thought last night. Now we've had two incidents, right? What do you think—if we do come across any suspects who can't account for their time, we put them in a lineup later today? And we ask in some of the people who were involved with the preparations for the parade, when *that* bomb had to have been planted, and some of the Music Hall people—ushers, cashiers, and the like—who were on duty yesterday and last night. If one of the suspects is our man, somebody may remember having seen him at one place or the other, or both. It's a long shot but we could conceivably get an ID. You know?"

"I like the idea," Tynan said. "I'll set it up."

"There are two guys you ought to contact about possible witnesses," Max Kauffman said. "One's the chief accountant at Macy's. Ernest Guthridge's his name. And there's an assistant manager at Radio City. I can't remember his name but Sergeant Tolkin'll know."

Tynan set his empty coffee cup down on the desk. "You finished with the note and envelope? Want me to send them to the lab?"

The note and envelope were in a manila file folder so if there were any prints on the paper they'd be preserved. The Inspector closed the folder and handed it to Tynan. "There's one other thing," Max Kauffman said. "Headquarters is sending over the tape of the bomber's phone call. I think everyone working on the case should hear it."

Tynan knew that all calls made to the 911 number were automatically taped. He nodded and left.

The Inspector decided he'd better start preparing an investigation report on the bombings for the Commissioner. He decided against calling in the policewoman who had been temporarily assigned to him and who sat at the desk just outside his office. He would use his dictaphone instead. The policewoman, Florence MacKay, was filling in for Sergeant Margaret O'Dell who was regularly assigned to him but who was on a month's leave of absence. MacKay was a buxom blonde in her late twenties who had a forceful manner that grated on his nerves. He tried to avoid her as much as possible since she would, thank God, only be there temporarily. He did, however, dislike this additional upsetting of his sense of order. He knew he would find Sergeant O'Dell's absence particularly disturbing if the bombings turned into a major case.

He began to compose his thoughts as he reached for the dictaphone. He was pleased with the idea for holding a lineup because, although he didn't really expect anything to come of it, it would help pad out his report to the Commissioner.

Shortly before 6 P.M. Tynan began assembling his witnesses in a room in the basement of the station house where the lineup would be held. There were nine witnesses present—Guthridge and two other men, Plower and Jackman, who had worked on the parade; the assistant manager from Radio City Music Hall, Hartz; two women cashiers, a Miss Weldon and a Mrs. Falk; and three male ushers at the theatre, Stone, Weiner, and MacLaine.

The room was long and narrow. At one end was a raised wooden platform which extended from one side of the room to the other. Directly in front of the platform were four spotlights, and behind the spotlights a number of folding chairs had been set up in rows. There was a door opposite one end of the raised platform through which the suspects would be brought into the room and taken out. Tynan seated the witnesses in the first row of chairs. Pennell, Braxley, and Manders of the 16th Bomb Unit drifted in and took seats in the rear rows. A detective named Robling manned the spotlights.

Max Kauffman came in, chewing on an unlighted cigar, and took a seat next to Tynan just before Robling turned off the overhead room lights and switched on the spotlights, focusing the harsh, glaring beams of light on the raised platform. There was a moment of hushed expectancy in the room, then the door opened and Detective Cohen of the bomb squad herded the suspects through and lined them up across the platform.

There were seven suspects in the lineup, six men and a woman. Mixed in among them were three 16th Precinct plainclothes detectives and two policewomen dressed in street clothes. All twelve people, suspects and police officers alike, blinked their eyes and seemed to cringe slightly, instinctively, when they were caught in the brilliant beams of the spotlights. Max Kauffman felt a twinge of sympathy as he studied the twelve faces intently. Goddamn if they didn't all look guilty—of something.

Tynan leaned close to the Inspector and whispered, "The third guy from the door, recognize him?"

Max Kauffman looked at the man, a stoop-shouldered individual with a puffy face who kept bobbing his head up and down, a vacuous, nervous smile flickering on his lips.

"Remember him?" Tynan asked.

Max Kauffman shook his head; he had no memory of ever having seen the man before.

"That's Demowski," Tynan said. "You remember: Teodor Demowski."

"Yeah, I remember," Max Kauffman said. It was the first case he and Tynan had worked on together. But the man had aged so that he hadn't known him.

"We bagged him in the roundup of suspects," Tynan whispered. "They just released him from Matteawan a week or so ago. He's on probation. They may try to bring him to trial but I doubt it."

There was another moment of silence in the room while the people on the raised platform shuffled their feet nervously. Tynan let the silence go on for another few seconds before he raised his voice and said: "Starting with the man nearest the door, I want each of you in turn to take one step forward, state your name in a loud, clear voice and tell us what you were doing on the night before last, the night before Thanksgiving, on Thanksgiving Day itself, and Thanksgiving night. All right, you, the first man."

Detective Cohen prodded the man nearest the door forward. He stood squinting out into the darkness of the room behind the spotlights and said haltingly, "Name's Frank Laughton. I was home alone night before last. Yesterday I went out and took a walk by myself. I ate my supper at a Beef and Brew place on Madison Avenue. Somewhere around Fifty-ninth, Sixtieth, I think. Then I went home. I was alone again."

After the man had completed his statement Tynan leaned forward and asked each witness in front of him if the man looked familiar. All of them said no. Tynan asked the next man to step forward.

One by one each of the people on the platform went through the same routine and each time the witnesses repeated that they didn't recognize the individual—until the last man in the lineup stepped forward and spoke. This time one of the cashiers from Radio City, Mrs. Falk, turned in her seat and whispered hesitantly, "I think—I'm not sure—but there's something about that man that looks familiar to me."

"You're *sure*, Mrs. Falk?" Tynan asked.

"I—it's—well, I'm *sure* there's something familiar-looking about him."

Tynan nodded. "Yes, thank you, Mam. We'll check into it."

"It's *something* about him, something. . . ." Her voice trailed off.

Max Kauffman had been listening in, and after Mrs. Falk turned back in her seat, he and Tynan glanced at the man in the lineup. Tynan looked at Max Kauffman and shrugged; the man the theatre cashier had thought looked familiar was Desk Sergeant Hanlon. Hanlon had just gone off duty and was on his way out when Detective Cohen grabbed him to go into the lineup. Hanlon's expression had been dour throughout the proceedings and Max Kauffman thought it was his expression that caught the cashier's eye and led to the misidentification. But there was no question about the misidentification; Hanlon had been on duty at the station house during the holiday period.

Tynan leaned close to the Inspector and whispered: "A good example of a civilian trying to be helpful." Tynan stood, ending the lineup, and Sergeant Cohen led the people off the platform. The spotlights were switched off and the overhead lights in the room turned on. While the witnesses were milling around, preparing to leave, a phone rang in the rear of the room. Detective Manders picked it up and, after listening, hurried toward Max Kauffman and Tynan. Tynan was thanking the witnesses for their time and Max Kauffman was nodding to them as they put on their coats and hats. Manders interrupted, pulling Max Kauffman and Tynan to one side. "The desk sergeant just called down," Manders said in a low voice. "There's a guy came in and says he wants to confess he's the bomber."

Max Kauffman and Tynan turned to go upstairs but were blocked by the theatre cashier, Mrs. Falk, who grabbed Tynan's arm. "It just came to me what it was that looked familiar about that man a few minutes ago. It wasn't *him* that looked familiar, now that I remember. It was what he was wearing. I mean it reminded me of this man I saw several times around the box office early last night. I'd forgotten all about it. But he kept hanging around the theatre, then he'd disappear and come back again. Finally he bought a ticket and went in. What made me think of him was that that fellow you showed us just a few minutes ago was wearing the same kind of coat, a black raincoat."

Max Kauffman and Tynan listened courteously, thanked the woman, and hurried away. Both of them were anxious to question the man who had just come in upstairs, and neither of them ever gave another thought to the woman's words.

"All right, have a seat," Tynan said to the man who wanted to confess. Tynan and the man sat on opposite sides of a small table in the interrogation room. Detectives Pennell, Manders, and Braxley were also in the room, leaning against a wall behind Tynan. Max Kauffman was silently prowling from one end of the room to the other. Tynan switched on a tape recorder.

"Would you please state your full name, age, address, and occupation."

The man nodded. "My name is Charles Frederick Pauker. P-a-u-k-e-r. I am thirty-three years old. I live in Apartment C at Eleven-O-Nine Barrow Street in Greenwich Village. I am unemployed."

"You know your statement is being recorded?"

"Yes."

"You've been advised that you have a right to a lawyer before you make any statement, and if you don't have a lawyer, you'll be provided with one?"

"Yes."

"And you understand that anything you say here can also be used against you in court?"

"Yes."

"All right, then," Tynan said, "what is it you want to tell us?"

Pauker closed his eyes for a moment. He was a tall, very thin man, with a narrow face that tapered down to an almost nonexistent chin. His eyes were pale blue and he had big ears and a large Adam's apple. He was wearing a white shirt, black tie, and blue serge suit that was shiny from wear and needed pressing.

He opened his eyes and said in a firm voice: "I want to confess that I am the bomber. I was responsible for those bombs."

"What bombs?" Tynan asked.

"The bomb in the parade. The bomb at Radio City Music Hall."

"Tell us about the bombs. What were they like?"

"They were bombs. Dynamite. I made them."

"Made them out of what?"

"Dynamite, I told you. Explosives."

"Gelignite, is that correct?" Tynan asked.

"Gelig—" the man hesitated, thought for a moment and said, "I'm not going to answer that."

"Why not?"

"You're trying to trick me."

"Trick you into what?" Tynan asked reasonably.

There was a kind of weary desperation in Pauker's voice as he said: "Why are you asking me all these questions? I told you I did it. *I'm the bomber.*"

"Where did you hide the bomb that exploded during the parade?"

Pauker looked bewildered. Then he said carefully, "I hid it inside the balloon, of course."

There was silence in the room.

Max Kauffman had stopped his pacing and was staring out a window, his back to the room. He could feel the cold seeping in around the edges of the window. Darkness had come sometime earlier. The day had been overcast but there'd been no snow, although

73

he'd been expecting it since early morning. There was a loud sob in the room behind him. He turned and saw tears streaming down Pauker's face.

"*Why won't you believe me?*" Pauker asked in a broken whisper. "God told me I am guilty. His voice came to me. He said I must be punished for what I did. I don't always remember what I do. But I must have done it if God said I did." He lowered his head to his arms which were supported by the table top and wept softly.

Max Kauffman crossed to the table and put a hand gently on the man's shoulder. "It's all right, Charles. We're going to get someone to listen to you, someone who'll believe you, someone who can help you."

Pauker suddenly flung Max Kauffman's hand away and came up out of the chair with a swiftness that surprised everyone in the room. His face was contorted as he sprang at Max Kauffman and clutched him around the neck with both hands. Max Kauffman stumbled backward, gasping for breath as the man's fingers closed around his throat. Pauker was amazingly strong for such a frail-looking man. The Inspector could feel the spray of saliva on his face as Pauker shouted obscenities at him. Max Kauffman was fighting for breath, fighting against losing consciousness, lashing out blindly with both fists.

Then Tynan and Pennell were on top of Pauker, trying to pull him away. Manders and Braxley joined them. Manders got a hammerlock on Pauker's head. It took the combined strength of all four of them to haul Pauker across the room while he clung to Max Kauffman's throat, dragging the Inspector with them. They finally wrestled the man down backward across the table and Manders grabbed a handful of Pauker's hair and pounded his head against the table top. It was only then that the man released his grip on Max Kauffman's throat.

The Inspector staggered over to a chair. He clutched it with one hand for support and rubbed his throat with his other hand, his chest heaving as he struggled to force air into his lungs. Pennell, Manders, and Braxley held Pauker pinned to the table while Tynan grabbed the phone, called the desk for additional men, and then phoned Bellevue.

Within seconds the interrogation room was filled with police officers. It took seven men to subdue Pauker long enough to handcuff his arms behind his back and put leg irons on him. When he still kept struggling, they lifted him bodily and carried him out of the room, his heels dragging across the floor, to lock him up in a cell.

"You all right?" Tynan asked, going over to Max Kauffman.

The Inspector could only nod his head. He was still rubbing his throat.

Tynan looked at him closely. "You want me to get you a doctor? Anything I can get you?"

Max Kauffman shook his head emphatically and managed to say hoarsely: "All . . . right . . . I'm all . . . right." He gestured for Tynan to follow him and they left the room.

They rode the elevator to the third floor in silence. When they got to his office, Max Kauffman went over to a cabinet behind his desk and poured himself a pony glass of Napoleon brandy. He filled a second glass for Tynan. They both drank. Max Kauffman emptied his glass in a couple of gulps, shuddered, and coughed. He unlocked his desk drawer, took out his .38 and jammed it back into the holster under his coat; like all police officers he was required to carry the weapon except when questioning suspects in the interrogation room where such a suspect might try to grab the gun. He'd locked the .38 in the desk before he'd gone down to the interrogation room.

He shook his head, cleared his throat and, still hoarse but now able to talk, said: "I know that poor son of a bitch is sick and all that, and I'm supposed to feel sorry for him. But he almost killed me. If I'd been wearing my gun, I'd have shot him dead on the spot. And of course he's not the bomber."

"No," Tynan said, "I think we can be sure about that."

Max Kauffman crossed to a tape recorder sitting

75

on a window sill. "I want you to hear that taped nine-one-one phone call from the bomber." He'd already threaded the tape into the recorder. He turned it on.

OPERATOR:	Police Operator.
VOICE:	I want you to know there's a bomb planted in Radio City Music Hall. It's there now and it's going to go off.
OPERATOR:	Radio City Music Hall?
VOICE:	That's it.
OPERATOR:	Hold on. Who—
SOUND:	Click
OPERATOR:	Hello. Hello.

Max Kauffman switched off the recorder. "It's not much," he said, "but have the men listen to it."

"Right," Tynan said. "Yeah." He unplugged the recorder and picked it up.

"I'm going to check out," Max Kauffman said. "If anything new comes up, we'll be in touch. Otherwise, I'll see you Monday."

After Tynan had gone, Max Kauffman cleared off his desk and put on his storm coat. He decided it hadn't been a completely wasted day. They'd eliminated a number of suspects, and there'd be others; the lab was sure to provide them with some leads and meanwhile, so far the Commissioner had stayed off his back, and they'd gone through a whole day with no new bombings or threats. If Kit Devereaux had been home he could have spent the evening with her. He was sorry she wouldn't be back until Monday.

On his way through the precinct lobby, Max Kauffman saw two white-jacketed attendants from Bellevue leading Charles Pauker out of the station house. They had strapped Pauker into a straitjacket. He went docilely, probably because they had also already shot him full of something, Max Kauffman decided. He rubbed his throat reflectively and went outside, pausing in the cold, clear air. He breathed deeply, then walked slowly toward his waiting car.

CHAPTER EIGHT

Monday morning Max Kauffman was late getting to the precinct. He had slept soundly the night before, but though he felt refreshed and well rested when he awakened for the first time at 6 A.M., he had stayed in bed for another hour and a half dozing. He seldom indulged in such a luxury. This morning, however, warm as he was under the covers, he could feel that it was a bitter cold day outside which made it even more pleasant to stay in bed, drifting between sleep and wakefulness, between dreaming and daydreaming, in the thin, washed-out light of what he knew was another sunless morning.

His throat had been tender on Saturday and showed faint bruise marks, but by Sunday he felt no discomfort and had forgotten all about the attack on him at the station house on Friday.

The weekend had passed pleasantly enough for him, if a bit dull. There had been no further bombings, for which he was thankful, and Saturday evening, after spending a few hours catching up on paperwork at the station house, he had gone with his wife, Belle, to the Metropolitan Opera where they had seen a performance of *Don Pasquale*. On Sunday he spent the afternoon with his father, had reassured the old man that everything was going to be all right with the family business and had promised, at his father's insistence, that he would have a talk with his two brothers-in-law. He felt both touched and a trifle ashamed of himself when his father repeated over and over again his gratitude for the visit. Nor did it matter that he knew full well that the old man was, as he always did, deliberately playing on his sympathy and sense of guilt.

All in all, he was satisfied with the weekend which had afforded him the opportunity to fulfill his familial responsibilities. Now he felt he could free his mind of them for a while.

Another reason for his reluctance to stir himself this morning was that he dreaded the day to come. He had what his kids would call "bad vibes" that there would be another bomb incident before the day was over. It was like waiting for the other shoe to drop.

At 7:30, however, he got up, shaved, showered, and dressed, then ate a large breakfast of juice, oatmeal, steak and eggs, toast and two cups of coffee which Anna prepared for him. Belle was still asleep and he ate alone in the dining room, skipped reading the papers, and instead looked out at the choppy East River below. The river was always busy at the beginning and end of each month, as it was now, with tankers heading north and south, in addition to the normal shipping, the freighters, a few private boats, the tugs, the constantly patrolling police boats, and, in the air, police helicopters. While he was eating, he watched three seaplanes land downriver at the Twenty-third Street and East River pier, bringing morning commuters into the city. Today the sky and water were the same slate gray color.

His regular driver, Detective Henry Lukin, was back on duty and waiting for him with the car when he got downstairs. It was after nine when he reached the station house. Policewoman MacKay was at her desk outside his office. She was talking on the phone and looked disheveled. She waved a batch of messages at him. Tynan, who had been waiting to see him, followed when Max Kauffman took the messages and went into his office.

"Looks like it's going to be one of those days," Tynan said.

Max Kauffman grunted and thumbed through the messages. The Commissioner had called at 8. Howard Williams, a reporter for *The New York Times*, called at 8:29, newsmen from ABC, CBS, NBC, and four local TV stations had called at 8:32, 8:35, 8:37, 8:39, 8:42, 8:45, and 9:00. The Commissioner called at 8:45, a reporter for the *Daily News* called at 8:30, and another reporter, this one from the *New York Post*, called at 8:50. There were also calls from three other precinct commanders. On both Saturday and Sunday, the media—television, radio, and newspapers —had carried big stories on the two bombings. Although Max Kauffman had made sure all the information on the bomb case came from the office of the Deputy Police Commissioner for Public Affairs, he, Max Kauffman, had been identified in the news accounts as being in charge of the case.

He knew the newsmen wanted to talk to him personally but he had no intention of dealing with them directly. He buzzed for Policewoman MacKay and when she came in, handed her back all the messages from the media people.

"I want you to return each of these calls," he said, "and tell them that there will be no statement from me. Whatever information they want must come from the Deputy Police Commissioner for Public Affairs."

Policewoman MacKay held up some more messages. "I have additional calls that have just come in from reporters for the radio stations. You want me to tell them the same thing; is that correct, sir?"

"That's correct," he said. "Plug in the coffee pot," he said to Tynan, and then began dialing the Police Commissioner. While he was dialing, he asked Tynan: "Any new developments for me to pass on to the Commissioner?"

Tynan shook his head. "Nothing earth-shaking. A couple of things I want to talk to you about first. The investigation is continuing. I'll have a progress report for you this afternoon which you can pass on to him."

Commissioner Hilliard came on the other end of the line. "Inspector Kauffman?"

"Yes, sir."

"Any new leads on this bomber thing?"

"The investigation is proceeding. I'll have an up-to-date report on your desk this afternoon," Max Kauffman said.

"I know you and your men are going all out on the case," the Commissioner said. "I wanted you to know, however, that I'm particularly eager to apprehend this individual before we get a panic situation in the city. You understand, with the holiday shopping period coming up, the Department is already under some pressure from the retail business community to stop the bombings. You can imagine, there's great concern that potential shoppers may be frightened away from the city if there are more occurrences."

Max Kauffman nodded to himself. "Yes sir, I can appreciate that." He could understand something else as well, not mentioned by the Commissioner; John Kenyan Hilliard had been appointed by Mayor Andrew Forester. There had been a mayoral election in Manhattan just a few weeks earlier and Forester had been defeated. Hilliard was, therefore, a lame-duck commissioner and certainly any chances he had for reappointment would go down the drain if the bombings continued until the new mayor took office in January.

"There's another reason I phoned you earlier," the Commissioner said. "I had several conversations over the weekend with Doctor Luther Myles. He has some theories about the bomber, about the kind of man he might be, that I think you and your men should hear. He can be at your precinct at three this afternoon. Is that satisfactory?"

"Yes, sir," Max Kauffman said: Dr. Luther Myles was the police psychiatrist.

"Good," the Commissioner said. "I'll be waiting for that report." He hung up.

"The Commissioner wants us to listen to some of Luther Myles' theories about the bomber," Max Kauffman said to Tynan. "He'll be here at three. We'll meet in the lineup room. Try to get as large a turnout as you can."

"Right," Tynan said.

Max Kauffman and Tynan conferred for the next hour on developments which had occurred during the weekend. Police had set up a special phone number for callers who had any information on the two specific bomb cases, and the number was being widely circulated by newspapers, TV, and radio. There had been seventy-five bomb-scare calls to the 911 number and the special phone number on Saturday, fifty-five on Sunday. Four more people had confessed to being the bomber and were undergoing psychiatric tests at Bellevue, and a check was being made on their backgrounds. "None of them appears to be our man," Tynan observed. The lab had definitely established that gasoline and black gunpowder had been used in the bombing of the parade balloon. The other components of that bomb were some kind of plastic bottle, a small metal can, a clock, probably a small alarm clock, and a transistor radio battery. There were no fingerprints on the shopping bag or the cake box. The bakery the cake box came from was on Ninth Avenue, in the Fifties, but there was no way of determining who had purchased whatever was in the box, or whether the box had merely been picked up by the bomber out of some garbage left on the street. The investigation was continuing.

"In other words, we're not too far from where we first started," Max Kauffman said philosophically.

Tynan agreed. "There is one other thing," he said hesitantly. "Over the weekend I went through every file I could find which might turn out to have some bearing on the case." He paused and added half-apologetically: "I always try to operate on the theory that you never know where you may get a lead, however unconnected it may appear to be."

"Go on, go on," Max Kauffman said impatiently.

Tynan frowned. "Well, this one is pretty far out. It concerns one of the 'converted' cars being used by members of the Intelligence Division."

Max Kauffman nodded. At almost any given time the Department had for its use over five hundred "converted" vehicles; that is, cars and trucks that came into police possession after they were abandoned in the streets or seized as evidence for having been used in criminal cases. Police frequently converted such vehicles for their own use because they were less easily recognized than even standard unmarked police cars.

"This particular car," Tynan went on, "is a five-year-old Mercedes sedan. It was found abandoned on the West Side Highway four weeks ago. It had a busted crankshaft and the license plates had been stripped off. The only reason there's any mention of it in bomb squad files is because when the Department first recovered it, the lab boys did a routine dusting job on it and found traces of black gunpowder on the floor of the back seat. What attracted my attention was that the gunpowder was composed of the same elements as were used in the gunpowder which set off the explosion in the parade balloon—charcoal, sulfur, and potassium perchlorate. They also lifted a dozen or more fingerprints from the interior of the car."

"Of course they tried to run a trace on the car?" Max Kauffman interjected.

"Sure," Tynan said. "But it didn't go anywhere. Somebody had done an expert job of wiping out the engine serial numbers. Evidence indicated it had been done recently. Because of the traces of gunpowder found, a flyer was sent out to all units. When nobody seemed interested, the Intelligence boys converted it for their own use."

"And the fingerprints?" Max Kauffman asked.

Tynan spread his hands in the air. "No check was made on them. It didn't seem important at the time. It may not be important now. But this morning I got a copy of all the prints found in the car and sent them on to the FBI Identification Division in Washington. Which means if we're lucky we may get an answer—eventually."

Max Kauffman smiled thinly, thinking, as he sometimes did, what a vast difference there was between the public view of the scientific efficiency of police work and the actual truth; knowing as he did that the FBI received over twenty thousand requests for fingerprint identifications a year, which meant that even, in this age of the computer, such checks of fingerprints where the person was unknown had to be made manually, and that could take weeks.

"It may be just another dead end. . . ." Tynan let his words trail off.

"So," Max Kauffman said encouragingly, "you try one thing and if it doesn't work out, you try another. That's the nature of our business."

On his way out the door Tynan said, "I'll see to it we have a large representation at the three o'clock meeting with Myles."

Max Kauffman phoned French Hospital and was informed that Patrolman Yost's condition was unchanged. He put in calls to the three precinct commanders who had phoned him earlier. Each offered whatever help he could give. The Inspector especially appreciated the offers because they were made outside official channels.

Just before noon his private phone rang. He took the instrument out of the desk drawer and answered it. Catherine Devereaux said: "Good morning. Can you talk?"

"I love you," he said.

Her delighted laugh came to him from the other end of the line. "I guess you can talk all right," she said. "I'm back, and I love you, too."

"How was your weekend?"

"I missed you most dreadfully. When will I see you?"

Now he laughed. "That's what I wanted to hear. I'm all yours after six."

"I'll be waiting," she said softly.

Tynan brought in his investigation progress report and left it. Max Kauffman sent Detective Lukin, his driver, over to Rosoff's Restaurant for a tuna fish salad plate and a bottle of beer and ate lunch at his desk while going over Tynan's report. As he finished each page, he passed it on to Policewoman MacKay for final typing. At ten to three the report was finished and on its way to the Commissioner and Max Kauffman went down to attend the meeting with Police Psychiatrist Luther Myles.

True to his word, Tynan had managed to gather together an audience of twenty-three men from the precinct, not all of whom were assigned to the case, although seven of the detectives working directly on the bombings—Raucher, Garibaldi, Walsh, Doheny, Cortez, Riggins, and Beelin—were present. The other five bomb squad detectives were out on the investigation. Max Kauffman decided that there were enough men present so he shouldn't get any gripes from the Commissioner about a lack of interest at the precinct in what the psychiatrist had to say.

The men sat in the folding chairs where the witnesses at Friday's lineup had sat, and Dr. Myles perched on the edge of the wooden platform where the bomb suspects had been paraded on Friday. Max Kauffman took a seat alone toward the rear of the room and lit a cigar.

The police psychiatrist was a man of medium height, in his late forties or early fifties. He had a strong face, firm chin and mouth, and dark brown hair graying at the temples. He was dressed conservatively in a gray suit of soft flannel. As he talked he chain-smoked king-size filter cigarettes through a long cigarette holder.

The psychiatrist told them that what he was attempting to do was to create a rough "psychological composite" picture of the kind of man the bomber might be, based on past behavioral patterns drawn from other bomb cases.

The bomber was, Dr. Myles said, likely to be a man between forty-five and fifty-five. He had probably recently suffered an injury to his ego, felt frustrated, persecuted, was likely to be seriously psychotically paranoid, although this would not necessarily be evident to those around him. The bombings were an attempt to gain both attention for himself and punish those—possibly all of society—he believed had wronged him. He was full of hostility. He probably had a serious sexual maladjustment—"the explosion of the bombs might easily provide him with a form of sexual gratification"—and a loner. He probably brooded a lot, particularly about his sexual inadequacies, and "in commiting the public act of bombing was demanding that he be recognized and acknowledged for having done something, even if it was reprehensible and destructive. Remember the way he signed the note 'The Bomber.' He has now shed his former self and assumed a new identity—'The Bomber.' "

Max Kauffman puffed on his cigar, his attention wandering now and then. When the phone rang in the back of the room, he knew that was what he had been waiting to hear. He walked quickly to the phone and picked it up. Dr. Myles had stopped talking, and it was quiet in the room. Most of the men had turned in their seats and were watching the Inspector.

"Inspector Kauffman."

The 16th Precinct dispatcher on the other end of the line said: "Inspector, we just got a report from Unit Twenty-seven Edward. There's what looks like the bombing of a car in front of address ten-zero-two West Fifty-first Street. Unit is on the scene and has called for fire equipment. Unit advises one man trapped in car—dead—is Detective Al Manders, this precinct."

"Tell Unit Twenty-seven we're on the way," Max Kauffman ordered. He hung up the phone and looked toward the front of the room. "Al Manders was just killed. It looks like his car was bombed over on West Fifty-first Street." He hurried from the room. The other men followed quickly behind him.

Max Kauffman, Tynan, and Detective Garibaldi rode together to West Fifty-first Street. Six other cars, carrying additional members of the bomb squad, followed them. The address on West Fifty-first Street was in the middle of the block. More police cars, two fire engines, and a Police Department ambulance clogged the street. The bombed car was pulled over to the curb with the driver's seat nearest the sidewalk. Its hood was up and firemen were hosing down the motor with water and chemicals through the clouds of smoke. The rest of the car was intact, which meant that the gas tank hadn't exploded.

When Max Kauffman got closer to the car, he saw that the windshield had been blown out and so had the front window on the passenger side. The door on

85

that side had also buckled and wouldn't open. The buildings on the street were a mixture of ancient brownstones and shops, grocery stores, shoe repair shop, a dry cleaner's, a candy store. People had come out on the sidewalks to watch, but police kept them well back from the smoking car.

The Inspector walked around to the driver's side of the car where two firemen and the two uniformed patrolmen from car 27 were trying to open the jammed door with a crowbar. Peering over their shoulders, Max Kauffman got his first view into the interior of the car and instinctively recoiled in shock.

The force of the explosion had wedged Manders' upper torso against the door in the space between the door and the steering wheel, on the driver's side of the car. His face was flattened against the rolled-up window, which hadn't shattered, and the dead eyes were open, staring blindly out through the glass. The eyes were still clear blue, untroubled, and they had a moist shine like the button eyes of toy animals.

"Jesus!" Max Kauffman said hoarsely. "Get him out of there."

One of the patrolmen working with the crowbar turned his head impatiently, opened his mouth to say something, saw it was the Inspector standing behind him, and went on with his work. They pried at the door with the crowbar for another minute or two and it finally gave, slowly, grudgingly, then swung wide open.

"Oh, my God!" one of the firemen yelled as a deep pool of blood which had been dammed up on the floorboards in the front seat of the car overflowed into the street soaking the bottoms of their trousers. Manders had been blown in half at the waist, with the upper part of his body wedged into the seat, while the lower half lay on the floor. Max Kauffman found himself absurdly calculating from his knowledge of physiology that the average human body, at a weight of 156 pounds, contains thirteen pints of blood. Therefore, the blood from Manders' roughly 190-pound-body equalled about sixteen pints, which accounted for the copious overflow into the street.

From the interior of the car police recovered pieces of white cardboard similar to the cardboard cake box found in Radio City Music Hall. Manders' .38 was also found on the floor of the car. It had not been fired.

The Inspector steeled himself against the grisly sight of the remains and began issuing terse commands. The sections of the corpse were swiftly removed from the car, wrapped in rubber sheets, and placed in the ambulance for the trip to the morgue. A radio call to the 16th Precinct brought a tow truck quickly. As it towed the car away, firemen were washing down the street with hoses and flushing the stained water down a curbside drain.

Max Kauffman then directed police officers from the 16th Precinct to fan out through the neighborhood and try to piece together the events which had led up to Detective Manders' death. He stayed on the scene, using a squad car as a command post, and questioned possible witnesses who lived on the block.

Within an hour Max Kauffman believed he had enough facts to surmise what had happened. His detectives, reporting back to him, had learned through the questioning of shopkeepers and others in a several-block area around the scene that Manders had been working his way up and down the streets around Coleman's Bakery, asking everyone he came across if they had noticed anyone in the neighborhood carrying a cake box or brown shopping bag recently. That was a fact. And what Max Kauffman and the other officers guessed was that Manders, while making his investigation, must have actually spotted just such a man carrying a cake box and ordered him over to the car. The man had apparently been the bomber and it appeared Manders had taken the cake box into the car. The bomb had either been wired to a time detonator or rigged to go off when the box was touched in some way. It had exploded and the bomber had escaped.

Although there was confusion and fear on the street when the bomb exploded, several witnesses testified that they saw a man running away from

Manders' car at the time of the explosion. They had been so shocked by the blast that none of them was able to give an accurate description of the fleeing man. Most were able to agree, however, that he was wearing a dark coat or jacket—one man thought it was a black raincoat. The witnesses were taken back to the station house to make statements. Max Kauffman and the other police officers also returned to the station house.

When they reached the precinct, the desk sergeant reported to Max Kauffman that he had just been notified by Headquarters that both the *Daily News* and the 911 number had had a phone call from a man who identified himself as the bomber. The message was the same in both cases: "It's the third day of Christmas."

Al Manders had been a bachelor who lived with his family in Riverdale. Tynan dispatched Garibaldi and Cohen to inform them of his death.

"Goddamn it," Tynan said sadly. "Al was a good man."

"I know it," Max Kauffman said, and then added softly: "We're going to nail this son-of-a-bitching bomber. I don't know how or when but we're not going to give up. I guarantee it."

The phrase "black raincoat" used by witnesses at the scene of the bombed car struck a responsive chord in Max Kauffman's memory. The same words had been used by the Radio City Music Hall cashier, Mrs. Falk, to describe the garment worn by the man she had noticed hanging around outside the theatre on Thanksgiving Day. The Inspector requested Tynan to have one of his men question the cashier again to see whether she could add to her description of the man.

While Max Kauffman and Tynan were still conferring in the Inspector's office, painters began arriving to start painting the office that night. Then the phone rang and the desk sergeant said the 31st Precinct had just called to advise they had in custody another man who wanted to confess that he was the bomber.

Max Kauffman hung up the phone and said to

Tynan: "I'm going to dictate a short report on Al Manders' death for the Commissioner. Then I'm getting out of this nuthouse for the night. I want you to leave, too, now! That's an order. We'll pick it up again tomorrow."

Tynan left gladly. He had an important date with Barbara Costa that evening and he was determined he wasn't going to let the events of the day spoil it.

Max Kauffman wrote out his report on two sheets of a yellow legal pad and gave them to Officer Florence MacKay to type and send to the Commissioner. Afterward, he phoned his wife and told her he was tied up on the bombing case and didn't know when he'd get home. As a precaution, before he left the station house, he got a signal beeper from the radio dispatcher to carry with him in his coat pocket. He'd be with Catherine Devereaux, out of touch with the precinct, and if there was an emergency—God forbid—the dispatcher could signal him with the beeper and he'd call in. He dismissed his driver and took a cab over to his barbershop at Times Square and Forty-seventh Street for a shave and facial massage before he continued on to Catherine Devereaux's apartment.

Soon after nightfall, an hour earlier, it had started to sleet and the street pavements were wet and slippery, reflecting dark, blurred images of the flashing electric signs of Times Square.

CHAPTER NINE

Tynan had been planning this night for the past couple of weeks. It was the anniversary of the first date he and Barbara Costa had had, and he wanted to make it a special occasion. The problem was solved for him when he read in the papers that Mel Torme was appearing at the Maisonette of the St. Regis Hotel. Both of them were Torme fans. Tynan would have liked to have made the evening a surprise for Barbara but that was impossible because he'd not only made a reservation for the dinner show but had also taken a suite in the hotel for the two of them for the night.

They had decided to make it a festive, dress-up evening and that morning when Tynan left home he brought with him an overnight bag containing his tuxedo. Barbara was going to wear an evening gown.

Tynan had driven over from the precinct at a little after six, left his car in the hotel garage, and registered for them, saying his wife would be along later. He had wanted to arrive at the hotel before she did because he had also ordered roses and champagne to be sent to the suite, and that *would* be a surprise for her. The roses were there waiting when he checked in, as was the champagne in a bucket of ice. He had time to shower and shave and put on his dressing gown before she came in with a bellhop carrying her suitcase.

As soon as they were alone, she came into his arms, shaking her head as she looked around at the roses and champagne.

"You know, John Tynan," she whispered, "you

may be a cynic, all right, but nobody can say you're not a sentimental cynic. I love the roses and champagne."

She kissed him, and as they stood pressed close together, she was surprised to feel him trembling. She didn't say anything, she just held him tighter. In the quiet they could hear the sleet beating against the windows.

"And a wise one, too," he said, making an effort to keep his voice normal. "Listen to that storm. And we're here inside, warm and dry and cozy, with nothing to do all evening except amuse ourselves."

He took a deep breath. He was all right now, but for a moment there despite his resolve not to let anything spoil the evening, visions of the ugly blood-splattered scene in the bombed car that afternoon had intruded on his thoughts. He had had, briefly, a strong unnerving premonition of his own death.

"Come on," Barbara said, taking him by the hand and leading him into the bedroom where her suitcase lay on the bed. She opened the suitcase and lifted out a flimsy pink negligee. She held it up in front of her. It was so sheer that it was like looking through spun glass. "All for you," she said. "For later."

She took her clothes out of the suitcase and, after kissing Tynan on the lips, went to the bathroom to shower and dress. Tynan put on his tuxedo, lit a cigarette, and opened the champagne. He turned the radio on low and found WTFM.

When Barbara came back into the room she was wearing a long, black evening gown that fitted her like a sheath. The gown had spaghetti-thin shoulder straps and she wore with it a thin, gold Christian Dior belt, a gold necklace and earrings, and gold evening sandals.

"Beautiful," Tynan said. "You're beautiful."

They drank the champagne and carefully talked of trivia, the music in the background. Later they went to the Maisonette and listened to Mel Torme sing while they had dinner. They thought he was, as always, just great. When the show and dinner were

92

over, they had coffee and brandy nightcaps. Tynan had always been a sucker for certain feminine gestures as now when, after they had finished their drinks, Barbara ducked her head for a moment, slipped on a pair of glasses, took out her compact and touched up her lipstick. Then she quickly removed her glasses, looked up, and smiled at him. Her gestures, her smile made her seem at that moment somehow femininely vulnerable. Tynan took a sip of his brandy and said: "I know it's probably against your principles, but—will you marry me?"

She almost choked on her drink but she managed to nod her head.

"Are you sure," she asked, looking at him searchingly, "you want to do this?"

"I'm sure," he said.

Her eyes had gone wide and soft, the way they did when she made love. She smiled at him shyly and asked in a low voice: "But what about your theory of the way marriage—uh, uh—" The four-letter word he had used to describe his theory seemed to be inappropriate to use at this time and place and, instead, she said: "—the way marriage, to say it as it would be censored on television, beep-s up beep-ing?"

He laughed. "You truly are *something* else. The answer is, of course, that we'll stay so busy beeping, it'll just never happen to us."

"Speaking of which," she said, that wondrous, sudden smile spreading over her face, "let's go upstairs. Now."

"I'll drink to that," Tynan said.

Max Kauffman reached Catherine Devereaux's apartment at about seven. She was waiting for him at the front door. The wind and sleet of the night gusted in behind him and he quickly shut the door and took off his hat and coat and hung them in the hall closet before he followed her into the living room.

Even after all the years they had known one another intimately there was always a moment when, if they had been apart for a length of time and came

93

together again, that they stood, not touching, simply looking at one another, each silently seeking reassurance of the unchanged existence of their love.

She was wearing this night a pale-blue chiffon cocktail dress, sheer hose, and black patent leather pumps with high heels. The dress was knee-length. He knew that she knew he liked to see her legs.

Still not speaking, they kissed, a long, lingering kiss.

"I don't need to ask now if you missed me," she said when she released him.

He smiled. "Nor do I. I'm glad you're back, Kit. Very glad."

She went to the sofa and sat and he sat beside her. "What would you like to do?" she asked. "Go out for dinner? Or have dinner here? Or just stay here and have dinner later? Out or here? I'm prepared for any eventuality."

"I—" he rubbed his face with his hand, "—whatever you'd like. I really hadn't thought about it."

She knew then that he was preoccupied and distracted but it didn't bother her now, except for him, because she knew that whatever it was it had nothing to do with them, with their relationship.

"I have a bottle of Dom Perignon and some black caviar on ice," she said. "Would you like that? We can just be quiet for a while and decide later about the rest of the evening."

"Yes," he said. "I'd like that."

She prepared the caviar and black bread and he opened the champagne. As they nibbled at the caviar and sipped champagne, she told him about her weekend in Delaware. She said it had been pleasant enough with her family, but he could tell that her estrangement from them—which had begun when the family first discovered her involvement with Max Kauffman nine years earlier, and disapproved—was still there. He gathered that she was tolerated by her family (once for a time they had disowned her), but that there were no longer any close ties between them. He'd always felt guilty about the situation, but it was beyond his power to alter.

As she talked on, he nodded his head from time to time and smiled when she smiled, but she soon knew he wasn't really listening to her. After a while she kissed him lightly on the lips and got up from the sofa.

"I want to be with you," she said. "Give me a moment and then come back."

He nodded. She left and he poured himself a glass of champagne and sat sipping it. Soon he heard her calling him from the back of the apartment. He went back and found her in bed, a spread pulled up over her. There was a single light on the bedside table and most of the room was in shadow. He closed the bedroom door behind him.

"Undress," she said, "and come here."

He took his clothes off, careful to remove the beeper signal from his pocket and put it on the bedside table where he could hear it. When he was standing by the bed, she pulled the spread down from around her so he could see her nude body. He stood for a moment watching her. She had a way of looking at him when he was naked, of fixing her eyes on the lower part of his anatomy which, when he watched her, always aroused him. Now she held her arms out and he went to her.

When he was in bed beside her, she reached out a hand and turned off the light. It was only then that he realized she had closed the drapes at the windows and the room was in total darkness. He could see nothing. It was the first time they had ever made love in such a fashion and he thought how wise she was as slowly, slowly, he lost all sense of the existence of any world beyond this moment and the next and the next in the close darkness where there were only murmurs, her tantalizing scent, the coolness of her flesh under his lips, her touch of fingers and lips on his body, the feel of the liquid silkiness of her. Her. Him.

The man came up out of sleep suddenly in the hotel room. For a moment he didn't know where he was and his fear was like a constricting band across his chest which wouldn't let him breathe. The fear, without a name or source, was very great in him. There was a whimpering, animal sound in the room. He didn't know it came from his own lips, and he turned his head from side to side on the pillow. He saw, in the dirty gray light from the window, the table, the chair, and the bed of the shadowy room, and finally knew where he was. The fear didn't leave him, though, because he was sure he could see a human form standing in the shadows. His mind was confused. He thought maybe he was dreaming. That happened to him. Sometimes he thought he was awake when he was dreaming; sometimes he thought he was having a dream when he was awake. Now, though, the table, the chair, the bed, the room, the gray light, were too real for it to be a dream. And the figure he saw in the shadows was moving, moving toward him. He cringed and was ready to cry out when the figure moved closer and he saw it was Adrienne. He almost wept with relief.

She came and sat down on the bed beside him, putting a soft hand on his forehead and whispering how proud she was of him. He felt strong then. They talked about all he had done. They both laughed about the way the newspapers were calling him "The Christmas Bomber."

She became serious and warned him he must be careful. People had seen him that day when he passed the bomb in the cake box to that detective in the car. He told her he'd be careful. He was going to get rid of the black raincoat. There was going to be one more bombing and then he was going to stay out of sight for a while. He knew the police were looking for him.

She told him how clever he was. All the talking made him drowsy and he kept drifting off to sleep but he knew it when she slid into bed beside him and they made love. He was soothed and soon he was asleep again. Sometime during the night he awakened and saw her head on the pillow beside him. He leaned over and kissed her and she stirred in her sleep. Just before he drifted off to sleep once more, he thought it wasn't Adrienne in bed beside him, but Felice, one of the prostitutes he used. He was too sleepy to rouse himself enough to look at her again. But he slipped his hand under his pillow to touch the chain and locket he had taken from around Adrienne's neck before they made love. The chain and locket were there, so Adrienne must be in bed beside him. He slept.

CHAPTER TEN

"Police operator."

"Listen carefully. A truck with the Christmas tree on it for Rockefeller Center is parked in front of Thirty Rockefeller Plaza."

"Yeah?"

"There's a bomb in the gas tank of that truck."

"A bomb? Who—"

"*Listen!* The time is now eleven-fifteen. The bomb is set to explode in exactly thirty-six minutes."

"Wait! Hang on. Hello? Hello?"

The police operator, Officer Howard Remsen, in the Headquarters Communications Center on the eighth floor at 1 Police Plaza, swore inaudibly even as his fingers moved rapidly punching the computer keyboard in front of him. Within seconds the information he had just received was coded by the most modern communications system in the world and flashed to police radio dispatchers—in Headquarters and Manhattan Central, also known as the 16th Precinct—which would, in turn, order sector cars to the scene.

There were seven police cars pulled into the block in front of 30 Rockefeller Plaza between Forty-ninth and Fiftieth Streets when the squad car, with Max Kauffman in the front seat next to the driver and John Tynan and the car's second patrolman in the rear seat, rounded the corner of Fiftieth Street at Rockefeller Center and slammed to a jolting stop with a scream of tires. Max Kauffman was on the radio, hunched over, clutching the microphone with one hand.

"All right, all right," he growled into the radio, "where are they now? Where are the units? K."

The dispatcher's voice came back quickly. "Car six-two. Units are now on Sixth Avenue crossing Thirty-eighth Street. You should be hearing their sirens any minute. K."

"What about traffic control on Sixth Avenue? K." Max Kauffman demanded.

"Car six-two," the dispatcher promptly responded. "Be advised traffic control units Sixth Avenue already in place or moving into place. K."

Max Kauffman grunted, leaned forward, and jammed the microphone back into place under the dashboard. He'd been on the radio ever since the squad car left the 16th Precinct in response to the bomb alert from Headquarters. First, he'd had the central dispatcher check with officials at Rockefeller Center for information about the installation of the famous Christmas tree, to make sure the thing wasn't a hoax. At the same time, while he was waiting for that information to come back, he began improvising a plan to move the truck as swiftly as possible out of the crowded midtown area, where casualties could be high if there was an explosion, to the closest spot where less damage would result. He had been coordinating this plan, which involved other police units in the city, through the central dispatcher.

While the Inspector was still en route to 30 Rockefeller Plaza, the dispatcher had informed him that somebody at Rockefeller Center said the Christmas tree had arrived in the city that morning, and that later that day it would be set up. There would be two more days while scaffolding was erected around the tree for the trimming, a week for the trimming itself, another day to take down the scaffolding. Then there would be the annual lighting ceremony, which was always televised.

Once Max Kauffman had this information, he knew he couldn't take a chance that the bomb call had been a hoax. He'd ordered in other police units to assist in the movement of the truck. The police dispatcher had just confirmed that such units were on the way.

The Inspector swung around in the seat toward Tynan. "How much time have we got?"

Tynan had his eyes on the watch strapped to his wrist. "Twenty-one minutes," he said tersely.

Max Kauffman shoved the car door open. "Let's go! Let's go! For Christ's sake." To the driver of the squad car he said: "Pull over in front of the truck. Keep your motor running and be ready to move!"

The Inspector left the squad car door swinging open as he stepped out into the street. The flatbed truck with the giant Christmas tree on it was parked in Rockefeller Plaza directly across the street from number 30, the only building in the block, which also housed NBC's offices and studios. Down below where the truck was parked was the Rockefeller Center skating rink and the restaurants that faced on the rink. Today, after the stormy night before, the sky was clear and the sunlight dazzling despite the subfreezing temperature. The flags on the tall poles lining the street above the skating rink flapped briskly in the chilling wind. Max Kauffman could hear the wail of sirens coming from downtown.

The police who had arrived on the scene earlier were standing warily around the truck, waiting for orders. As usual, a large crowd of people, drawn to the scene by the arrival of the police, stood everywhere along the block, looking on.

"Get those people back!" Max Kauffman shouted to the police. "Get them out of here! This is no circus!"

Tynan sprinted across the street to the front of the truck and yanked up the hood. He'd brought an ignition "jumper" with him from the station house. It took him only a matter of seconds to attach the jumper, a coil with three wires, to the engine. Now he didn't need an ignition key to start the motor. He slammed the hood shut, ran around and climbed into the cab of the truck.

The squad car that had brought Max Kauffman

and John Tynan from the 16th Precinct shot forward down the middle of the street and nosed in ahead of the truck. One front door of the car was still swinging open. Tynan gunned the truck engine. As Max Kauffman hurried toward the waiting squad car, a dozen blue-helmeted police on motorcycles roared around the corner from Fiftieth Street with a deafening scream of high-pitched sirens. Max Kauffman paused only long enough to wave the motorcycle detail on toward Forty-ninth Street and then jumped into the squad car.

Patrolmen on foot stopped all traffic on Forty-ninth Street before it reached Rockefeller Plaza. The motorcyclists swept around the corner of Forty-ninth in the direction of Sixth Avenue, followed by the squad car carrying Max Kauffman. Behind the squad car was the truck, with Tynan driving, which was followed by another police car.

Streaking toward Sixth, the motorcycle detail opened up with the sirens. At the intersection of Forty-ninth and Sixth, the twelve motorcycles executed a sweeping turn, leading the two police cars and the truck uptown on the one-way avenue. In the front seat of the squad car, Max Kauffman gripped the radio microphone in his hand and made a small silent prayer that all the other police units were in place on the street ahead as he'd ordered.

Once the motorcade had completed the turn onto Sixth, the formation of motorcyclists spread out in a line across the street and accelerated. The squad cars and the truck between them kept pace. Max Kauffman watched the speedometer needle in his squad car climb steadily to sixty, sixty-five, and keep going.

The vehicles flashed by intersections in a blur of speed—Fiftieth Street, Fifty-first, Fifty-second, Fifty-third—each intersection on both sides of the street blocked off to all traffic leading into Sixth Avenue by two or three prowl cars, angled across each side street, at every corner.

Max Kauffman kept glancing back at the truck following them, and at his wristwatch. They now had less than fifteen minutes before the bomb in the gas tank of the truck was supposed to blow up. And the noise was horrendous—the sirens, the horns of irate drivers blocked on the side streets, snatches of the Headquarters radio dispatcher's voice chattering to units involved in the operation. "I read you car eight-zero, hold position" . . . "car one-four . . . car one-four . . . this priority excludes all traffic movement Sixth Avenue. Con Edison emergency truck no exception. K. . . ." "Car six-two, request position. K. Car six-two—"

"Car six-two," Max Kauffman yelled into the microphone. "Approaching Fifty-eighth Street. K."

Oh dear God, Max Kauffman thought, *let this work*. He knew he hadn't had time to really think through the problem of where to move the truck in the city, as quickly as possible, to the safest possible area if it did explode. Now that it was too late, he was beginning to have second thoughts about the location he had chosen.

The time left was now less than seven minutes.

The motorcycles, the squad car, the truck, and the second prowl car now shot across the intersection at Central Park South and went careening up the winding road inside Central Park.

"Five minutes!" Max Kauffman groaned aloud.

Up ahead he could see the cyclists performing balancing acts as their big bulky machines swayed dangerously from side to side on the narrow curving road. The motorcycles and the three vehicles had had to reduce their speed once they were on the park's zigzagging roads, but they were still traveling so swiftly that they were all rocking sickeningly from side to side. Max Kauffman clung to the side of the seat.

They were deep into the park now, well up into the sixties. The Inspector spotted one of the motor-cyclists motioning with an upraised gauntleted hand as the formation went into a curve up ahead.

"Slow down!" Max Kauffman ordered the driver of the squad car. "Signal with your blinker lights to Tynan!"

A few yards beyond, the squad car itself went

into the curve and as it came around, Max Kauff-man saw that the motorcyclists had pulled their ma-chines off to either side of the road and left a large gaping space between them leading off the road to-ward the west side of Central Park. The Inspector in-stantly saw why they had chosen this spot to stop: there in the park was a large clear area, with few trees around, extending all the way from the road to the stone wall that ran alongside Central Park West.

"Pull over! Pull over!" Max Kauffman ordered the driver of the squad car. As the car pulled over to the shoulder of the road and while it was still rolling, he jumped out.

Tynan, in the truck, was just rounding the curve. Max Kauffman signaled frantically with his arm to the open clearing off the road. The truck swung around, left the road, and went bouncing across the uneven ground. Max Kauffman glanced at his watch. Three minutes to go . . . two minutes and fifty seconds. . . .

The truck plowed across the clearing, rolled down a steep dip in the ground, then climbed a rise.

"Jump!" Max Kauffman shouted. "Jump!" He cupped his hands, even though he knew Tynan couldn't hear him, and shouted again: "Jump!"

The truck topped the rise and stopped. Max Kauffman saw the door open and, an instant later, Tynan hit the ground running hard away from the truck toward the road. He sprinted down the dip in the ground and up again, ran for another three or four yards, then flung himself flat on the ground a split second before there was a brilliant orange flash and the truck disappeared in a sheet of flames. Sec-onds passed before the shockwaves and the thunder-ous roar of the explosion carried to the policemen standing at the edge of the park road. They felt like they were being buffeted by a scorching wind.

Max Kauffman stood, not moving, until he saw Tynan stand and start walking slowly toward the road. The Inspector turned then, went to the squad car and, using the radio, called in fire equipment.

"I don't guess it was a hoax after all," Tynan said drily when he reached Max Kauffman. Despite the cold of the day, Tynan had to wipe the sweat off his face with his hand.

A short while later the fire engines arrived and the firemen, using chemical sprays, quickly put out the flames. All that remained of the truck was a heap of black, twisted metal which, to the Inspector's eyes, curiously resembled a piece of oversized sculpture by the artist Giacometti.

"One thing about it," Tynan said as he and Max Kauffman walked toward the waiting squad car, "there's not much scattered around this time for the lab to pick up."

"There's another thing about it," Max Kauffman added, "the guy's pushing his luck too hard, setting off one explosion on top of another, like this. We'll get him soon."

CHAPTER ELEVEN

The first real snow of the year fell in the city on December 16. Max Kauffman stood at the window of his office in the 16th Precinct and watched the soft, feathery flakes driven by a hard north wind splatter against the glass pane. It was a wet snow which didn't stick when it hit the ground but foreshortened the view beyond the window into a hazy frost in which was reflected the Inspector's image, the lights in the office, and the fire in the fireplace behind him. The snow had started falling soon after midday. It was now 4 P.M.

Max Kauffman turned from the window and went back and sat at his desk. He loosened his tie and unbuttoned his collar. Then he stood and took off his suit jacket. He took the jacket over to the closet, hung it there, and came back and sat in his chair. He picked up the cigar he'd left smoking in the ashtray and stuck it in his mouth. Leaning forward, he reached for the report he'd been reading before he'd wandered over to the window to look out at the snow and, finding the spot where he'd left off, began to read again.

Tynan's report was a summary of the investigation to date on the "Christmas Bomber" case. The investigation had continued even though twelve days had passed since the last bombing incident, in which the truck and the Rockefeller Center Christmas tree had been destroyed, thirteen days since Detective Al Manders had been killed.

Detective Albert Francis Manders had long since been buried, on December 6, in the family plot in

107

Farmingdale, Long Island, after a full-dress, ceremonial P.D. funeral. Over four hundred police officers had attended the services, including out-of-state delegations from New Jersey, Pennsylvania, Connecticut, and Boston, Chicago, and Washington, D.C., in addition to members of the 16th Precinct and other N.Y.P.D. officers. All the uniformed patrolmen had worn black mourning bands over their shields. Max Kauffman had been there, in a place in the front row, along with the Police Commissioner, the Mayor, and several other ranking officers, and had felt acutely uncomfortable because for the first time in years he had changed into his inspector's uniform for the occasion.

A second Christmas tree had been trucked into Rockefeller Center and trimmed and the annual lighting ceremony had gone off smoothly, only four days later than the usual date.

Meanwhile, during the past twelve days, members of the Bomb Investigative Unit had worked day and night to run down all possible leads on the bomber. Coleman's Bakery on Ninth Avenue had been checked out again and again and again, and the employees repeatedly questioned about a man wearing a black raincoat who might have made purchases there. No one had any clear recollection of such a man.

Detectives had spent days canvassing the neighborhood of Coleman's Bakery and West Fifty-first Street, where Al Manders had been killed in the car, asking everyone whether they had seen a man wearing a black raincoat and/or carrying a white cake box. Police had no real faith that they would actually collar the bomber with these two slim pieces of evidence but they had to try. All they succeeded in doing was locating five men in the West Side neighborhood who owned black raincoats. None was their man.

Nor were they any more successful in getting a useful description of the man the Radio City Music Hall cashier said she had seen wearing a black raincoat nor from the people who had been out on West Fifty-first Street the day Manders was killed. At best, the descriptions these witnesses provided were too conflicting, far from specific; they could have fit hundreds of men in Manhattan.

In addition, police had kept an around-the-clock watch on the West Side neighborhood in the hope of spotting a man in a black raincoat—this despite the fact that Max Kauffman and John Tynan believed the bomber would have gotten rid of his raincoat by now. He must have suspected he'd been seen on the street at the time Manders was killed. He had probably also gone into hiding.

The only physical evidence the police had in their possession—the pieces of metal can, clock, plastic bottle, and radio battery recovered from the Thanksgiving Day parade bomb—had likewise led to a dead end. No fingerprints had been found on the note from the bomber, nor on the cake box found in Radio City Music Hall, nor on the pieces of cake box removed from Detective Manders' bombed car. Police were holding the tape recording of the bomber's voice for future use, including the last phone call he had made to the 911 number, after the truck and Christmas tree had been dynamited, proclaiming it "The fourth day of Christmas."

There had been no report back from the FBI Identification Division on the fingerprints found in the abandoned Mercedes.

Bomb squad detectives had checked back through an accumulation of twenty years of files on bomb cases in the city and had questioned over a hundred people who had had any connection with bombings over the years. Again, these efforts came to nothing. Details on the three bomb incidents in Manhattan had been sent to every police department in the country, in case the bomber had operated in another city before coming to New York or had moved on to another city. But this, too, led nowhere.

In twelve days eight more people had confessed to being the bomber, bringing the total to fourteen, twelve men and two women, who swore that they had planted the bombs in the parade and at Radio

109

City Music Hall, that they had blown up the truck, and were responsible for Detective Manders' death. Police questioning and psychiatric tests had eliminated all of them as the probable bomber, although nine men and one woman were still being confined at Bellevue.

There had been four hundred bomb scare calls to the 911 number and the special phone number set up by police during the twelve-day period. But by the previous day—December 15—such calls had leveled off to the normal average of twenty-five.

Tynan had concluded his report with the words: "Investigation continuing. . . ."

About the only cheering news connected with the bombing cases was that Patrolman Ralph Yost, though still in French Hospital, was recovering. Most of the civilians who had been injured or burned in the parade bombing were also recovering or had been released from the hospital.

Max Kauffman made a couple of minor notations on the report. He suggested that the West Side neighborhood be kept under surveillance and that one of the psychos being held at Bellevue, a man named Luther Cargill, be questioned again. He buzzed for Policewoman MacKay to return the report to Tynan. When she didn't answer, he swore softly, shaking his head. These days, it seemed to him, life was unusually abundant with minor irritations.

Sergeant Margaret O'Dell's absence was certainly one of the irritations. The disarray of his office—the painting and redecorating still hadn't been completed —was another, but the lack of progress in the bombing case was, of course, the major source of irritation. Because, though in the past eleven days six murder cases falling within the jurisdiction of the 16th Precinct had been solved and there had been arrests made in twenty-one burglaries, nineteen assault cases, eleven rapes, and thirty narcotics cases, the unsolved bombing incidents still took top priority. The case was never far from the thoughts of Max Kauffman.

The Inspector got up from his chair, went over to the fireplace and placed another couple of logs on

110

the flames. Then he went back to his desk and again buzzed for Officer MacKay. When she still didn't answer, he picked up the file and decided he himself would take it down to Tynan. The lieutenant's office was on the second floor, in the front of the building, and Max Kauffman used the inside fire stairs instead of the elevator since at this hour the shifts would be changing and he knew he'd probably have a long wait.

Tynan wasn't in. The plainclothes policeman who did the clerical work for the Bomb Investigative Unit said the lieutenant had gone to the lab, and Max Kauffman went into the office and put the report on the desk.

Tynan's office was, in contrast to Max Kauffman's, almost totally impersonal. There was a desk, a chair, and a small filing cabinet. There was a rug on the floor but no pictures on the walls. The top of the desk was bare except for a glass ashtray full of cigarette butts and a black picture frame containing the photograph of a dark-haired girl. Max Kauffman studied the photograph curiously. Tynan had told him just within the past week that he planned to be married on Christmas Day and that he hoped, if the bombing case had been solved by then or if the incidents had stopped, he could take a ten-day honeymoon. Looking at the photograph of the girl, Max Kauffman decided she was quite pretty. He silently wished them *mazel* —good luck—and went back up the stairs to his office.

Florence MacKay was back at her desk, busily typing. She didn't notice him until he passed by her desk and then she looked up, startled, and said accusingly, "I didn't know you'd left your office."

"You weren't here and I went looking for you. Now you're here and I'm here and I can't remember why I wanted you."

He felt in a better humor when he closed his office door and sat down at his desk again and pulled toward him another batch of reports dealing with other crimes within the precinct's jurisdiction. Outside, the snow was still falling silently in the last, darkening light of late afternoon.

The man who was now known to the police as the Christmas Bomber crossed the street at the intersection of Park Avenue and Fiftieth Street and hurried into the recessed shelter outside the entrance to the Colgate-Palmolive Building on the west side of Park Avenue directly across from the Waldorf Astoria Hotel. He stood there, facing the street, and brushed the snow off the sleeves of his jacket. The jacket was a faded blue denim and under it he wore a bulky cable knit sweater, with the jacket buttoned up to the neck and the collar turned up. His trousers were dark blue and he wore no hat and no overshoes or rubbers over his black blutcher shoes. He was warm enough; the snow and the cold were more a nuisance than a discomfort. But he'd walked a long way, and he could feel the dampness through the soles of his shoes and his socks.

It was getting close to 5 P.M., the hour when most businesses in New York ended work for the day, and the streets were already beginning to fill with people hurrying to subways, buses, and trains, to get out of the weather, to get out of the city. About a dozen people were standing in the entranceway to the building near the man in the denim jacket. None of them gave him more than a passing glance.

He fished a cigarette out of his jacket pocket and lit it while he studied the street. Park Avenue was divided down the middle by a concrete island and traffic moved uptown on the east side of the island, on the far side of the street from where the man stood, and moved downtown toward Grand Central Terminal five blocks south on the west side of the street in front of the Colgate-Palmolive Building. Both uptown and downtown lanes were jammed with early rush hour traffic, mostly taxicabs, and pedestrians scurrying from one side of the avenue to the other. Dusk had already come but the street was well-lighted by the illumination from the windows of all the office buildings in the area, by the Waldorf across the street, and by the overhead street lights set at close intervals in each block along Park Avenue. In addition, with Christmas only nine days away, many of the buildings had already decorated their fronts with electrical displays and—as was a tradition in Manhattan each year—out in the center concrete island there were several small lighted Christmas trees within each block along the length of Park Avenue, all of which supplied more light.

Wet snow was still falling, spilling down across the avenue with the transparency of swirls of gauze through which the man could clearly see the street. He flipped away the cigarette which he'd smoked down to a butt and lit another one. He had purposely not looked at his watch while he was standing there and yet he could tell from the growing crowds on the sidewalk and the increase in traffic out on the Avenue that it was after five. On the other side of the street a long line of taxicabs stretched for a block or more waiting to pull up in front of the Waldorf to pick up or discharge passengers. He could feel the excitement growing inside of him. He *had* to look at his watch.

It was exactly 5:14 and five seconds. His heart began to pound in synchronization with the watch's second hand as it ticked off the seconds . . . fifteen . . . twenty-five . . . thirty-five . . . forty-five . . . fifty. . . .

He looked up from the watch. His heart pounded, and pounded again—and then the explosion came: a burst of flame, a shattering blast, and the Christmas tree nearest the corner of Fiftieth Street, out in the center island of Park Avenue, blew up. Flames shot into the air and cascaded down into both sides of the street.

Almost immediately a second Christmas tree out on the island in the same block blew apart, followed by a series of explosions, block by block up Park Avenue from Fiftieth to Sixtieth Streets, as one or two trees in each block burst into flames and blast after blast rumbled back down the street. Following the blasts, the whole area suddenly erupted in sound. Cars along both sides of the concrete divider jerked to a stop with a shriek of brakes. Some cars piled into the rears of the cars ahead of them. Other cars, attempting to swerve out of the way of the flames falling into the

113

street, ran up onto the curbs and stalled, bringing on a blare of car horns. Adding to the din were screams and yells from frightened pedestrians who had been caught midway in the street and were now trying to make their way through the jam of cars to the safety of the sidewalks.

Back in the doorway of the Colgate-Palmolive Building the man in the denim jacket was barely aware of the shocked, scared look on the faces of all the people milling around him in the entranceway and out on the sidewalk. He moved carefully through the crowd to the corner of Fiftieth Street, turned and walked swiftly west.

The first call about the bombing of the Christmas trees on Park Avenue came into the 16th Precinct at 5:29 P.M. Max Kauffman was in his office preparing to leave for the day when the call was relayed to him from the Communications Division in Police Headquarters on Chambers Street and Park Row downtown. The information was sketchy; all he could learn was that there had been a series of explosions in the vicinity of the Waldorf Astoria Hotel on Park Avenue somehow involving Christmas trees and it was suspected bombs were involved. He paused only long enough to call the precinct dispatcher, ordered him to send Tynan and his bomb squad to the scene, then headed over to Park Avenue himself in the limousine which had been waiting outside the station house to take him home.

The Inspector's car, with Detective Lukin at the wheel, was only able to proceed to Fifth Avenue and Fiftieth Street. There traffic was hopelessly backed up for two blocks solid eastward to Park Avenue. Max Kauffman walked the rest of the way. There were sounds of sirens all around him, coming from every direction, as major emergency equipment, fire-fighting apparatus, police vehicles, and a couple of ambulances converged on Park Avenue.

At first when the Inspector finally reached the block in front of the Waldorf, the situation looked appallingly hopeless: The street was full of cars stalled, jammed together, angled sideways, nosed in either to the curbs or to the center divider, and wedged in, all along Park Avenue above and below Fiftieth Street. The sidewalks were clogged with people. Most of the fires caused by the explosions had gone out but the stumps of the smoke-blackened Christmas trees still smouldered and from time to time red-hot embers fell from the tree branches and sputtered out on the wet pavement. The wet snow, too, helped extinguish the flames.

A dozen prowl cars, the first to respond to the central dispatcher's call, had already reached Park Avenue and patrolmen were checking out the damage in each block from Fiftieth to Sixtieth Streets. Taking over the radio in one of the police cars parked in front of the Waldorf, Max Kauffman contacted the other units. All reported that damage in the ten-block area appeared to be minimal; there were no real injuries, most of the fires had gone out, and the main problem was to unsnarl traffic and get it moving again.

Once he had that information, the Inspector radioed Headquarters Communications and directed that all emergency equipment, except for the bomb unit, be recalled. The job to be done was now in the hands of traffic control. It took the police another three-quarters of an hour to clear both sides of Park Avenue. Once the last car was gone, Max Kauffman instructed the patrolmen to block off Park Avenue from Fiftieth to Sixtieth and as soon as that was done, he ordered John Tynan and the members of the Bomb Investigative Unit to start collecting specimens of the rubble so it could be examined in the lab. Unlike the limited amount of debris collected by the bomb squad after the parade explosion, tonight Tynan and his men would need trucks to cart away the debris they would recover from the ten-block area. The Sanitation Department agreed to send several trucks when Max Kauffman radioed in his request for help in carrying out the project.

The Inspector stayed until the first three trucks had been filled and had left for the police lab. He and Tynan stood on the island between Fifty-sixth and

Fifty-seventh Streets and watched them go. It was almost 8 P.M. Heavy snow was falling now, covering the street and the ground solidly an inch or more deep. The soft, thick snow made it feel warmer and a kind of peaceful stillness settled over the city. The worst of the snow had held off long enough for the bomb squad to begin filling the last truck.

"Whatever we might have hoped before," Tynan said wearily, shaking his head, "I'd say it looks for sure like we've got a full-blown madman on our hands."

Max Kauffman nodded. "And whatever this is all about it's keyed in somehow with Christmas." He took a couple of impatient steps forward and came back. "But what—what—what *is* it?"

Both men were silent for a moment and then Max Kauffman said, "Look, we'll talk tomorrow. Soon as that last truck leaves, get some rest tonight and let the lab boys run with the ball for a while."

The Inspector crossed to the nearest squad car. He radioed Headquarters, gave them a terse report on the bombings of the Park Avenue Christmas trees to pass on to the Commissioner, and asked the driver of the squad car to drive him home. As the car turned the corner on Fifty-sixth Street and started east, Max Kauffman glanced out the rear window. Traffic was moving again on Park Avenue and all traces of the day's ugly, explosive violence had disappeared under the clean, white snowfall.

CHAPTER TWELVE

"There must be *something* we can do to stop this madness."

The words, which were meant to be a statement, came out sounding like a question because of the lack of conviction in the voice of the man who spoke them. The man was Police Commissioner John Kenyan Hilliard. He glanced expectantly at each of the men sitting in a semicircle of chairs in front of his desk at Police Headquarters. Present were outgoing Mayor Andrew Forester; Mayor-elect William Angleton who had been invited by Forester to attend the meeting; Deputy Police Commissioner for Public Affairs Robert Harlow; the director of the FBI's New York office, Martin Eberhard, who was there because although the FBI had not officially entered the case, it was cooperating with the N.Y.P.D.; Captain Joseph Briggs, head of the Police Academy bomb squad; and Deputy Chief Inspector Max Kauffman.

No one attempted to reply to the Commissioner's words for a moment. Max Kauffman had just finished making a lengthy verbal report on the Christmas Bomber case, after which he had passed out typewritten copies of a progress report on the case, including the previous day's bombing of the Christmas trees on Park Avenue. The report included the information that, following the incidents on Park Avenue, the police had received another phone call from the bomber who said: "It's the fifth day of Christmas."

The first, incomplete reports from the lab on the debris collected at the sites of the bombings on Park Avenue indicated that sticks of TNT wired to small alarm clocks had caused the explosions. Both the morning's *Daily News* and *New York Times* carried front-page stories on the latest bombings.

Robert Harlow, Deputy Police Commissioner for Public Affairs, cleared his throat and said tentatively: "Perhaps more men should be assigned to Inspector Kauffman. It might have a salutary psychological effect on the case."

"I don't think at the moment," Max Kauffman answered, "that it's a question of a lack of manpower. So far we've had sufficient men to do the job that needs to be done. Our problem is primarily a lack of clues, a lack of leads." He frowned. "I can't see how assigning more men to the case would change these basic facts. I'm satisfied that the present force is keeping pace with the developments in the case."

"That was not quite what I meant," Harlow said, a trace of impatience in his voice. "I was thinking of the psychological aspect as far as the public is concerned. The reassurance they'd get if the Department announced that a, well, a small army of police had been assigned to the case. You know, something like 'the greatest manhunt force ever assembled in the history of the New York Police Department.' That kind of thing."

Max Kauffman had it straight now what Harlow was suggesting: PR gimmicks. He shrugged and remained silent.

"Well, Inspector?" Harlow demanded.

"I really can't add to what I've already said," Max Kauffman said mildly. "I'm concerned with solving the case. What you're suggesting is outside my area of knowledge or responsibility. Someone else will have to judge the merit of your plan."

Harlow pressed the others in the room for an endorsement of his suggestion and for the next half hour there was an animated discussion in which it soon became apparent that Commissioner Hilliard, Mayor Forester, and Harlow favored taking some kind of dramatic action in the case and—in the absence of other suggestions—believed that a large force of police should be assigned to the investigation. FBI agent Eberhard and Captain Briggs of the bomb squad remained noncommittal. Mayor-elect Angleton listened interestedly but gave no opinion. Max Kauffman, having already expressed himself, remained silent.

The Inspector had quickly concluded that all the present Mayor, the Commissioner, and Harlow were interested in was the *appearance* of activity. To him it was an indication of the frustration of the case that the best any of them in the room could do—including himself—was waste time on a meaningless discussion of a plan with no real substance. He was smoking a cigar and his attention wandered.

The Commissioner's office was on the 14th floor of the new Headquarters building at 1 Police Plaza. Max Kauffman could see that outside the window the sky was partially cloudy with drifting banks of dark clouds which from time to time obscured the sun while a blustery wind sent the snow still piled along the bottom of the window ledge swirling into the air high above the street.

During the night there had been a four-inch accumulation of snow in the city. The temperature hovered around sixteen degrees through the morning and now in the early afternoon was still only twenty degrees. Max Kauffman squinted his eyes and studied the partially overcast sky, trying to decide whether or not it would snow again before night.

The Inspector forced his attention back to the group in the office when Mayor-elect William Angleton interrupted the others who had been talking endlessly and said: "If I may, I'd like to put a question to Inspector Kauffman?"

Max Kauffman nodded. "Yes, sir?"

"Let me see if I understand correctly," Angleton said. "At the moment you feel you have adequate help in handling this investigation?"

"Yes sir."

"But you do foresee a time when it might be advantageous to assign more men to the case?"

"That's correct," Max Kauffman agreed. "If and when we do get a lead or some kind of real pattern

119

begins to emerge, so that there's a possibility we could conceivably head off the bomber before he strikes again, then I would want more men, would need them, would request them."

"And in the meantime," Angleton went on, "it is your considered opinion that there isn't anything we can do beyond what we're already doing to—in Commissioner Hilliard's words—'stop this madness'?"

Max Kauffman leaned forward and said earnestly, "That's about right, sir. Except that the odds are on our side; sooner or later we will most surely pick up a lead. The problem is that lead will probably come from somewhere completely outside our investigation and we're more or less hamstrung until that happens. But when it happens—if it happens—that's when we really go into action. Meanwhile, of course, we keep digging."

Martin Eberhard said, nodding at Angleton, "That's almost always the way it happens, in our experience with bombing cases similar to this one."

Briggs agreed.

"I see." Angleton looked at the others in the room. "Perhaps," he said gently, "Mr. Harlow's suggestion, which is a very sound one, is premature."

Mayor Forester, Hilliard, and Harlow hastily agreed. Max Kauffman understood: they felt they were off the hook now. The responsibility had been passed to him. It reminded him of a poker game he'd once played at college, a variation of seven-card stud. In the game seven cards were dealt face down to each player. Each player, after looking at his cards, picked out what he considered to be the three worst cards, then passed one of them to the player on his right and two to the player on his left, each player receiving cards rejected by players on either side of him. The game was called "Fuck Your Buddy."

However, since in any event he was in charge of the case already, he didn't mind. In fact, he preferred it that way. There were handshakes all around and assurances from everyone that when the time came that he needed help on the case, all he had to do was ask.

Driving back uptown to the precinct in his limousine, Max Kauffman couldn't prevent himself from thinking that there was only one word, a Yiddish word, which precisely described the meeting in the Commissioner's office: *bubkes;* absurd, foolish, nonsensical.

Less than thirty minutes later when Max Kauffman arrived at his office, John Tynan was there waiting for him, pacing the floor.

"I was hoping you'd get here soon," Tynan said hurriedly. "We just received a call to the special police number. Someone says he thinks he may have seen the bomber yesterday screwing around with the Christmas trees on Park Avenue. Actually, the citizen didn't say 'screwing around'—he's a retired Presbyterian minister. It could be the break we've been hoping for."

"Yes," Max Kauffman said. "Did he see the man, get a good look at him?"

"I didn't get all the information. I was just on my way over to question him. I thought perhaps you'd like to come along."

"I would." Max Kauffman hadn't taken his hat and coat off and he and Tynan walked back to the elevator.

"The man who called in is a Reverend Clarence Norris. He lives in an apartment building at Park and Fifty-eighth. He may really have something for us because he's cooperated with the police before. He's a 'neighborhood watcher.' The 19th Precinct gave him a pair of binoculars. They say he's reliable."

Max Kauffman nodded. Scattered over Manhattan were certain citizens who acted as unofficial neighborhood watchers. These individuals, usually elderly persons or shut-ins, spent a large part of their time each day keeping an eye on the streets and surroundings near where they lived. Whenever they spotted an accident, a fire which might otherwise be undetected, or any suspicious activity, they reported them by phone to the police or other authorities. The N.Y.P.D., in turn, encouraged such civilian surveillance and sometimes supplied these citizens with binoculars or other equipment to help them keep watch, especially since law enforcement studies have shown that two-thirds of big city crimes are solved when police are able to respond within two minutes of the commission of a crime, while if the police response was delayed five minutes or longer, less than one crime in five was solved.

When they got downstairs, outside the precinct, Max Kauffman decided they'd use one of the bomb squad station wagons. Tynan drove, Max Kauffman sat in front beside him, and Detective Lewis Braxley, who took shorthand faster than any other man on the squad and would record the interview with the witness, sat in back.

Most of the snow that had fallen the night before had been churned by the heavy flow of traffic into dirty gray slush. Tynan drove fast. He didn't use the siren but he kept cutting in and out around other cars and jumping stop lights. As they drove swiftly up Park Avenue Max Kauffman noted that employees of the city's Parks Department were out in the center island replacing the damaged Christmas trees.

Reverend Clarence Norris lived on the fifth floor front of a twelve-story apartment building on Park Avenue between Fifty-eighth and Fifty-ninth Streets. A young black woman wearing a starched white uniform met them at the door to Norris's apartment, took their coats, and led them into a small, dark living room. The room was sparsely furnished with a brocaded sofa and four arm chairs of cane with cushioned seats and backs of brocade that matched the sofa. Next to the sofa on an end table was an open Bible. The man they had come to see was waiting for them in the center of the room, in a wheelchair.

Reverend Norris was in his eighties. He had white hair, fine and soft as a baby's, and neatly parted from crown to temple. His skin was like porcelain, skeins of bluish veins showing through the translucent flesh, his eyes bright blue behind steel-rimmed bifocals. His advanced age was most pronounced in the shrunken jaws of what had probably been a powerful, square-shaped face. He was wearing a wine-colored

122

smoking jacket, a white shirt with a jaunty argyle bow-tie, dark trousers and dark socks. His feet, resting against the floorboards of the wheelchair, were encased in black house slippers.

"Don't let the wheelchair fool you," he said, shaking hands with the three policemen. "It's not because I'm too feeble to get around by myself. I had a stroke, and it left my legs paralyzed. But thank the good Lord it didn't affect my eyesight. I know you're busy, I won't keep you."

He turned in his wheelchair, propelled himself over to one of the front windows, and beckoned them to follow. He pulled back the curtains from a window where a pair of binoculars sat on the sill and pointed to a section of the Park Avenue center island just up the block from the apartment house toward Fifty-ninth Street, where there was still a bomb-blackened tree standing.

"Three-thirty or around that time yesterday afternoon I was taking a look at the street with the glasses there. It was snowing some so I didn't have a clear view. The first time I noticed this fellow, he was right there stooping over that Christmas tree. I didn't pay any particular attention. I thought it was a city worker fixing the tree. Later I noticed he'd moved down the block to another tree. I took another look at him then. I still didn't think anything."

He paused. "Until of course there were the explosions later on, and I read the stories in the newspaper. I think, on reflection, he must have been this bomber you're looking for."

"Did you get a good enough look at him to give us a description?" Max Kauffman asked.

"Not as good as I'd like to have," the old man said. "But I can try to describe what I saw of him."

Detective Braxley had taken out a pad and pencil and began to scribble as the Reverend Norris spoke.

"He was, I'd guess, about five feet, ten or eleven inches tall. Not too heavy, looked a little underweight was my impression. I really didn't get a clear enough view to judge his age with any accuracy but—and

123

again this is just an impression—I'd say late forties, fifties. Because of the snow, even though he was bareheaded, I couldn't tell precisely how much of his hair, which was dark, was gray. He was wearing a jacket, not a coat, and dark pants. I had only one quick glimpse of his face. I know he had a moustache but I have no clear memory of the rest of his features. I think I might know him though if I ever saw him again. Maybe not."

"Anything else distinctive about him you remember?" Tynan prompted. "A big nose, ears? The cast of his eyes? The way he stood or walked? Anything at all?"

The Reverend shook his head. A trifle sadly he said, "I'm sorry, no. After the fact, you wonder how you could look straight at a man and not really see him. It could be that it's the way of the city; so many small things go wrong each day, we get so used to seeing somebody out there trying to fix them that they just blend into the landscape."

There was a moment of silence in the room before Max Kauffman said: "Reverend Norris, you said you might know this man if you ever saw him again."

"Yes. I might."

Max Kauffman smiled encouragingly. "I have an idea, then. Down at Police Headquarters we have a new kind of machine for creating a composite photo of a subject. It's called the Minolta Montage identification system. As perhaps you know, in the past we've had to depend upon police artists to draw sketches, based upon witnesses' descriptions of suspects, to create such composites."

"Yes," the old man said, "I did know about that."

"This new system," Max Kauffman explained, "now does the same job electronically. A photo of a blank face, hopefully generally similar in shape to the suspect's face and head, is flashed on a TV screen. Then, as the witness tries to recall various specific facial features, they are added one at a time to the face. You understand?"

"I understand," Norris said.

"Good." Max Kauffman smiled again. "The photo synthesizer can keep changing the features quickly. The point I'm getting at, as you've probably already guessed, is that by the process of elimination of features and expressions, you just might be able to arrive at an approximate likeness of the bomber. I think it's worth trying if you're willing."

"Oh, yes," the old man said quickly, "I'm perfectly willing to try. If you don't think it will be a waste of the Police Department's time."

Max Kauffman shook hands with Norris. "Don't you worry about that. Is tomorrow convenient for you? We'll provide you with transportation. We can send one of our station wagons to pick you up, which might be more comfortable for you. In the afternoon?"

"Two o'clock tomorrow afternoon would be fine." The old man was still shaking hands with the Inspector and now he said shyly, "There is one thing I'd like very much."

"What's that?" Max Kauffman asked.

"Could I—would it be possible to make the trip in a squad car? My wheelchair's collapsible so it would fit. I've always wanted to ride in a police car. If it's not against regulations."

Max Kauffman, Tynan, and Braxley all grinned. "There'll be a squad car here at two P.M. to pick you up and it'll bring you back," the Inspector assured him.

Driving back to the precinct, Max Kauffman suddenly sat bolt upright and said: "My God! I just thought of something!"

The Inspector's sudden movement and loud exclamation distracted Tynan enough so that he almost ran a red light. He jammed on the brakes, and all three of them were thrown forward in their seats. The station wagon stalled. The traffic light turned green. Horns began to blow behind them.

"What? What is it?" Tynan asked, ignoring the horns.

"Today's December seventeenth, correct?"

"Yes," Tynan said.

Max Kauffman spread his hands in the air. "After the Christmas trees blew up, the bomber called it 'the fifth day of Christmas,' correct?"

Tynan nodded.

"Well, starting tomorrow there are exactly seven days until Christmas. Which means that if he really means to set off a total of twelve bombs—and we've already had five—we'd better brace ourselves for a bombing a day from here on."

Tynan got the car started again. They drove back to the precinct in silence, each preoccupied with his own grim thoughts of the next seven days.

CHAPTER THIRTEEN

On December 18—another cold, bleak day with no sun and piles of sooty slush at the street curbs and patches of glazed ice on the sidewalks and pavements —the fifth bomb exploded in the city. The time of the explosion was 4:30 P.M. and the location was the east side of Fifth Avenue between Forty-first and Forty-second Streets, across from the central branch of the New York Public Library.

As police reconstructed the event, one of the city's numerous derelicts, an alcoholic panhandler, wandered uptown from his usual haunts on Third Avenue below Tenth Street in the Bowery. He was a tall, emaciated man of indeterminate age, with wiry gray hair that needed cutting and a face covered with bristly whiskers. He was shabbily dressed in a worn navy peajacket, a grimy, patched blue shirt, and dark trousers which were too large for him and were held up by a piece of rope tied around his waist. His black shoes were cracked and scuffed on top, had a hole in the sole, and he wore no socks.

Shoppers, shopkeepers, and passersby who were in the vicinity at the time and noticed the man recalled, when later questioned by police, that the derelict had been trying to cadge handouts and, as was a common practice among the city's human scavengers, had been poking through the refuse in the large wire wastebaskets set along every block on Fifth Avenue.

At one of the wastebaskets, in the block between Forty-first and Forty-second Streets, he apparently spotted a package wrapped in colorful Christmas paper and tied with red ribbon. When he snatched it up

127

and ripped off the ribbon and paper, the package exploded in his hands. His right arm was blown from the shoulder at the socket and his left hand was severed at the wrist. The force of the blast blew him back across the sidewalk and left him, unconscious, in a bleeding, crumpled heap in the entrance of an office building two doors from the corner. The repercussion from the blast shattered the glass windows in the four shops nearest to the explosion and several people inside those shops and passing by on the street received minor injuries from the shards of flying glass.

Police cars and ambulances quickly responded to the calls to 911. Those who required medical attention for their injuries were taken to University Hospital and Beth Israel; the derelict, still unconscious, was removed to Bellevue.

As soon as word of the bomb reached the 16th Precinct, John Tynan and several members of his bomb squad went immediately to the site of the explosion, while Max Kauffman sped to Bellevue in the hope that he might learn something from the derelict. Perhaps the panhandler might have seen the individual who deposited the package in the wastebasket. But the pathetic old man never regained consciousness. Two hours from the time he was admitted to Bellevue, he died from shock and loss of blood.

The body was removed to the hospital morgue, which was also the city morgue, where it would be held temporarily. Max Kauffman accompanied the two attendants who wheeled the sheet-covered corpse through the dark subterranean tunnel that connected the main hospital building with the pathology building. It was no sentimental journey on the Inspector's part but rather an admittedly unreasonable reluctance to give up the best possible clue, if the old man had actually seen the bomber and lived to talk, that they'd had so far.

But of course he learned nothing from the corpse as he stood by and watched the attendants lay the body out in a refrigerated drawer. The Inspector took out a cigar and chewed on it as he reflected upon what would undoubtedly be the eventual fate of the derelict's remains.

The body would be kept at the morgue for fifteen days in case anyone showed up to claim it. Police would meanwhile try to track down the identity of the derelict. They would question scores of individuals in the Bowery, other panhandlers, operators of skid-row flophouses, missions, and soup kitchens. The man's fingerprints would be checked in police files. The newspapers and television would carry photographs and descriptions of him. But despite all this, unless the Inspector missed his guess, no one would come forward to claim the body. There'd possibly be an autopsy at the end of the fifteen-day wait. Afterward, the head might or might not be severed from the torso and the skull retained in the pathology department. Either way, the body would be placed in a rough pine box at the morgue. It would be transported by morgue wagon up to the Bronx and beyond, to City Island, north of Manhattan. From City Island there would be a ten-minute ferry ride across the Long Island Sound to Hart's Island, the city's Potter's field. There the body, wrapped in a paper shroud, would be buried with no gravestone to mark the spot; only a death certificate printed on treated paper listing all information the authorities had on the corpse—in case the body had to be recovered, as sometimes happened—would be attached to the box to distinguish it from the other more than 650,000 bodies which had been buried on Hart's Island since 1869.

Max Kauffman watched the morgue attendants slam shut the drawer with the body in it. He supposed that in death the derelict would remain as anonymous as he'd been in life, his only claim to fame that he was the second fatal victim of the Christmas Bomber.

Rain was falling as the Inspector rode back to the precinct in his limousine. In the early evening, it was now 7:30, and with only six shopping days left before Christmas, many of the department stores were still open, and on the sidewalks shoppers hurried along under bobbing umbrellas. Some stores and apartment buildings had strung their fronts and lobbies with electric Christmas lights which, seen through the rain, had the look of multicolored abstract blobs drip-painted on the darkness.

At the station house, Max Kauffman went straight to John Tynan's office. The lieutenant was at his desk talking on the phone to Barbara Costa. He concluded the conversation hastily when the Inspector appeared, saying: "I don't know how long I'll be yet. I'll give you a call about half an hour before I'm ready to leave and then I'll come pick you up and we'll go out to dinner."

Max Kauffman lit a cigar and perched on the edge of the window sill. He exhaled a mouthful of smoke and said: "The old bum never regained consciousness. Did you get anything?"

"The lab's still processing and will have to confirm it," Tynan said, "but it looks like sticks of TNT again, wired to a clock." He shook his head. "There was another phone call from the bomber. Nine-One-One's got it taped."

"The 'sixth day of Christmas'?" Max Kauffman asked.

"What else?" Tynan said. He looked at the Inspector questioningly. "We agree, don't we, that the wastebasket wasn't the original target for the bomb?"

Max Kauffman rubbed his eyes with the thumb and forefinger of his left hand. "We agree. He must have been on his way somewhere to plant the package and he got scared and dumped it in there. Maybe all the prowl cars and men we've got out on the streets scared him into getting rid of it in a hurry. Once that old bum picked up the package and it went off, it served the bomber's purpose, anyway, if I understand his purpose; to create panic and disrupt the city during the holiday season."

Tynan picked up a photograph from his desk and looked at it. It had been sent over from Headquarters and was a reproduction of the composite picture put together by the Department's Minolta Montage identification system based on the sketchy description supplied by the minister, Clarence Norris. Tynan sighed. "Our reverend friend is just too conscientious a citizen to hazard a guess at what the suspect looks like, except for what he *knows* he saw." The photograph he held showed a face, angular in form, with all the features missing except a thin, black moustache under where the nose should have been. "At least," he added, "we know the son of a bitch we're looking for has got a moustache."

Max Kauffman pushed himself up from the window sill. "I wouldn't be too sure about that. He also *had*, if he's the same man, a black raincoat. Remember? But he wasn't wearing it when the minister saw him. By now he may not be wearing a moustache, either."

He always thought of that particular autumn as the golden days—the happiest time of his life—when the light, day or night, seemed to have a special color that was soft and comforting and there were no dark shadows at the edges of the color. The light extended to the infinity of his vision, indoors or out, and he knew it was because of Adrienne:

The house had once been a mill. The original timber and beams which had formed the structure of the mill now did the same for the house. What had been the main floor of the mill had been below ground and had become the basement of the house, and the rooms had been built above it, a large living room, two bedrooms, a kitchen, and two baths under the peaked roof. The wooden walls of the mill had been replaced with glass, so the sun could pour in, and a wooden sundeck had been added, encircling the house. There were woods all around but the house stood in a landscaped clearing, with a swimming pool in back, and a high chain link fence enclosing the property. The nearest neighbors were miles away. They had the guard dogs, too, to keep out unwanted visitors. And the surrounding woods added to the sense of privacy without being threatening.

But for him the sense of golden light came of course from Adrienne. It was the color of her body, for one thing, the body which she delighted in expos-

131

*ing to the summer sun and to him. He had never ex-
pected that there would ever be a time when he could
be so alone with her, with no one else around, that she
could be so completely his and he could be so completely hers—not after all they had been through.*

*The sheer physical, sensual pleasure of their days
and nights together was almost unbearable. But the
time he had had her completely for his own, as she
had had him for her own, was so brief. And forever
after, the pleasures of that time became symbolized
for him in the gold chain and locket with the tiny
portraits of her and him which she always wore when
they made love....*

He shook his head stubbornly, knowing that was
a dream of another time now gone—a dream. Still, the
presence of Adrienne was there with him in the tiny
hotel room. He couldn't see her but he felt she was
very close, trying to tell him something. He shook his
head stubbornly again. No, she wasn't there. No! No!
No!

He stood up, impatient with himself, and paced
the room. He said aloud: "Adrienne is not here. Adrienne—is—dead. *Adrienne is dead.*" It was important
for him to remember or he wouldn't be able to finish
what he'd started out to do.

Dead. The bitter memory came back, flooding
his mind: the blood, the broken body lying askew, the
smashed face and crushed skull, nothing remaining of
her that was recognizable. And she lay there, the life
leaking out of her, lay there for an eternity until finally, when help came, it was too late. All the while
that song went on and went on in the distance, "Jingle
bells . . . jingle bells." He blamed *them,* all of *them*
—the city; *they* let her die.

The gold necklace and locket were all that was
left. He'd managed to retrieve them when the necklace snapped and fell from around her throat. He'd
managed to do that. And her pocketbook, too; he'd
taken it and what little there was in it. There had been
nothing he could do, do for her. He knew she'd understand. Just as he knew she understood what he was

132

doing for her now. Exacting revenge. For himself, yes, but for her, too.

He put his hand in his coat pocket and touched the necklace and locket. He could hear her somewhere nearby whispering. Whispering something, something. The voice seemed to be drawing him across the room. He moved toward the bathroom, went in, and turned on the light. He was standing in front of the mirror. He remembered then; the moustache. That was what she was trying to tell him. He'd thought of it himself, at the time, but had then forgotten. Someone might have noticed him when he was putting the bombs around the Christmas trees on Park Avenue. The moustache would be a way of identifying him. He had forgotten until Adrienne reminded him. He picked up his razor.

It was after midnight when Max Kauffman arrived home. His wife and daughter had gone that morning up to Cambridge, Massachusetts, to visit the boy, Lawrence, for a few days and the Inspector was surprised to see the lights turned on in the living room. As soon as he closed the door behind him, the maid, Anna, appeared from the back of the apartment. She was still dressed in the uniform she wore when she was serving in the day and evenings.

"Sir," she said, "I waited up to tell you your sister, Mrs. Katz, has been phoning all night, trying to reach you. She sounded very upset and she asked me to tell you it was very urgent that you call her back tonight. She said I should ask you to please phone her no matter how late you came home."

Max Kauffman could see the worry on Anna's face.

"Thank you, Anna," he said gently. "I'm sorry you had to wait up for me. It's all right; you go on to bed now. I'll phone my sister right away."

She nodded. "Is there anything you'd like me to fix you?"

"No, nothing, thanks."

As he walked down the hall, Anna turned off the

133

lights in the living room and went toward the quarters she shared with her husband in the back of the apartment, saying, "Good night, sir."

"Yes, good night, Anna," he said, "and thank you for waiting up for me."

Earlier, around nine, when he'd left the precinct, he'd stopped by Catherine Devereaux's apartment. They had dinner together there, and then had sat in her living room, she curled up in his arms, and listened to records. It had been a quiet, gentle evening, the kind they sometimes shared when, even though they didn't make love, they felt as close as if they had.

Max Kauffman went on into his bedroom now, took off his Chesterfield coat, suit coat, shirt and tie, sat on the side of the bed, and dialed his sister's number. His sister, Rachel, and her husband, Marvin, lived in Jamaica Estates, Long Island.

She answered the phone on the first ring and as soon as she heard his voice said, tearfully, "Oh, thank you so much for calling tonight, dear Max." She paused and he could hear her weeping.

"All right, Rachel," he said soothingly; "whatever it is, tell me about it."

"It's—" she paused again and he could hear her struggling to get her voice under control "—it's about Marvin. He's in trouble, serious trouble. He *has* to talk to you. He was afraid—he wouldn't call you himself—so I did."

"You were right to call me," Max Kauffman said. "Is Marvin there now? Can I talk to him?"

"Yes," she said. "Wait a minute. Here he is."

"Hello Max? This is Marvin."

Max Kauffman lay back on the bed, holding the receiver to his ear. "Rachel says you have a problem. Do you want to talk about it now, or what?"

"Not now," Marvin Katz said quickly. "I need to see you. I'd like it to be as soon as possible. Tomorrow if you could, if it's not asking too much."

"Do you want to have lunch?" Max Kauffman asked. "That would be the best time for me."

"Well," Marvin said, uncertainty in his voice, "it can't be in a restaurant. Too public. And it can't be at

134

your office," he added quickly, and then: "How about my office?"

"Sure," Max Kauffman said. "How's twelve-fifteen?"

"Good. Twelve-fifteen's fine. I'll order us a spread sent in. What would you like? Just name it."

The Inspector had to tighten his hold on the telephone to control his impatience. The stupid son of a bitch; one minute he was groveling on his belly and the next he was the munificent host ready to lay on a banquet.

"A hot pastrami on rye and a beer'll suit me," Max Kauffman said brusquely.

"Yeah, yeah, Max," Marvin said hurriedly. "And listen," his voice was almost choked up. "Oh, God, thank you, Max. I really, really appreciate this."

"Don't thank me yet. Wait until I hear what you have to say. See you tomorrow. Let me talk to Rachel again for a minute."

His sister came back on the wire, still weeping and trying to thank him.

"Take it easy, kid," he told her. "Marvin and I'll talk tomorrow and try to get whatever it is straightened out. Meanwhile, I don't want you to worry. I'll call you."

Still weeping, she said good-bye and hung up the phone.

Max Kauffman took a pair of pajamas out of the bureau drawer and went into the bathroom to take a shower. Whatever his brother-in-law's problem was, he figured it couldn't be as bad as the problem he himself had with the Christmas Bomber.

CHAPTER FOURTEEN

It was 11 A.M. the following day, December 19, and for the past hour Max Kauffman had been in his office studying the file the police had amassed so far on the Christmas Bomber. On his desk were the reports from the police lab on the material collected from the sites of the bombs, the transcripts of testimony by various witnesses, the first note the bomber had sent to the *Daily News*, and the composite photograph. The Inspector also had a Hagstrom street map of Manhattan spread out across the top of his desk. Using a felt-tipped pen he began marking large red Xs at the locations in the city the bomber had chosen as targets for his explosives. While he was working he reached over and turned on the recorder sitting at the edge of his desk into which he had threaded all the taped exchanges between the bomber and 911 in sequence as they'd occurred.

OPERATOR: Police operator.
VOICE: I want you to know there's a bomb planted in Radio City Music Hall. It's there now and it's going to go off.
OPERATOR: Radio City Music Hall?
VOICE: That's it.
OPERATOR: Hold on. Who—
SOUND: Click.
OPERATOR: Hello. Hello.

There was a soft whirr of blank tape and then:

OPERATOR: Police operator.
VOICE: This is the Bomber. It's the third day of Christmas.

137

SOUND:	Click.
OPERATOR:	Police operator.
VOICE:	Listen carefully. A truck with the Christmas tree on it for Rockefeller Center is parked in front of Thirty Rockefeller Plaza.
OPERATOR:	Yeah?
VOICE:	There's a bomb in the gas tank of that truck.
OPERATOR:	A bomb? Who—?
VOICE:	*Listen!* The time is now eleven-fifteen. The bomb is set to explode in exactly thirty-six minutes.
OPERATOR:	Wait! Hang on—Hello? Hello?
SOUND:	Click.
OPERATOR:	Police operator.
VOICE:	This is the Bomber. It's the fourth day of Christmas.
OPERATOR:	Police operator.
VOICE:	This is the Bomber. It's the fifth day of Christmas.
OPERATOR:	Police operator.
VOICE:	This is the Bomber. It's the sixth day of Christmas.
OPERATOR:	Listen—
SOUND:	Click.

Max Kauffman turned off the recorder. The voice was the same on every tape; there was no question about that. A couple of times, in the two longer messages, the voice had betrayed nervousness. Otherwise the words in all of the messages had been spoken without any particular inflection in the voice. The police lab had made voice prints of all the taped messages, but, essentially, the voice didn't tell Max Kauffman any more than did the composite photograph with most of the features of the man's face missing.

The Inspector laid down his pen and looked at

138

the six Xs he'd marked on the map: Forty-seventh Street and Broadway; Sixth Avenue and Fiftieth Street; Fifty-first Street west of Eleventh Avenue; Fiftieth Street and Rockefeller Plaza; Park Avenue from Fiftieth to Sixtieth Streets; and Fifth Avenue and Forty-first Street. He calculated that if he drew lines on the map running uptown and crosstown to encompass the Xs, he would have a rectangular area roughly nine blocks wide by nineteen blocks long in midtown Manhattan.

He was still trying to decide what that could mean to the investigation when the buzzer on his intercom sounded.

He pressed the intercom button. "Yes?"

"Inspector," Policewoman MacKay said, "I have a Mr. J. T. Spanner on the line. He says you know him. He wants to speak with you."

Max Kauffman glanced at his watch. It was 11:40. He ought to be leaving now for the meeting with his brother-in-law.

"Tell him I'm tied up," Max Kauffman said. "Ask if you can take a message."

The Inspector stood up to put his coat on and the intercom buzzer sounded again. Goddamn it! he thought as he pressed the button and said, "Yes, what is it?"

"Sir," Policewoman MacKay said, "Mr. Spanner's quite insistent that he speak with you. He says he has some very important information for you concerning one of your major cases. I have him holding on five."

"All right," Max Kauffman answered. "I'll talk to him."

The Inspector shoved his arms into his coat sleeves and sat back down at his desk. J. T. Spanner was a private investigator who had once worked in the Homicide Bureau under Max Kauffman and had once before involved himself in one of the Inspector's cases. At the successful conclusion of the previous case, an investigation of a robbery at the Metropolitan Museum of Art, during which Spanner had been of enormous help to the police, Max Kauffman had told the private investigator that he, Spanner, had a favor

139

coming to him from the N.Y.P.D. if he ever had to ask. The Inspector assumed that Spanner was now calling to make a request. He punched extension five and picked up the receiver.

"Yeah, Spanner? Inspector Kauffman here."

"How are you, Inspector?" Spanner asked conversationally.

"Harassed, as usual," Max Kauffman said quickly. "What can I do for you?"

Spanner's voice was, the Inspector was certain, deliberately casual as he answered: "I think I may have a lead for you on this Christmas Bomber thing. A witness who may be able to make a positive I.D. on your man."

"I'm interested," Max Kauffman said. "Who's the witness? Give me a name and address."

"No, no," Spanner said. "It can't be done that way. There are conditions. But you'll get your I.D."

"All right, all right," the Inspector said impatiently. "Spell it out."

"The witness is a client of mine. The conditions are that this person be kept out of the case publicly. The witness may be in some danger, and I'm asking that you, and you alone, talk to the witness. Here at my office. You can do it now if you'd like."

Max Kauffman glanced at his watch again. "I can't do it right now, Spanner. How about a couple of hours from now? Say two o'clock."

"Hold on a moment," Spanner said and, after a pause, "Two o'clock's fine. Do you have my address? The Graybar Building, Four-twenty Lexington Avenue, Room Thirteen-o-nine."

Max Kauffman scribbled down the address, hung up the phone, and put the address in his wallet as he left the office.

He decided to take a cab instead of his limousine for the meeting with his brother-in-law since the streets were always so crowded with traffic down in the garment district. He caught one outside the station house and they headed east across town. After the bitter cold of the past several days, the temperature had moderated overnight and there was a weak sun which could be spotted at times through the patches of gaseous haze that had formed over the city. The Christmas trees and decorations along the streets and avenues looked out of season in the sudden thaw of the day.

Kauffman and Son, the family garment firm, was on the sixth, seventh, and eighth floors of an ancient sandstone building on Seventh Avenue a few doors north of Thirty-seventh Street. Max Kauffman left the cab at the corner. He had to climb out in the middle of Thirty-seventh Street because the delivery trucks and handcarts with racks of clothes on them blocked both curbs on the side street. The sidewalks as well as the streets were virtually impassable during noontime in the district, with a steady flow of people hurrying to and from lunch, or lunching while standing on the sidewalk from hot dog stands pulled up to the curbs, and the stream of handcarts moving across the sidewalks from buildings to waiting trucks. Max Kauffman worked his way through the crowds, went into the building and rode the decrepit freight elevator up to the eighth floor where Marvin Katz had his office.

There was a company guard at the elevator door on the eighth floor, an old man named Abe Schechter who had worked for the firm ever since Max Kauffman could remember, back into the days when Grandfather Asa ran the business. The two men shook hands and then Max Kauffman walked down an almost block-long aisle between rows and rows and rows of women's dresses. The close, dusty smell of fibers he remembered so well—and remembered so well disliking —from the days when he had visited the place as a small boy was very strong now in his nostrils and he kept feeling like he was going to sneeze. For a moment he experienced a breathless, choking sensation of the kind that years before when he was a youngster signaled the onset of an attack of asthma from which he periodically suffered through childhood and until he was in his twenties. He took out his handkerchief, blew his nose, and the feeling passed.

At the end of the aisle, Marvin Katz was waiting for him in the doorway of his office, a cubbyhole of a room with a single grimy window that let in little light, and the compensating light in the office, from fluorescent tubing set in the ceiling overhead, was much too harsh and bright. The office was cluttered with swatches of material, stacks of tissue patterns, ledger books, and piles of dresses draped over the two filing cabinets. The only other furniture was a scarred wooden desk with a swivel chair behind it and another wooden chair on the opposite side of the desk.

Marvin Katz pumped Max Kauffman's hand enthusiastically, saying, "You just don't know how much I appreciate this, Max. I know how busy you are."

He led the Inspector into the office, carefully closed the door behind them, and pulled the visitor's chair out for Max Kauffman to sit.

"Really appreciate it," Marvin Katz repeated and went behind the desk and took a seat in the swivel chair.

He had cleared off the top of the desk to make room for two paper placemats, one in front of Max Kauffman, one in front of himself, on which sat a dish of cold salad and a bulging sandwich of pastrami, both wrapped in cellophane. He had ordered the lunch from The Governor, at Broadway and Thirty-ninth Street, one of the favorite eating places for people working in the garment district. Next to Max Kauffman's sandwich was a brown paper bag in which were six bottles of Michelob beer.

Marvin Katz was approximately the same height as Max Kauffman. He was heavier, though, carrying an additional fifteen to twenty pounds, and was ten years younger than the Inspector. His hair was black and wavy. Max Kauffman remembered that once people frequently remarked that his brother-in-law had a widow's peak identical to the widow's peak of the movie actor, Robert Taylor. But now the hair had receded at the forehead and there was a bald spot at the crown the size of the bottom of one of the Michelob beer bottles. His eyes were blue and he had a well-formed nose, mouth, and chin. He was in his shirt sleeves, the shirt a white-on-white fastened at the wrists with large onyx cufflinks, and wore a wide, green polyester tie with bold black squares on it, brown double-knit wool trousers, and narrow black Italian-made shoes.

"Well, now," he said, glancing at Max Kauffman, then leaning down, and opening a desk drawer and bringing out a pint of Cutty Sark scotch and a stack of paper cups.

"Not for me," Max Kauffman said. "I'll just have a beer."

His brother-in-law uncapped one of the Michelobs with a bottle opener from his desk drawer and poured himself a cupful of scotch; he swallowed a mouthful of it. Max Kauffman drank his beer from the bottle and waited while Marvin lit a cigarette.

Max Kauffman settled back in his chair. "All right, let's hear it, Marvin."

"Uh, yeah." Marvin took another drink of scotch, refilled the paper cup, and said: "Max, I sure hope you can help me. I got a real problem."

The Inspector nodded encouragingly.

"What it is, you see," Marvin said slowly, "is a while back I started gambling." He paused again and took another large gulp of scotch.

Max Kauffman leaned forward. "Let's knock off the booze, okay, Marvin? Just say what you've got to say."

"Sure thing." Marvin moved the cup and bottle of scotch over to the side of the desk. "What I started to say was a while back I began playing the horses. For a while I won and then I hit a losing streak. I mean bad. I kept thinking I'd recoup my losses. I don't know what came over me. Instead of laying back I plunged in heavier, hoping to win big. Soon it wasn't just horses; it was football, basketball, hockey. And always losing. Between one thing and another, I got in deep. I mean *deep*, and now I'm in over my head." His hand holding the cigarette was shaking.

"Where'd you get the money?" Max Kauffman thought he already knew the answer but he hoped he was wrong.

Marvin laid his hands flat on the desk, his eyes avoiding Max Kauffman. "That's just it. I didn't get the money. My bookie carried me." He paused to swallow painfully. "I'm into him for a lot of money."

"How much money?" Max Kauffman asked in a cold, flat voice.

Marvin swallowed again before he answered. "Twenty-two thousand, five hundred dollars, God help me."

Max Kauffman sat motionless and silent. Marvin looked at him and flushed. "And that's not even the worst of it." His hands trembling, he pulled the bottle of Cutty Sark back to him and took a deep drink straight from it. "Now," he said in a shaky voice, "the guy won't settle for the money. Assuming I could raise it."

"Who's this guy? Who's your bookie?" Max Kauffman asked.

"Moe Blum." Marvin shifted his eyes away and then back to the Inspector. "You know, 'Moe the Undertaker,' they call him."

Max Kauffman was seething with anger, which he concealed when he spoke. "You knew he was backed by the Gallano family? Everybody in the district knows that."

Marvin nodded.

"So, all right, what *does* he want if he won't settle for money?"

"Oh, Jesus, Max, you're going to kill me." Marvin's voice was full of anguish. "He wants a piece of the business. *This* business. Tomorrow."

"You don't even own a piece of the business. Where would he get an idea like that?" Max Kauffman asked as if he were puzzled. When Marvin just shook his head and didn't answer, the Inspector said: "He got it from *you*, of course. That's why your credit was good, that's why he carried you for twenty-two thousand five hundred dollars' worth of gambling losses."

Max Kauffman was up on his feet so fast that he almost turned the desk over on top of Marvin. His brother-in-law tried frantically to scoot backward in his swivel chair, but before he could move beyond reach the Inspector flung himself across the desk top and grabbed a handful of white-on-white shirt and polyester tie. Max Kauffman's other hand was upraised in a fist.

"You miserable, fucking *shmuck!*" he raged, bodily dragging Marvin over the desk toward him until their faces were only inches apart. "You thought Papa was going to die! You were figuring on it, that's the only way you'd have a share of the business. I ought to—"

"Help me, Max. Think of your sister, Rachel, your nieces, Andrea and Betsy, *Oy, Gottenyu!*" Oh, dear God, Marvin pleaded. "*Oy, Gottenyu! Oy, Gottenyu! Oy, Gottenyu! Oy, Gottenyu! Oy—*"

The Inspector struggled to control his terrible anger. He lowered his fist and shoved Marvin away from him, back across the desk where he flopped into his chair. Max Kauffman took several deep breaths and sat down.

"All right," he said, "pull yourself together. You're supposed to meet Blum tomorrow with an answer, is that right?"

Marvin nodded miserably and whispered: "He said if we don't make a deal, they're going to kill me."

"Where are you supposed to meet him?"

"The same place I make my bets every day. He's always down at the corner at eleven A.M. sharp in his car. I get in, we drive around the block, once, twice, whatever time it takes to talk, and then he lets me out."

Max Kauffman could visualize Moe Blum from other times he'd seen him operating in the garment district. He was a slim, saturnine old man, maybe sixty, maybe seventy, maybe even eighty, who had been known to the police for years as a member of the city's "Jewish Mafia." He was always dressed in a black suit, complete with vest, summer or winter, which was where he had gotten his name, "the Undertaker."

"Tomorrow," Max Kauffman said, "when you meet him you're going to be wired up with a tape recorder under your clothes—"

"Oy—"

"Shut up!" The Inspector stood and began pacing

145

short steps back and forth in front of the desk. "I'll get somebody to give you the equipment and tell you how to use it. You're going to tell Blum you're willing to pay him the money you owe him plus the going rate for interest on the street. If he agrees, we'll work out some way to raise the money. If he doesn't, you'll have a tape of what he says."

Marvin shook his head. "I don't understand. And then what?"

"If he doesn't agree, then it's extortion."

"But what good does that do me?" Marvin asked. "I'm still on the hook."

Max Kauffman started to tell him the plan he had in mind but instead said: "You and the tape will go into court."

Marvin looked disbelieving. "You'd do that to me, your sister's husband—testifying in court about his gambling debts?"

"I'd do it," Max Kauffman said grimly. "You'd better believe I'd do it."

"Max! Max! Max! I'll get *killed.*" The sweat was pouring down Marvin Katz's face. "One way or the other, I'm going to wind up dead. There's no way I'll be able to bring this thing off tomorrow. He'll know."

The Inspector leaned over the desk. "You have no choice, you son of a bitch. If you don't do what I tell you, you're going to get killed. You just better bring it off tomorrow." He swung around toward the door. "Be home tonight. All night. I'll have to make some arrangements. Stay there till I call."

"What about your sandwich and beer?" Marvin wailed as Max Kauffman went out the door. The Inspector didn't answer. He slammed the door behind him so hard it shook the walls.

He was furious—at his brother-in-law, at Moe Blum, at the crazy bomber, at all the fuck-ups of the world who couldn't handle their own lives and had to have somebody follow along and clean up behind them. For a moment he believed he'd had a bellyful of all of it, especially police work. And then he thought, of course he'd never leave the Police Department. It was like that old joke about the guy who had a job with the circus sweeping up behind the elephants, and who was always complaining. When somebody asked the guy why he didn't quit, he answered "What, and get out of show business?"

CHAPTER FIFTEEN

Out on Seventh Avenue again, Max Kauffman caught another taxi. There was still time for him to eat lunch before his meeting with Spanner at 2 P.M., and he remembered he'd always enjoyed the food at the Oyster Bar at Grand Central Station, which would be convenient, too, since it was next to the Graybar Building where Spanner's office was located. He got out of the cab on Forty-second Street opposite Grand Central and crossed the street.

The Oyster Bar was on a lower level of the station. The restaurant was crowded. It was a popular place for business lunches, and there were several large groups waiting. Because he was alone, however, he was lucky and was seated as soon as he entered the room. He ordered a large oyster stew and drank two bottles of beer with it.

While he was eating, he pondered the best way to handle the problem his brother-in-law had with Moe Blum. He already knew what he wanted to do but he had to figure out exactly how to do it. To bring off what he had in mind he'd have to go outside the precinct, keep it away from himself. That meant asking one hell of a big favor from somebody in the Department. It had to be someone he trusted absolutely, and even then the whole thing could backfire. He didn't like what he had to do but he couldn't think of an alternative. So be it. Painful as it was to him he knew there was only one man he could call upon: Leo Morgen of the Headquarters Public Morals Division. He and Leo Morgen had started out as rookies, training at the Police Academy together. They had been close friends for a quarter of a century, and he had been best man when Leo and Beatrice Morgen were married. Over the years Leo had risen to the rank of captain in the Morals Division, with primary responsibility for the Department's antigambling investigations.

Max Kauffman finished his lunch and went upstairs. He called Headquarters from a phone booth on the main level of the station. He had to wait several minutes before Leo Morgen came on the line.

There was genuine pleasure in Leo's voice when he answered: "Max! For God's sakes, how are you? And Belle and Lawrence and Debbie?"

"Fine, Leo; we're all fine. And you and Bea and Sammy and Joel?"

"All well, thank God," Leo said. "When are we going to get together? I know you've got a sticky case going now; I've been hearing things down here. You know."

"Yeah," Max Kauffman said. He cleared his throat. "Actually, Leo, the reason I'm calling is I need to see you. It's urgent."

"If you say it's urgent, Max, just name the time and place."

"Tonight?" Max Kauffman asked. "At my place? Belle and Debbie are away visiting Lawrence up at Harvard. Would it be possible for you to meet me there at, say, about nine?"

There was the briefest hesitation before Leo said, "Sure, sure, Max. Nine P.M. I'll be there."

Max Kauffman made one more phone call from the booth, to his apartment to tell Anna that she and her husband, Gustave, should take the night off. Then he walked quickly across the concourse of Grand Central Station, through the connecting entrance to the Graybar Building next door, and rode the elevator to the thirteenth floor, arriving outside J. T. Spanner's office at a couple of minutes past two.

There was a young woman, a strikingly pretty brunette, sitting behind a small walnut desk in the outer waiting room of the office. She had a smooth ivory complexion, and dark brown hair that swung loosely around her face and was curled under softly at the ends, shoulder-length. Her eyes were large and brown and had a saucy glint in them. She had a nice mouth that smiled easily. Her dress was a wool jersey with a high neck and long sleeves, the color a seashell pink that accentuated her dark hair and eyes. Max Kauffman had met her before and knew she was Spanner's ex-wife but Spanner had two ex-wives and both of them still worked for him. The Inspector could never get straight which was which.

"Good afternoon, Inspector," whichever ex-wife it was said, coming around the desk. "J. T.'s waiting for you." She moved across the waiting room and opened a door.

Spanner was sitting behind his desk in the inner office. It was a light, airy room, not all that large, but the four windows facing on Lexington Avenue and forming a fourth wall behind the desk gave it the appearance of spaciousness. The furniture was Danish modern. In addition to the desk and the chair Spanner was sitting in, there were four other chairs arranged in front of the desk, a sofa against the wall next to the door, and a coffee table in front of the sofa. The room and its furnishings had a not unpleasant, functional look. The ex-wife went out, closing the door behind her.

Spanner got up from the desk and shook hands with Max Kauffman.

"Thank you for coming, Inspector."

"Yeah, Spanner."

They both sat, Spanner taking a chair in front of the desk next to the chair the Inspector sat in. Spanner was thirty-eight years old, five feet ten inches tall, and weighed one hundred and seventy-two pounds. His black hair was cropped close to the skull and he had brown eyes. His features were regular and whatever character his face had came from the lines and creases around the corners of his eyes and mouth and across the lower part of his forehead. He was wearing a charcoal gray worsted suit, a yellow

151

shirt with button-down collar, and a black knit tie.

Spanner lit a cigarette and Max Kauffman took out a cigar and began to unwrap it.

"I'll bring in my client in just a minute," Spanner said. "First, I'd like to give you a little background. Okay?"

Max Kauffman nodded and lit his cigar.

Spanner leaned forward. "As you know, I do a lot of investigative work on a regular basis for the law firm of Hogarth, Whittaker, Macauley. The other day John Macauley phoned me and said one of their clients had a daughter who might have some information about who this bomber was who's been terrorizing the city. The only thing was, the daughter was afraid to talk to the police, afraid of getting involved, afraid the bomber might kill her if he found out she could identify him."

The Inspector stirred impatiently in his chair. "And you want me to assure you I'll keep her out of it publicly? All right, I give you my word I will—if it's possible. As long as she understands that if there's a trial and we need her testimony, she'll have to appear."

"Yes, she understands that," Spanner said. "She's not concerned about later on. We're talking about now—before you apprehend him."

"No problem there," Max Kauffman said. "For now nobody needs to know about her. All I'm interested in is what she's got to tell me in confidence about who she thinks is the bomber."

Spanner flicked his cigarette ash into an ashtray on the desk. "Good! Good! Now there're just a couple of other things. This client of Macauley's, the girl's father, is pretty important to Macauley's firm. He's a stock broker. Macauley had to stick his neck out to assure the guy you'd handle the daughter gently after I had to stick my neck out to assure Macauley you'd handle the daughter gently."

"So everybody gets it in the neck if I don't, huh?" the Inspector couldn't help interjecting.

"Something like that," Spanner said easily. "But of

course as I pointed out to Macauley, you'd have no reason to treat her roughly since, after all, she's come forward of her own free will to cooperate with the police when she could have remained silent."

Max Kauffman exhaled a plume of smoke. "A real public-minded citizen, in other words. Fine, that's fine. I get the message. I'll keep it in mind. You said there were a couple of other things, but you only told me one. What's the rest of it?"

"It's like this," Spanner said, "the story she's going to tell you sounds, uh, well, weird. But I believe her story and I believe this guy she's going to tell you about is the bomber."

"All right, all right, already," Max Kauffman said. "I believe you believe her. This is the Goddamnedest preamble I've ever listened to before I even hear anything of substance. For Christ's sake, can I meet her and hear her story now?"

Spanner grinned and stood up. "Sure." He went to a side door in the office, opened it, and said, "Come on in, Carrie."

The young woman who came into the office was in her mid-twenties. She had long blond hair framing a pretty, carefully made-up face—eye shadow, powder, fresh lipstick—and a well-put-together body. She was about five feet six inches tall in high heels and was dressed in a soft blue cashmere jacket and skirt. Under the jacket was a white silk blouse with pearl buttons down the front. There was a string of baby pearls around her neck matching her tiny pearl earrings. She seemed poised and self-possessed.

The Inspector stood and shook hands with her as Spanner said: "Caroline Harger, Inspector Max Kauffman." Standing close to her, the Inspector could see the dark circles under her eyes which the makeup couldn't hide.

Spanner turned her toward the sofa and she sat there while the two men pulled their chairs around and sat across the coffee table from her.

Max Kauffman gave her an encouraging smile. "Spanner tells me you may have some information for

153

us about the bomber. I have assured him I will keep everything you say in confidence insofar as I'm legally allowed."

She nodded. She had crossed her legs and the Inspector didn't fail to notice that her right foot began swinging back and forth under the coffee table; she wasn't quite as poised as she tried to appear.

"It was about six months ago," she said. "I went to this bar on First Avenue to—just to have a drink. The Velvet Swing, it's called. On First, in the Sixties. I was alone and I met this man—oh, before that, I'd had several drinks. I mean in the bar before I met him." She laughed nervously. "I don't usually drink that much. I don't know what came over me that night. I was really woozy by the time I met him—uh. I mean you have to understand I was woozy because of what comes next."

Max Kauffman nodded. He was sitting back in his chair. His cigar had gone out and he'd put it in the ashtray on the table. His arms were folded across his chest. So far it was a familiar story. New York was filled with single girls like Caroline Harger, lonely, restless, who frequented the so-called singles bars, looking for somebody to buy them a drink, or provide them with companionship, or lay them. From what he knew, sometimes it was one or the other but most times, men being what they were, such girls wound up getting laid, which was all right or, worse, getting beaten up or murdered, which wasn't all right.

"So, anyway," Caroline Harger went on, "I met this man—it's all kind of blurred—and he said I needed some air so we left the bar. And the next thing we'd taken a taxi and we were at his place. It was all kind of still blurred, you see." She paused and ran her tongue over her lips, then said quickly, "He, uh, tried to make love to me. He tried and he tried and he couldn't. I guess I fell asleep and then I was awake again." Her foot was swinging violently now under the coffee table. "He'd tied me to the bed, arms and legs."

She stopped again, her voice breaking.

Spanner stood. "Do you want me to get you a

glass of water or something?" When she shook her head, Spanner patted her shoulder and said, "You're doing fine."

She kept her eyes on the far wall of the room as she continued: "On the table next to the bed was this —this contraption. He kept making me look at it and telling me what it was. It—it was a bomb. It was sticks of dynamite wired to a clock, and he kept telling me it was going to go off and blow us both up in a matter of minutes. And then he tried to make love to me again, and this time he did. And all the time he was making love to me he kept calling me by another name: *Adrienne*. Blurred as everything was, it was like a tr—like a nightmare, and I thought it was. But it wasn't."

"And all this time you were still, uh, woozy?" Max Kauffman asked in an even voice.

"High," Caroline Harger said.

"From the drinks," Spanner quickly prompted.

"From the drinks," she said, picking up his words. "We kept—I guess we kept drinking after we got to his place."

Aha! Max Kauffman thought, understanding. She wasn't high, she was stoned, and it wasn't from drinks, it was from grass or something stronger. With that in mind, her story made more sense, the whole buildup by Spanner before he'd brought the girl in made more sense. Christ, he couldn't care less what she'd been doing. That was somebody else's problem in the N.Y.P.D.; his problem was the bomber. "Yes, I understand," he said.

Spanner, watching the Inspector and the girl, relaxed in his chair; the worst was over now. Caroline Harger thought she'd conned Max Kauffman, but Spanner knew better. The Inspector had read her like a book, understood now why she had been "woozy" and was vague about her experiences that night, and he obviously didn't give a damn. She had nothing to worry about for whatever she'd taken that night and Spanner and Macauley were off the hook for having encouraged her and her father to tell her story to the police.

"Please go on," Max Kauffman said gently.

"Well, the next thing," the girl said, "we were in a taxi and he was taking me home. I lived down in the Village at that time—I'm back living with my family now. We talked in the taxi. I remember I asked him who 'Adrienne' was and he was kind of vague and said something about she was his wife and she'd been killed last Christmas Eve by a city bus. He wouldn't say anything else."

Max Kauffman felt his heart skip a beat. "You're sure he said she was killed last Christmas Eve?"

Caroline Harger nodded vigorously.

The Inspector took out a notebook and wrote in it. "And her name was 'Adrienne'?"

"Yes."

"And his name?"

"Paul was all he told me that night," Caroline Harger said. "But later, several days later, I went back to the house—I'd remembered the address. The whole thing was so unreal I wanted to see if there really was such a place. I was scared but I had to know. I didn't see him, or anybody around the house. The place looked deserted. It's a nice-looking town house. But his name was on a little metal plate below the mail slot in the front door. Paul Driner. D-R-I-N-E-R."

Max Kauffman's pulse was racing. "And the address?"

"Twenty-one West Seventy-ninth Street," she said very carefully. "Just off Central Park West."

"This could be very helpful," the Inspector said.

Spanner said quickly, "That's not all."

Max Kauffman looked up. "Oh?"

"Yes, there's more," the girl said. "Recently, when the bombings started in the city, I wondered if this man, Paul, could be behind them. It worried me. But for a while I didn't tell anybody. And then, just a week ago, I was in a taxi coming across West Forty-eighth Street—it was between either Sixth Avenue and Broadway or Broadway and Eighth Avenue—and I saw him again. At least I think it was him. He was with a girl. She looked like a, you know, a hooker. She was a tall redhead in a miniskirt, boots, and a fur jacket. They went into this hotel together. I jotted down the name: the Hotel Sydney."

She uncrossed her legs and sat up very straight on the sofa. "When I saw him again, after all the terrible bombings were going on, I knew I had to talk to somebody. I told my father—not everything, you understand—and he told his lawyer, and then I talked to his lawyer, and then to Mr. Spanner, and now to you. I just felt I had to tell somebody."

"I know this couldn't have been easy for you to do," he said kindly. "You're very brave."

"Thank you," she said, her voice barely audible.

"Please, one more thing, Miss Harger," he asked; "do you think you could help us by trying to give us as complete a description of this man as you can?" He explained to her about the Headquarters composite photo identification system and told her he would arrange to have her taken to Headquarters and back again in his own limousine. Spanner could accompany her. The sooner the better.

She looked at Spanner and when he nodded, she said, "Yes, I'll go whenever you say, this afternoon if you'd like. I don't know how accurate my description will be but I'll try."

The Inspector closed his notebook. "Good! I'll phone my chauffeur right now and he can be here in fifteen, twenty minutes." He stood. "I'm curious. Do you recall any one significant feature about this man?"

She frowned and said, "Um, well, he had a moustache, I know."

Max Kauffman smiled. "That's what I was curious about. Thank you again, Miss Harger." He turned to Spanner. "May I use a phone for a few minutes?"

"Use the phone on my desk," Spanner said, and walked Caroline Harger back to the adjoining office.

Max Kauffman called the 16th Precinct and asked Detective Lukin to come immediately to Spanner's office, pick up Spanner and the girl, take them to Headquarters, and bring them back. Then he talked to Tynan, quickly summarized what he had learned of the possible identity of the bomber, and directed Tynan to get a search warrant for the police to use at the West Seventy-ninth Street address—in case they needed it—to run a check through the records on the name "Paul Driner," and a check through the accident reports for Christmas Eve of the previous year to find whether a woman named Adrienne Driner had been killed by a bus in the city.

"I'm headed back to the precinct now," the Inspector added. "As soon as we get a search warrant, we'll take some men and go up to his house."

"You think this is the guy, Inspector?" Tynan asked.

"I think it could be. She also mentioned he had a moustache."

Max Kauffman hung up the phone and Spanner came back into the office and walked him out to the elevators.

"Look, I appreciate your help, Spanner," the Inspector said. "Don't worry about the girl. I'll see that she's protected, no matter what comes up. Let me know if she needs any help. And thanks again."

"Sure," Spanner said. "We'll be in touch."

They shook hands as an elevator stopped at the floor. Max Kauffman got on the elevator and Spanner headed back to his office.

CHAPTER SIXTEEN

It was 4:45 that afternoon when the line of six squad cars turned off Central Park West into Seventy-ninth Street and pulled up silently in front of the house at Number 21. Max Kauffman stepped quickly out of the lead car, followed by John Tynan and Detectives Cohen and Garibaldi, and started across the sidewalk toward the house. Detectives Braxley and Raucher, who had been riding in the second car, were right behind them. Then all six squad cars emptied as uniformed patrolmen, twelve of them, stepped out on the street and stood waiting at the edge of the curb while the Inspector and the five detectives approached the house.

Number 21 was a three-story building, a cheerful-looking town house with white stone steps leading up to the vestibule and front door. Max Kauffman led the way up the steps. The door was painted black. Half-way down it, just as Caroline Harger had described it, was a mail slot and a small metal plate embossed with the name "Paul Driner." The Inspector pressed the doorbell and heard chimes echoing inside the house. He rang a couple of more times, pounded on the door with his fist, then stepped aside and Detective Ray Braxley took his place, a ring of keys in his hand. It took Braxley less than five minutes to unlatch the three locks on the door. The door swung back slowly, creaking on its hinges, and the six detectives moved through quickly, coats unbuttoned and pulled back so they could draw their guns easily if necessary.

There was a small foyer inside the door, with mail scattered across the floor where it had been

159

dropped through the slot in the door. Beyond the foyer was a large, high-ceilinged living room. On one side of the foyer were stairs leading to the upper two floors. The living room was deserted and virtually empty of furnishings. There were no rugs on the floors, and the only things in the room were a piano and a long, curving sofa. The interior of the house smelled musty, as if it had been closed up for a long time. Max Kauffman signaled with his hand and the detectives moved away soundlessly to search the rest of the house. The Inspector stayed in the living room and lit a cigar. He wandered around the room, not touching anything, but observing that there was a heavy layer of dust on the window sills, the piano, and the top, seat, and arms of the sofa.

One by one, the detectives came back and reported there was no one in the house.

"The second floor is just about as empty as it is in here," Braxley said. "Most of the furniture's gone, except for a couple of beds."

"It's the same on the third floor," Cohen reported.

"The place looks like it's been all but cleaned out," Tynan said. "I don't think anybody's been here in months."

Max Kauffman grunted. "Yeah." He was back in the foyer, moving the mail around on the floor with the toe of his shoe. Most of the letters were junk mail addressed to OCCUPANT. A couple of the envelopes, which also looked like advertising circulars, were addressed to Mr. Paul Driner.

The Inspector looked up. "I'd say if he is our man, he's flown the coop." He pointed to Tynan. "Radio the precinct. Tell them to get some lab boys up here. I want the whole place dusted for fingerprints and whatever else they can find."

Tynan nodded and went outside to one of the squad cars.

Max Kauffman walked through the house from top to bottom, looking over the rooms curiously. As the men had reported, most of the rooms were bare except for a piece of furniture here or there. Nothing significant caught his eye. Back in the living room again, he selected Garibaldi and Braxley to stay on at the house until after the lab men had finished their work there. Then, he instructed, the house was to be locked up again, and he ordered Tynan to post a twenty-four-hour-a-day surveillance of the house from the street until further notice.

By the time the Inspector came outside a small crowd had collected in the block and was watching the police activity. Max Kauffman assigned Detectives Raucher and Cohen to question residents along the street and see if anybody had any information on Paul Driner. The Inspector left one prowl car at the scene and the rest of the group started back to the precinct.

The sun had set and the wind was freshening. After the warming thaw of the day, Max Kauffman could feel the cold that had come again with the darkness seeping into the squad car. He looked back at Tynan sitting in the rear seat. "I want to start trying to run down who that girl is, that hooker, at the hotel on West Forty-eighth." Earlier he had filled Tynan in on the story Caroline Harger had told of seeing the man she thought was the bomber with the girl. "She may be our best bet. Get some men on it tonight. If they locate her I want her brought in for questioning."

"Right," Tynan said. "Also, I'm going to put men to work digging into every possible record, municipal, state and federal, Social Security lists, business incorporation records, real estate records, bank accounts, and the like to see if we pick up a Paul Driner or an Adrienne Driner. I'll need some extra men."

"Yeah, good," Max Kauffman said. "I'll see to it."

At 6:30 they were back at the precinct. Tynan accompanied Max Kauffman up to the Inspector's office. Policewoman MacKay had a message from one of the assistant medical examiners at the city morgue, a Dr. Howard Wallstein, who said he might have some information on the female accident victim the police had inquired about.

"Hang on," Max Kauffman said to Tynan, and phoned the assistant medical examiner. Dr. Wallstein told him that a careful check had been made through the files for Christmas Eve of the year past and that there was only one fatal vehicular accident victim in the city on that date: a Caucasian female, believed to be in her early thirties, who had been struck by a number 4 bus and killed instantly on Fifth Avenue at Fifty-third Street at approximately 7 P.M., December 24. She had died of a crushed skull and massive internal hemorrhaging. She had carried no handbag and no identification could be found on her. The body had been brought to the morgue by a City Hospital ambulance. Police had attempted to establish her identity through her clothing but had failed. A description of her had been circulated and the missing persons reports were carefully watched, but no one had reported anyone missing who came close to fitting her description. Her identity was never established and no one claimed her body, which was held at the morgue for thirty days, longer than normal. It was finally buried in Potter's field on January 24 this year. Max Kauffman told Dr. Wallstein that he wanted the body exhumed as soon as possible and returned to the morgue and a cast made of all the bones and teeth. The assistant medical examiner assured him that an order for disinterment would be drawn up immediately and the body should be recovered and returned to the morgue the next morning. The Inspector would be notified.

Max Kauffman hung up the phone and told Tynan what he'd learned, concluding, "This Driner tells Caroline Harger that his wife, Adrienne, was killed by a bus last Christmas Eve. Everything he said matches with the unidentified female corpse they bring into the morgue that night. But why didn't Driner identify the body or claim it?" He shook his head.

"At least," Tynan said, "it looks like it was her death last Christmas Eve that set him off on the bombing spree this Christmas. It looks like it all ties in. The Twelve Days of Christmas and so on."

"That, yeah," the Inspector agreed. "But it still doesn't explain why he didn't identify her body."

Tynan frowned. "Maybe her death drove him

over the edge at precisely the moment it happened, and he was incompetent."

"Maybe." Max Kauffman leaned back in his chair. "Anyhow, now that we've got a possible name to go with the corpse, we'll circulate the name and descriptions of any peculiarities in her skeleton and teeth to doctors and dentists. As long as we can't turn up Driner, I want to nail down for a fact that this corpse was his wife, Adrienne."

Tynan nodded in agreement and then said: "I'm going to get moving on the rest of the investigation."

"That reminds me," Max Kauffman said. "I don't know where I'll be tonight. But I'll have the beeper with me. If you manage to pick up that hooker, I want to be notified."

The desk intercom buzzed. Tynan gave a wave and left the office.

Max Kauffman pressed the intercom switch. "Yes?"

"Commissioner Hilliard on five," Policewoman MacKay said.

"I have it." Max Kauffman picked up the phone. "Hello, sir, this is Inspector Kauffman. I was just getting ready to dictate a report to you on some possible new developments in the Christmas Bomber case." He quickly related the information that had been uncovered that day.

"Glad to hear it," John Hilliard said. "Everybody's getting uptight on this thing. I understand the *Times* and the *Daily News* are both going to run strong editorials tomorrow calling for swifter police action. Maybe this information you have now is the break we've been waiting for."

"I'd like to believe that," Max Kauffman said. "But of course we agree that this information must not be made public until we see what it's all about."

"Absolutely," the Commissioner said.

"We're going to need some extra men to help comb the files."

"You've got them," Hilliard answered. "I'll get you a hundred. Tomorrow morning."

"Tell them to report to Lieutenant John Tynan here at the precinct," Max Kauffman said.

"Right," the Commissioner said.

Max Kauffman hung up, took his private phone out of his desk drawer and dialed Catherine Devereaux.

As soon as she heard his voice, she said, "Please tell me you're calling to say I'll see you tonight."

"There's no way you can get out of it," he told her and was pleased when she laughed happily.

"The only thing is," he said, "it's going to be a while. Not before ten, ten-thirty. I'll tell you what; why don't you get all dressed up and I'll take you out for a late supper?"

"I'd like that." She paused, then asked, "And what about later?"

He smiled to himself. "That, too."

He put the phone back into his desk drawer, pulled the dictaphone over and began his report to the Commissioner. His eyes roved around the office while he dictated into the machine. Some progress had been made in redecorating the office, the painting of the walls and ceiling had been done, and the new wall-to-wall carpeting had been delivered and lay rolled up in wrapping paper in the back of the room. There was still some painting to be done around the woodwork in the office, and his new drapes hadn't arrived yet. When he finished his report, he dictated a separate reminder to MacKay to check the decorator on when the new drapes would arrive and when all the work would be completed.

It was 8:15 before the report was typed and he'd read it over and sent it on to the Commissioner's office. In forty-five minutes he was due to meet Leo Morgen. He called down for his car, called Tynan to tell him he'd have a hundred men reporting to help the following morning, and went home.

In the apartment he took off his hat and Chesterfield coat and his suit coat and hung them in the closet. He made himself a stiff drink of Chivas Regal and water at the pantry bar in the hall, drank some of it, and carried the glass with him into the bathroom. He doused his face with cold water and combed his hair. He finished the drink in the bathroom and carried the empty glass back to the bar. Then he got fresh glasses from the bar, put them on a tray along with an unopened bottle of Chivas Regal, a pitcher of water, and a bucket filled with ice. He took the tray into the living room and put it on the coffee table, then got a box of cigars from the den and placed them next to the tray on the coffee table.

Leo Morgen arrived promptly at nine.

"You old son of a bitch," Morgen said in greeting, giving Max Kauffman a handshake and bear hug.

"Same to you," Max Kauffman answered, grinning. He took Morgen's camel's hair overcoat and brown snapbrim hat and hung them in the closet.

Leo Morgen was a stocky man, a couple of inches shorter than the Inspector, with a thick neck, broad shoulders, and a muscular body. His hair was very light auburn, and he wore it combed across his head with no part. His eyebrows were the same color as his hair and formed thick tufts above his eyes which were smoky gray. He had on a glen plaid suit and vest, a red wool tie, white shirt, and black shoes well shined.

The two men made small talk about their families while Max Kauffman fixed them drinks, lit Morgen's cigar and one for himself. They sat across the coffee table from each other.

Morgen raised his glass. *"L'chayim!"*

"L'chayim!" Max Kauffman answered.

Both men drank. Leo Morgen lowered his glass and rattled the ice cubes in it. "So how's it feel to have the whole city waiting breathlessly for you to catch this madman bomber?"

"I can think of situations I'd rather be in," Max Kauffman answered. "What can I tell you, Leo? You've sat in the same kind of hot seat a few times yourself."

Morgen nodded. "Yeah, yeah, I guess I have, come to think of it." He looked up levelly at the Inspector. "Any way I can help, Max?"

Max Kauffman shifted uneasily in his chair. "I—uh—what I wanted to talk to you about is something entirely different."

"Okay, shoot." Morgen took another swallow of his drink and sat back in his chair.

Max Kauffman, speaking quickly, told Morgen the whole problem his brother-in-law had with the bookie, but omitted both names.

"These bastards never learn, do they?" Morgen said. "I mean both parties."

"No," Max Kauffman agreed, "they never learn."

"So what do you want from me, Max?"

"The bookie is Moe Blum," the Inspector said. "The other guy's agreed, at my urging, to wear a tape recorder when he meets Blum for the showdown, at which he'll tell Blum he's willing and able to repay the money, with interest, but there'll be no piece of the business turned over."

Morgen whistled through his teeth, sitting very alert in the chair. "Moe Blum, huh? 'Moe the Undertaker.' Jesus, Max you don't know how long I've been waiting to put that old fucker behind bars. If we nail him on an extortion rap, he's gone."

"There's a catch," Max Kauffman said. He drained his glass and set the empty glass down on the coffee table. "The other guy, the victim, is my brother-in-law, Marvin Katz. You remember, he married my sister, Rachel."

Leo Morgen's face was expressionless. "I remember."

There was a long, uncomfortable silence in the room. Finally, Morgen leaned forward. "Let me freshen the drinks." He fixed them both strong drinks and remained seated forward on his chair.

"You'll have to put it into words, Max—what you want me to do," he said in a toneless voice.

"I know." The Inspector stood, walked over to the window and back again. "I don't like it, Leo, but he's family. These things can get awfully messy in a courtroom."

Morgen raised a hand. "Just say it, Max, you know you have to say it."

166

"All right." Max Kauffman sat down and leaned forward. His voice low, he said, "I want somebody to wire my brother-in-law up tomorrow. If Blum won't take the money, persists in his extortion and it's on the tape, I'd like somebody to take the tape and talk to him, point out the error of his ways, and give him an opportunity to act like a reasonable man, and, not so incidentally, avoid going to jail."

Morgen sighed. "Yeah, I thought you had something like that in mind. The answer is, yes, I'll help."

Max Kauffman could see the brief shadow of ness that flickered across Morgen's face and then was gone. Morgen's smile was artificial and his voice strained when he said, "It's all right, Max. Sometimes these things happen. Sometimes the only way to handle them is a way like this."

"No, it's not all right," Max Kauffman answered. "I don't give myself that out. You do—well, what you think you have to do, I suppose. But doing a thing like this is never all right. I'm sorry, Leo."

Morgen stood. "Knock it off, Max," he said, his voice kinder. "You've been a good cop. You're still a good cop; you'll always be a good cop. Maybe once you're entitled to a personal favor from the law. Guys like Moe Blum are vermin. Besides, even if I got him into court, with the tape and everything else, he'd probably manage—with the Gallano family behind him—to slip free. He always has."

"Talking about that," Max Kauffman said, "Marvin, my brother-in-law, doesn't know the whole plan. He thinks he's going to have to go to trial against Blum, with the tape. I'm not going to tell him different, just in case Blum is obstinate and won't back off."

"I think that's a good idea," Morgen said. "But Blum'll deal once we get him on tape. I'm pretty sure about that. He's venal but no fool. Give me your brother-in-law's phone number and office address."

The Inspector took out a notebook and a pen and wrote out the information. He tore the page out of the notebook and passed it to Leo Morgen.

The other man stuck it in his wallet. "Tell your brother-in-law to be in the office early—8 A.M. Two

167

guys'll call on him. They'll identify themselves. Arnie and Milt. They'll wire him up, wait in the office until he meets with Blum, then take the tape. I'll see it's handled from there."

The two men had walked out to the foyer and Max Kauffman helped Morgen on with his coat and handed him his hat.

"Leo—"

"Don't say anything, Max." Morgen gave the Inspector an awkward pat on the shoulder. They shook hands, and Morgen left. Max Kauffman knew it would never be the same with them again, even though Leo Morgen had made the whole thing as easy for him as possible. He was profoundly depressed. He went back into the living room. Both of them had left their last drinks untouched. Max Kauffman gathered up the glasses and bottle and carried the tray back to the pantry bar. He took his own full glass into the bedroom with him, sat on the side of the bed, picked up the phone and called his brother-in-law.

Marvin answered on the first ring. "Is that you, Max?"

"Yeah, it's me. Look, tomorrow morning be at the office at eight o'clock. Be there. Two guys are coming to see you. They'll identify themselves as Arnie and Milt. You do exactly as they tell you to do. Understand?"

"Max, I—Max—"

"*Do you understand?*" Max Kauffman demanded, his voice like ice.

"Yes. But listen, Max, can't we talk for a minute. I—"

"Marvin, I don't, I do not, want to talk to you any more tonight. I'll call you after your meeting, after eleven tomorrow."

"Rachel wants to say something. Hang on," Marvin said quickly.

Max Kauffman shook his head and downed a large swallow of scotch.

"Max," his sister said, and dropped her voice to a whisper; "Marvin's so miserable. He's scared to death. He's just gone into the other room, so I can talk without him hearing. Max, what's going to happen to him?"

"He's going to be all right, Rachel," the Inspector said in an even voice. "It can't be helped that he's suffering; he got himself into this."

"Please don't be bitter, Max," Rachel pleaded. "It's not easy for Marvin—or Seymour, either, for that matter—being under Papa's thumb all the time. You just don't know. Have a little pity, a—"

"Rachel, Rachel, Rachel," Max Kauffman said in a patient voice, "I know you're upset but I'm very tired. There's nothing to be gained by talking any more tonight. I promise we'll have a long talk in a day or two. All right? All right, Rachel?"

"Yes, all right," she said. "And I know you'll do what's right. Good night, Max."

"Good night, dear Rachel."

He sat on the bed for a while after he'd hung up the phone, and finished his drink. Finally he roused himself and began undressing so he could shower and shave and put on fresh clothes before he went to pick up Catherine Devereaux.

When he arrived in a cab at Catherine Devereaux's apartment forty-five minutes later, she opened the door, ready to leave, her mink coat draped around her shoulders. Under it she had on a frothy, tangerine chiffon evening gown with a cowl neck and long sleeves. Her handbag was the color of her black peau de soie pumps; except for small, delicate tourmaline earrings, she wore no jewelry.

"*Elegante*—and then some," was the Inspector's compliment to the way she looked.

She, delighted with his reaction, kissed him spontaneously and then had to wipe the circle of lipstick from his mouth before they got into the waiting taxi.

They went uptown to the Cafe Carlyle for their late supper and to listen to Bobby Short play the piano and sing, mostly Cole Porter.

Max Kauffman felt edgy. He supposed it was a reaction to the drinks he'd had earlier—he didn't usually drink so much so quickly—as well as the accumulation of worries about the bomber and the mess his brother-in-law was in and had involved him and his friend, Leo Morgen, in. He ordered a bottle of Dom Perignon with their supper, although he sipped it sparingly. The encounter with Leo Morgen had disturbed him far more than he had anticipated when he had first come up with the solution of how to dispose of Moe Blum. Then it had seemed like a simple, pragmatic answer to a petty problem, and nothing more. Now, because of the way he felt after meeting Leo Morgen, he wasn't so sure.

"Rough day, Max?" Kit asked him from across the table, her face sympathetic.

"Yes."

She smiled and covered his hand with hers. "But nothing you can't handle, huh?"

He thought for a moment with great seriousness and then he smiled at her. "Oh, I suppose not."

They hadn't talked much so far that evening. He realized how unfair it was to her, and to himself, to spoil the evening by worrying over problems which, as she had so accurately put it, he *could* handle. There was a time and place for everything, and this was the time and place to enjoy the music and the look of her. He gave himself over to the Cole Porter–Bobby Short artistry—"Too Darn Hot," "Miss Otis Regrets," "From This Moment On," "You're the Top"—and the seductive playfulness of her mood, which, he recognized, she was signaling to him by the way she touched his hand and arm, by her smile and the way she looked at him.

Sex was not everything between them; in fact, he reflected, they were together many more times when they didn't make love than when they did. And in every way that was possible for him he had given her more of himself—his concern, his support, his attention, shared with her his deepest thoughts, than he had with all the other people in his life combined—just as he believed she had done with him. At the same time, however, he believed they were both honest enough to recognize that their sexual coming together was the strongest bond in their relationship,

170

and the strongest reassurance of their love, one for the other, and that it should be that way.

"Listen," she said to him now, her eyes mischievous, "they're playing our song."

Bobby Short was singing, "Let's Do It."

For all her teasing, it was such an unexpected thing for her to say that Max Kauffman had to smother his laughter with a napkin.

"That's the best offer I've had all day," he said. "Let's. Go home, that is."

He got the check. Before he could pay it, the beeper in his coat pocket began to buzz insistently. The waiter looked startled and several people at tables nearby turned to look curiously. The Inspector switched off the buzzer and stood hurriedly. "I'll be right back," he said to both Kit and the waiter.

He went out to the lobby of the Carlyle Hotel and called the precinct from a phone booth. He supposed Tynan wanted to let him know they'd picked up the hooker at the hotel. He'd been expecting the call all evening. When he got the station house on the line, however, the switchboard operator put him through to the dispatcher who said: "Sir, there's been a report of some kind of explosion in front of the Plaza Hotel, at Fifth Avenue and Fifty-ninth Street. I've already contacted Lieutenant Tynan. He's on his way there."

"Yes," Max Kauffman said, "I'll be there in fifteen minutes."

He went back into the cafe, paid the check, and led Catherine Devereaux out.

"There's been some kind of an incident in front of the Plaza Hotel. I'll have to check on it. You go on home and I'll be along shortly. If it looks like I'm going to be tied up too long, I'll phone you."

He put her into a cab on Madison Avenue, kissed her, and took a second taxi for himself. The driver cut across to Fifth Avenue and when they reached Fifty-ninth Street, the Inspector could see several squad cars and a police emergency van parked around the square in front of the Fifth Avenue entrance of the Plaza. The bomb wagon, red lights on the top blinking, and siren growling, was just pulling away from the curb. He could see several figures moving around the Pulitzer Fountain in the center of the square. The fountain was strung with blue Christmas lights which still twinkled cheerfully in the darkness. A small crowd stood watching from across Fifth Avenue in front of the General Motors Building.

He paid the driver and quickly crossed the sidewalk to the fountain where he spotted John Tynan. There were a couple of detectives from the 16th Precinct with Tynan, as well as several uniformed patrolmen. Max Kauffman approached them and asked, "What is it, Tynan?"

"It was another one," Tynan said, "but it's okay, Inspector. A bomb, but this one more or less fizzled. It was another clock, a primer, and some dynamite. This time we were lucky; only the primer went off. It made a noise but didn't do any real damage except to put a couple of small chinks on the inside of the fountain. It must have short-circuited. The two sticks of TNT didn't blow, and I sent them up to Disposal in the bomb wagon."

One of the patrolmen who had been on the radio in a squad car parked on Fifth Avenue now came hurrying up. "Sir," he said to Max Kauffman, "the dispatcher just sent word that nine-one-one got another call a minute or so ago. A guy said he was the bomber and that it was the Seventh Day of Christmas."

Max Kauffman turned and looked around the street, not really knowing what he was looking for. His eye took in the crowd still standing on the sidewalk. As his gaze moved on, he saw the sidewalk telephone booth at the far corner. He remembered that when he'd first arrived and gotten out of the taxi, he'd noticed the crowd and the phone booth. There'd been a man in the phone booth at the time. Now it was empty. Perhaps it was nonsense, but he couldn't help but believe that the man had been the bomber.

Tynan touched his arm and said: "I guess we're finished up here. Okay, sir?"

Max Kauffman nodded. "Yes, sure."

The other detectives and patrolmen began to leave.

Tynan fell into step beside Max Kauffman. "Inspector, if you've got a second, I'd like you to meet my fiancée. She's right there." He pointed to a red Porsche parked by the square, on Fifty-eighth Street.

"I'd be pleased," Max Kauffman told him.

"Barbara and I were down at her parents' place in Gramercy Park making preparations for the wedding next week when the call came," Tynan said. "Incidentally, to bring you up to date on the investigation: the vice squad thinks they know who the girl at the Sydney Hotel is. A hooker by the name of Felice Morrissey. She keeps a room there. She hasn't been in it tonight so far but they've got a stakeout on the place. Also I drew up assignment lists for the checks I want to run through the various records to trace this Paul Driner and Adrienne Driner. First thing in the morning, when the additional men report in at the precinct, I'll put them to work."

"Good," Max Kauffman said.

When they reached the red Porsche, Tynan leaned down and opened the door. "Honey, I want you to meet Inspector Kauffman," he said.

Barbara Costa slid out of the car. As Tynan introduced them, she and Max Kauffman shook hands.

"Jack's told me the good news." Max Kauffman smiled at her. "He's a lucky man. I wish you both a long life of great happiness."

"Thank you," she said.

Tynan looked around the street. "Do you have your car, Inspector? Can we drop you some place?"

"No, thank you," Max Kauffman answered. "You go on along. It was very nice to meet you, Miss Costa."

He watched them get into the car, waved to them, and after they drove away walked to the corner of Fifth Avenue and Fifty-eighth Street and hailed a cab to take him to Catherine Devereaux's apartment.

The seventh day of Christmas, he thought. Five days to go.

CHAPTER SEVENTEEN

Catherine Devereaux had been awake for the past half hour but she had laid quietly in bed, her eyes closed, listening to the comforting sounds of Max Kauffman moving around in the apartment, showering in the bathroom, and getting dressed. She kept her eyes closed because she knew that if he thought he had awakened her and was disturbing her, he'd only hurry and he'd be gone that much sooner.

It was morning. The last time she'd peeked at the clock on the bedside table it was five minutes past seven. She could feel the cold in the room even though she was warm under the bed covers. She knew it had snowed during the night because once she had gotten up in the darkness and looked out the bedroom window and seen the big white flakes falling, muffling the familiar night sound of the foghorns of boats signaling each other on the East River. It was December 20, a Friday, and she wondered if they'd have a white Christmas.

She was concerned about Max Kauffman. Sometime during the night she had awakened and found the bed beside her was empty. He was at the window, looking out. He didn't know she was watching him and he had sat at the window for over an hour. She knew he was worried about something—she supposed it was this bomber case—and she couldn't go back to sleep until he had returned to the bed. It was then, after a time when she heard his deep, even breathing and knew he was finally asleep, that she had gotten up herself and looked out the window and seen the snow.

Now she heard him come out of the bathroom. She could smell the pleasant, soapy steam of the shower which followed him into the room. He was trying to be quiet but she could hear the small, rustling sounds, the jingle of coins in his pants pockets, as he dressed. She wished she could slow him down, that he wouldn't leave so soon. Being alone, what she thought of as the absence of other people around her, seldom bothered her. But the absence of a specific person, *him*, was what she thought of as loneliness. It was what she knew she would feel today when he was gone.

With her eyes still closed, she could tell that he had crossed to the bed and was looking down at her. Then she felt his lips lightly brush her forehead. She could hear him moving quietly away from her. He was gone from the room. She could hear him moving quietly toward the front hallway, the front door open and close. And then he was gone from the apartment. Tears ran from between her closed eyelids and she rolled over on her stomach and buried her face in the pillow.

It was 8:15 A.M. when Max Kauffman walked into the 16th Precinct. He could feel the electricity in the station house. The lobby was filled with men moving in a file up and down the stairs to the offices where the bomb squad were located. The desk sergeant saluted Max Kauffman and called to him: "Sir, Lieutenant Tynan asked to be told as soon as you arrived. He wants to see you. Shall I send him up?"

"Send him up," the Inspector said. He continued on up to the third floor. Policewoman MacKay wasn't at her desk yet. Max Kauffman went into his office, turned on the lights, and hung his hat and coat in the closet. Crossing to the desk, he telephoned a coffee shop down the street and ordered breakfast, a pint of orange juice and two fried egg sandwiches, and two containers of coffee. He preferred fresh-made coffee in his own percolator in the office but he didn't have the patience to fool with it this morning.

A couple of minutes later Tynan knocked on the

door and came in. He had a piece of paper in his hand and a big smile on his face.

"Good news this morning, sir." He sat down in one of the chairs in front of the Inspector's desk.

"I can stand some good news," Max Kauffman said. He started to take a cigar from his pocket and then decided to wait until he'd had breakfast.

Tynan held up the piece of paper in his hand. "The FBI report on those prints picked up in that abandoned Mercedes Benz just came through. A positive match-up. Guess whose?"

"Paul Driner?"

"Right! Right! Right!" Tynan said exuberantly. "And that's not all. The prints came from army records. The file of one Captain Paul Verrick Driner, army serial number one-one-one-three-four-zero-zero-five-five-six. Active duty: Korean War, U.S. Corps of Engineers—*Demolitionists!* Discharged, April, Nineteen-Fifty-Two."

For a moment both men were silent. Then Tynan said softly, "I ask you: isn't that beautiful? Isn't that just plain downright gorgeous?"

Max Kauffman could feel the excitement building, too. "Yes, yes, it's all that."

"I've asked them for any other information they can find," Tynan said. "They're combing the files. And I've got all those men the Commissioner sent over going through other files. Son of a bitch, this could be our day."

"We've still got to find the bastard, though," Max Kauffman pointed out.

"We'll get that hooker, Felice what's her-name, today," Tynan promised. "The vice guys have got an iron ring around that hotel where she lives. She must have had an all-night stand somewhere else. She'll show up sooner or later."

Tynan left. Soon after the breakfast Max Kauffman had ordered came. While he was eating, he got out the map of the city he'd been working on the day before and made a new red X at the location on Fifth Avenue between Fifty-eighth and Fifty-ninth Streets where the bomb had been planted the previous evening. After he'd marked the new spot on the map, he saw that nothing had changed: the bomber was still working within the rectangular boundaries of nine blocks wide by nineteen blocks long in mid-Manhattan. Within that area was the spot where the woman, Adrienne Driner, was alleged to have been killed by the bus on Christmas Eve. Within that area, too, as the Inspector well knew, were most of the public displays of the holiday season in New York. Either, or both, could be the key to why the bomber chose these particular targets.

The Inspector was just finishing his breakfast when Policewoman MacKay tapped on the door and said, "Good morning, sir. I just wanted you to know I'm in." She had a small artificial Christmas tree in her arms. "I wonder, sir, you wouldn't mind if I put this up on my desk and decorated it, would you? A little holiday cheer?"

"No," Max Kauffman said, waving his hand. "I don't mind."

At 10:15, while the Inspector was working on the precinct duty roster for the coming Christmas week, Tynan phoned and said tersely: "They just brought the girl in. She's on her way to interrogation."

"I'm on my way." Max Kauffman put the papers he'd been working on aside and went downstairs.

The first impression Max Kauffman had of Felice Morrissey when he walked into the interrogation room where she sat in a chair, looking unconcerned, was of her uncanny resemblance to Caroline Harger. Felice Morrissey had long red hair while Caroline Harger's was blond, but their faces—the features, the bone structure, the prettiness of each—were remarkably alike. And like Caroline Harger, this girl had a shapely body and was about the same height. She was wearing a brown leather miniskirt which, while she was seated, barely covered her crotch, and a taupe satin blouse unbuttoned down the front except for one button just above the waistband of the skirt. It was obvious that she wore no bra and equally obvious from the way she kept purposely crossing and uncrossing her legs that she wore nothing under the skirt except panty hose. She was quite clearly putting on a show for the detectives who were in the room with her.

Tynan had just started to question her. He wasn't using a tape recorder and he walked in a circle around her as he asked questions. Detectives Cohen, Pennell, and Garibaldi were ranged around the room listening, and there were also two vice squad plainclothesmen present, Brodeman and Chavez. Max Kauffman pulled a chair over and sat straddling it backwards, his arms resting on the wooden back, a couple of feet from the girl.

"We want to ask you about a man you may know," Tynan said. "We think he's about five feet, ten inches tall, not too heavy, and he has a small black moustache—or did have. Maybe he's shaved it off recently. His name is Paul Driner, although he may not call himself that. Do you recognize anyone fitting that description?"

"I don't know any men," she said defiantly. "And I don't have to answer any of your questions. You want to charge me with something, charge me. And then I want to call my lawyer."

"You could help us a lot," Tynan said patiently, ignoring her words. "You were seen entering your hotel with this man a week or so ago."

"I don't know any men," she repeated in a toneless voice. "I don't enter any hotels with men. You want to charge me—"

"All right! *All right!*" Tynan said disgustedly. He started to say something and then looked at Max Kauffman.

The Inspector pushed his chair closer to the girl. "Now, Miss Morrissey," he said in a quiet voice, "we'd really appreciate it if you'd cooperate with us. This is a very important police matter. It would make it easier for all of us, you included, if you'd help us."

"I'm not helping," she answered flatly. "Not cops, I'm not. Why should I?" She stopped talking. Max Kauffman could see that she was calculating something. She looked up at him. "Anyhow, who's this guy that makes it such a 'very important police matter'?"

Max Kauffman considered for a moment before he said, "We have reason to believe he's the Christmas Bomber, the man who's been setting off bombs all over the city for the past several weeks."

"Yeah?" the girl said. The Inspector saw a quick flash of something in her eyes before she shook her head. "Well, whoever he is, I don't know anybody like that. I don't know—"

"—any men," Max Kauffman completed the sentence for her. "Yeah, we know. You told us."

He got up from the chair and motioned to Tynan to join him over by the window.

"Have Brodeman and Chavez take her to one of the offices upstairs and question her about her prostitution activities," he told Tynan. "I just want her delayed for twenty or thirty minutes. The rest of you stay here. I want to talk to you."

Tynan nodded and went over and conferred with the two vice squad men. They led the girl, protesting, from the room.

When they were gone, Max Kauffman looked around at Tynan, Cohen, Pennell, and Garibaldi. He nodded his head. "She knows something. My guess is she'll try to get to Driner. She may figure she can try to sell this information to him, or perhaps blackmail him. But she's a clever, street-wise little bitch. She'll guess we're watching her. She may not try to contact him right away. But I want a tail on her twenty-four hours a day from now on. Also, I want her rousted at regular intervals two to three times a day. Pass the word to Brodeman and Chavez. I want her brought in every time she approaches a man, or even if she doesn't. I want her rousted on a suspicion of prostitution, whether she gives us any proof or not. I want her business screwed up to the point where she's forced to either talk to us or to him. Got it?"

Max Kauffman went back up to his office. A composite photograph based on Caroline Harger's description of Paul Driner and sent over by the Headquarters identification system was lying on his desk. The photograph showed a man with dark hair with some gray streaks in it, a sharp nose, thin mouth and pointed chin, and a small black moustache. The Inspector looked at the face thoughtfully. He had misgivings—an instinct that this was not an accurate portrait of the bomber. He telephoned Spanner.

"Look," he said when Spanner was on the line, "I'd like an opinion from you."

"Ask it," Spanner said.

"You saw the composite photograph based on Caroline Harger's description, right?"

"Yeah, right."

"Do you think she could have been dissembling when she gave that description? You were there."

"Hmm," Spanner said. "I'll be frank with you. It's possible, yeah. Either because she's still scared shitless of this creep or possibly because she honestly drew a blank and is afraid to admit it because she thinks you'll think she's lying."

"I appreciate your leveling with me, Spanner. In every other respect her story seems to check out. I'm pretty sure we're onto something here."

"Glad to hear it," Spanner said. "Oh, and listen. Something I want to ask you. Caroline Harger's old man wants to take the family, her included, to Bermuda for Christmas. They're all pretty stretched tight over this business. I'll know where they'll be and we can get her back in a hurry if you need her. Harger says he won't go if you say no. Any objections?"

"No," Max Kauffman said. "I can't think of any. Except that if anybody's thinking of pulling a fast one, like whisking her into hiding, they'd be a fool."

"It's nothing like that," Spanner said quickly. "I guarantee you. You don't know Mr. Upright Harger. He's Law-and-Order itself."

"You have my permission," Max Kauffman said.

He hung up the phone and glanced at his watch. It was 11:20. All morning long, behind all his other preoccupations, he had been thinking of his brother-in-law's meeting with Moe Blum and waiting until he thought it was time to call. He took out his private phone and dialed the office of Kauffman and Son.

Seymour Greene, his other brother-in-law, answered. The Inspector knew that the two men had an arrangement so that when one was unavailable the other answered.

"Jesus, Max," Seymour Greene said, "I'm glad to hear from you. Something fishy's going on here today and I'm worried. Marvin's been locked up in his office with some men all morning, guys I've never seen before, and then he went out and came back, and they're locked up in there again. He's not taking calls."

"It's all right, Sy," Max Kauffman said. "Bang on the door. Tell him it's me. Tell him to get on the phone."

The Inspector waited and then Marvin Katz said, "That you, Max?"

"Yeah. How'd it go?"

"All right, I think," Marvin said, uncertainty in his voice.

"Well," Max Kauffman demanded, "did he go for the deal or didn't he?"

"No. He held out for his original proposition."

"But you got it all, huh?"

"Yeah," Marvin Katz answered. "They're listening to it now in my office. Those two guys, and Leo Morgen—"

"Leo's there?" Max Kauffman asked. "Put him on the line. Hurry up, Marvin."

He had to wait again and then Leo Morgen's voice said: "You wanted to talk to me, Max?" The voice was flat, impersonal.

"Did Marvin get it all down? Clean and clear?"

"Straight out of the horse's mouth," Leo Morgen said. "That old man's a fool."

"Then listen to me carefully, Leo," Max Kauffman said, "He's all yours. 'The Undertaker.' Pick him up. Take Marvin into protective custody. Take him now. And Leo, would you pick up my sister and the children, too? She's out in Jamaica Estates. Marvin'll give you the address. I'll call her now to get ready. I want protective custody for them, too. Just to be on the safe side. We're going to court."

"Max, are you sure this is what you want to do?"

"Do it," Max Kauffman said. "And, look, Leo,

182

would you please tell Marvin to tell my other brother-in-law, Seymour, what's going on."

"Max, I can't tell you how I feel," Leo said, his voice shaking. "You—you're—"

"You're a sweetheart yourself, Leo," Max Kauffman said gruffly. "We'll have a drink soon."

The Inspector made another call to his sister, quickly explained to her what was happening, and was relieved when she took it calmly.

"You'll be fine," he assured her. "They'll find a nice place for you to stay for a while. It'll be like you and Marvin and the kids are on vacation. And there's nothing to worry about, Rachel. You have my word on that. And I'll talk to Papa."

"I trust you, Max," she said. "I know whatever you do, it's right for everybody. I'll go pack now."

The Inspector felt better than he'd felt in days. He'd almost made a misstep but he'd pulled back in time. He'd forgive himself this one time. As he put his private phone back in the desk drawer, his other phone rang. It was Tynan.

"There's been another bomb," Tynan said. "I don't have any of the details but apparently it blew up in one of those sidewalk Santa Claus kettles on Fifth Avenue by the Channel Gardens in front of Rockefeller Center. No serious injuries but the report is that there's panic in the area."

CHAPTER EIGHTEEN

The snow that had fallen on the city during the night and in the early hours of the morning had ended before 9 A.M. that day. An hour later most of the clouds that had been massed over the city had blown out to sea. There was a sun and the temperature climbed to above freezing. The snow melted from the sidewalk on the west side of Fifth Avenue between Forty-ninth and Fiftieth Streets, in front of the Rockefeller Center Channel Gardens. By 11:45 the only evidence of the storm was small puddles of dirty water in the street gutters.

Max Kauffman stood in the middle of the block, with his back to the street, and surveyed the area where the latest explosion had taken place. The sidewalk had been cordoned off at either end. Members of the 16th Precinct bomb squad had just finished sweeping up whatever they found along the one-block stretch of sidewalk and stuffed it into plastic bags. There were four squad cars parked along the block, a police emergency van, and two bomb squad station wagons. Crowds watched from across the street in front of the Saks Fifth Avenue store, and from the windows of surrounding buildings.

The bomb had exploded inside a large black kettle that hung from a metal tripod. A man dressed in a Santa Claus outfit, a volunteer working for one of the city's charity organizations, had been soliciting donations from people passing by. The force of the blast had blown the kettle and tripod several feet in the air. The sides and bottom of the kettle were punctured in a dozen places as if it had been struck by buckshot.

Based on the superficial evidence found at the scene, John Tynan had already given a tentative opinion that the bomb had consisted of a tin can packed with gunpowder and nails. He believed a fuse inserted in the gunpowder had been lighted before the can was dropped in the kettle.

The volunteer Santa Claus wasn't much help in providing information about what had happened. The man, a retired bank security guard named Sam Burlingame, had been badly shaken by the incident. While Inspector Kauffman and John Tynan questioned him, other members of the bomb squad checked by radio through Headquarters with the charity organization until they were assured that Sam Burlingame was a legitimate volunteer.

Burlingame explained that just before the explosion, he had emptied the kettle of money, a few dollars and some change. For a moment his attention had been distracted by a woman who had brought a little girl over to say hello to "Santa Claus," and he had turned away from the kettle briefly. Soon after the woman and little girl left, the bomb exploded. "It scared the be-Jesus out of me," Burlingame said. "And everybody else on the block. There were people screaming and yelling and crying and running every which way, even out into the street. And cars and buses were slamming on their brakes. I tell you, it was scary and just a miracle that nobody was hurt or killed."

Burlingame said that he'd remembered something afterward which had made no particular impression on him before the bomb went off: There'd been a man standing not far from the kettle who had a package in his hand and was smoking a cigarette. The man had been standing near the curb and had his back turned. Burlingame assumed at the time that he was waiting for a bus. After the explosion, despite the confusion, he did notice that the man was gone although no buses had stopped in that interval of time. Tynan was satisfied that the man was the Christmas Bomber and that he could easily have taken the tin can of gunpowder from a package, lit the fuse, and dropped it in the kettle, then strolled away without having been noticed. Burlingame was not able to provide an accurate description of the man beyond the fact that he was tall, probably close to six feet.

Now, as Max Kauffman stood on the sidewalk, he noticed several cars and station wagons arriving, bringing newspaper photographers and reporters and television cameramen. He made a beckoning signal to Tynan and when the lieutenant came over, Max Kauffman asked, "You all finished?"

"Yeah," Tynan said.

"Then let's get out of here before those newsmen surround us."

He and Tynan got into one of the bomb squad station wagons. As they drove away, Max Kauffman could see the photographers and TV cameramen crowding around Sam Burlingame in his Santa Claus suit. Better him than me, the Inspector thought with a sense of relief.

"You want to have lunch somewhere before we go back to the precinct?" Max Kauffman asked.

"Sure," Tynan said. "Where?"

Before the Inspector could answer, the dispatcher came in on the radio, calling: "Car seven-two, car seven-two. I have a ten-three for you. Do you read me, car seven-two? Do you read me? K."

"That's us," Tynan said. "Why do they want us to call in by phone, I wonder." He picked up the microphone and answered: "Car seven-two to dispatcher. Ten-three message received. K."

"Roger, car seven-two. K."

Tynan spotted a phone booth at the next intersection, pulled over and double-parked, and left the motor running while he called the precinct. When he returned, he sat behind the steering wheel, his eyes on the notebook which he'd scribbled in while he was talking to the dispatcher.

"It's a message from one of the guys who's been going over the business incorporation records down at City Hall. He's found the papers for a Paul Driner

Construction Company which was in existence in the city for ten years and then went out of business two years ago. It has to be the same guy. His home address was listed as Twenty-One West Seventy-ninth Street."

"No more company, though, huh?" Max Kauffman asked.

"No," Tynan said, "but listen: in the incorporation papers Driner is listed as the president of the company, a guy named Everett Cragle as treasurer, and a woman, Millicent Lauder, as secretary. The home addresses of both are included in the papers. I've assigned Garibaldi and Pennell to try to run them down and ask them to come in and talk to us. Maybe before the day is over we'll know more about Paul Driner." Tynan put the notebook away and swung the station wagon out into the street. "What do you want to do about lunch?"

"Oh, hell," Max Kauffman said, "let's get back to the precinct. Maybe we're going to see some action."

Max Kauffman ate lunch at his desk, a steak sandwich, a green salad with Roquefort dressing, a bottle of beer, and two cups of coffee which he'd had his chauffeur bring him from the Old Homestead on Fourteenth Street and Ninth Avenue. While he was eating he used the dictaphone to make a report to the Commissioner on the fizzled bombing of the Pulitzer Fountain the night before, the bombing of the Santa Claus kettle on Fifth Avenue, and the information they'd uncovered so far that day on Paul Driner.

After he finished lunch he took the dictation tape out to Officer MacKay to transcribe and forward to Headquarters. She was busy outside his office putting the finishing touches to the Christmas decorations. She had draped strands of tinsel on the walls behind her desk and around the top and sides of the doors to the Inspector's office. She'd trimmed the Christmas tree with ornaments and more tinsel and it stood in the center of her desk. Max Kauffman gave her the dictaphone tape and asked her to type up the report immediately.

"Yes, sir," she said, and nodded toward the Christmas tree on her desk. "I hope you like it."

"Very nice," he said. The truth was he loathed plastic Christmas trees, loathed all plastic artifacts.

He went back into his office and phoned Catherine Devereaux on his private line.

"I was thinking about you," he said. "I miss you."

"I miss you, too," she told him. She said she was just getting ready to go out and do a little Christmas shopping and that she'd been hoping he'd call. Her voice sounded husky.

"Is everything all right?" he asked.

"Yes," she said. "Why?"

"You don't sound like yourself. You sure you don't have a cold?"

"No, no, I'm fine," she assured him.

"Well, okay," he said. "Uh, listen, Kit, there are some things going on today and I don't know what it's going to do to my evening. Also, I have to see my parents for at least a little while tonight, so I don't know what to tell you about later on."

"It's all right, Max. I'm not going to be doing anything. Do you want to leave it that you'll call me later, whenever you can?"

"Yes, if that's all right with you. Even if I can't make it, I'll phone you. And, Kit, are you sure everything's all right?"

"I'm fine, Max." She paused and added, "I love you very, very much."

"I love you, too, Kit, you know that."

He hung up the phone and shook his head, knowing that when she said "I love you very, very much" it was her way of asking if he loved her. He knew something was wrong and supposed she had gotten a phone call from her parents or her sister, Anne, who was married and lived in Washington, D.C., and it had upset her. He wished to Christ people would learn to manage their own lives even half as successfully as they thought they could manage other people's lives.

He picked up the phone again and called his parents. His mother answered and said his father was tak-

189

ing a nap. Max Kauffman said he'd like to come by for a visit that evening. His mother was delighted and told him his father would be, too. Since his father's heart attack, the family no longer gathered at his parents' place for their ritual Friday night dinners as they had done for at least the twenty-eight years Max Kauffman could remember. He hadn't given much thought to the fact that of course his mother and father must miss the weekly gathering of the family. Now he felt somehow guilty for not having even considered the loneliness they must feel on Friday nights. He told his mother he'd try to be there at nine and if he was delayed he'd phone later.

He lit a cigar and, while he was thinking about it, took from his desk drawer the map of Manhattan which he was using to keep track of the bombing incidents. He marked another large red X on the map where the bomb had exploded in the Santa Claus kettle. There were now eight Xs on the map.

Although he was keyed up about the bombing case because of the day's developments, he forced himself to put the map away, to put all thoughts of the bombings out of his mind, and get back to the work he'd interrupted earlier—when Tynan had called him about the bomb on Fifth Avenue—preparing the duty roster for the next week. It had to be posted before the end of the day shift so that the men going off duty would know who had to work over the Christmas holidays. It was the kind of son-of-a-bitching administrative chore he hated, especially since with the bombing case as active as it was he'd have to order most of the men in the precinct to report in. But it had to be done.

Fifteen minutes after he'd started work on the duty roster, Officer MacKay buzzed him to say that Dr. Wallstein was calling.

"I wanted you to know that, as you requested, we've recovered that unidentified female body and it's here at the morgue," the assistant medical examiner said. "We're starting work on casting the bones and teeth. I'll get back to you."

The Inspector hung up. John Tynan rapped on

the door and came in. "This case gets curiouser and curiouser," he said, shaking his head.

Max Kauffman tilted back in his chair. "What now?"

"I just got a report from one of the men I assigned to check out bank records for an account in Driner's name. He struck pay dirt at the National Deposit and Savings Bank."

"Yeah, so?" Max Kauffman asked.

"Well," Tynan said, "Paul Driner—same guy, same address on West Seventy-ninth—had an account there dating back ten years. Then eighteen months ago he closed out the account." Tynan paused and took a deep breath. "It was a hefty account—slightly over eight hundred and fifty thousand dollars, almost a million bucks."

"Um," Max Kauffman grunted softly.

Tynan held up a hand. "Wait, it gets curiouser. On the same day Paul Driner closed out his account, a Mrs. Adrienne Driner, same West Seventy-ninth Street address, opened an account, depositing slightly over eight hundred and fifty thousand dollars."

"Driner didn't want the money in his name," the Inspector said. "Huh?"

"Apparently." Tynan nodded. "But there's more. National Deposit and Savings records show that subsequently two withdrawals were made from the Adrienne Driner account, one in the amount of fifty thousand dollars on September fifteenth last year and a second in the amount of twenty-five hundred on—now get this—December twenty-fourth, last Christmas Eve. Since then the account has been inactive. I instructed the bank to notify us if there's any activity on the account."

Both men were silent. Max Kauffman shook his head slowly. "No, I know what you're thinking. It's too simple. All that money's in her name and she gets killed, and he can't get the money and it flips him out." The Inspector shook his head stubbornly. "No. He was her husband so he had a legal claim on it."

"But how," Tynan asked, "could he claim it if for

some reason he didn't want the money in his name? Couldn't it be that because of that, *and* the accident, he flipped?"

The Inspector frowned. "I just don't think so. Oh, I don't know. We're just going to have to wait until we get more of the pieces together."

Tynan turned to leave and Max Kauffman said, "Jack?"

"Yeah?"

"I know you're busting your ass on this case. And I just want to say that I'm more than satisfied with the way you and the men are conducting the investigation. Despite the fact that we haven't caught him yet."

"I appreciate that, Inspector," Tynan said. "But, as you say, we haven't caught him yet."

After Tynan was gone, Max Kauffman went back to working on the duty roster. Policewoman MacKay interrupted him once to get an okay on the report she'd typed for the Commissioner. Max Kauffman caught two typos—she'd left the "r" out of Driner's name in one place and the "e" out of Pulitzer in another—and he gave the report to her to correct and then send on to Headquarters.

At 3:40 Tynan phoned and said: "Garibaldi and Pennell have located both of Paul Driner's ex-associates, Everett Cragle and Millicent Lauder. Cragle's wife and Millicent Lauder's mother were both home at the addresses listed in the Driner Construction incorporation papers. They told Garibaldi and Pennell where each worked, for different companies, here in Manhattan. Garibaldi and Pennell have already contacted both subjects, and both promised to be at the precinct today between five and five-thirty."

"Splendid," Max Kauffman said. "When they get here, we'll interview them separately, here in my office."

Millicent Lauder sat rigidly upright in the chair across the desk from Max Kauffman, her knees pressed primly together even though the skirt of her black shirtwaist dress covered her legs more than adequately. With the dress, she wore gray stockings and black

192

leather oxfords which had low heels. She was close to fifty, if not in her fifties, a bony woman with little flesh on her and what there was anemically pale. Her hair was too black not to have been dyed and proper makeup could have helped some to soften the unfortunate angular unprettiness of her face, but she wore none.

She and Everett Cragle had arrived at the station house at about the same time and Tynan had brought them upstairs together. Max Kauffman and Tynan had decided to question her first and now Cragle waited outside the office while she settled herself in the chair in front of the Inspector's desk. Tynan sat in a chair at the corner of the desk, with three empty chairs between them.

"The two officers who spoke to me didn't tell me what this is all about," she said to Max Kauffman, "except that you wanted to speak to me with regard to my former employer, Mr. Paul Driner. Has anything happened to him?"

"How long did you work for Paul Driner?" Max Kauffman asked.

"For ten years," Millicent Lauder said. "The entire time the company was in existence. I was Mr. Driner's office manager and he made me an officer of the company; secretary. Please, can't you tell me what this is all about?"

"When," the Inspector asked, as if she hadn't spoken, "was the last time you saw or heard from Paul Driner?"

"On March twenty-first, year before last. In fact, tomorrow it will be exactly twenty months ago to the day," she said precisely. "The Driner Construction Company was officially dissolved on that date."

"And you've had no contact with Paul Driner since that time?"

"No." She sat up straighter in the chair. "Inspector Kauffman, you haven't answered my question. Has anything happened to Paul Driner?"

"We don't know," Max Kauffman said. "We want to question him, but so far we haven't been able to locate him. Or his wife."

193

"Adrienne, you mean?" Millicent Lauder asked.

The Inspector nodded. "Have you seen or heard from *her* in the past twenty months?"

"No." She was frowning now. "You say you want to question him. Why?"

Max Kauffman considered for a moment before he said carefully, "We want to question Paul Driner in connection with the recent series of bombings in the city. His house at Twenty-One West Seventy-ninth Street is deserted. We were hoping you might be able to give us some information that would help us find him."

"You mean you think Paul—Paul Driner—might know something about these *bombings?*" Her voice was incredulous.

"I mean," Max Kauffman said, "we have reason to believe Paul Driner is the man behind the bombings."

For the first time during the interview Millicent Lauder seemed to lose her rigid composure. She slumped slightly in the chair and remained silent.

"You see," the Inspector said, "we have some information which indicates that Mrs. Driner, Adrienne Driner, may have been killed when she was struck by a bus on Fifth Avenue last Christmas Eve. There was just such an accident at that time but the body was never identified. We are now trying to establish that that body was the body of Adrienne Driner. We are also attempting to locate Paul Driner to question him about the accident as well as the recent bombings. For example, we already know that Paul Driner served in the army as a demolitionist and has had experience with explosives."

Millicent Lauder sat, blank-faced, staring at the Inspector.

"Miss Lauder," John Tynan asked quietly, "do you know whether or not Paul Driner owned a Mercedes automobile?"

She looked sideways at Tynan, nodded, and said, "Yes." She looked down at her pocketbook. Almost as if talking to herself, she whispered, "She was always a jinx to him, that one."

"You mean Adrienne Driner?" Max Kauffman asked softly.

Millicent Lauder's head shot up and her eyes flashed angrily. "Yes! He was fine until she came along. She drove him crazy, before she married him and afterward. She did that to him, obsessed him with her pretty face and wanton body. He couldn't see, didn't want to see or hear, anything else about her." Spittle flew from her mouth as she made the pronouncement: "She was nothing but a common *slut!* If Paul Driner is doing these terrible bombings then she drove him to it. She was responsible!" Millicent Lauder pointed a finger at the door to the office. "Him out there, Everett Cragle, he could tell you about her if you could get him to talk. Yes, indeed. She had him hooked to her, too, with her sex. Paul Driner knew it. He never said anything, but it drove him crazy. If you ask me, that's why he closed down his business. Obsessed with her, he was."

Max Kauffman and John Tynan had remained silent during the woman's outburst. Now when she stopped talking she became aware of their silence. She pursed her lips, then lowered her head and shook it miserably.

When she raised her head her eyes were wet. "I've said too much. Inspector, I can't help you. I don't know anything. I don't know where that poor man is, or anything about him, or her. Can't I please leave now, please? You can get in touch with me again if you need me. But I want to go now."

Before the Inspector dismissed her, he explained about the composite photo identification system at Headquarters and asked if she would cooperate in giving the police a detailed description of Paul Driner. When she agreed, reluctantly, they worked out an arrangement for an unmarked police car to pick her up at her house the following morning at ten. "And thank you, Miss Lauder," Max Kauffman said. He made a motion with his hand and Tynan led Millicent Lauder from the office.

Max Kauffman lit a cigar and leaned back in his chair thoughtfully to wait for Tynan to return with Everett Cragle.

CHAPTER NINETEEN

"Nice to meet you, Inspector," Everett Cragle said smoothly, and sat in the chair Millicent Lauder had just vacated. Tynan sat again in the chair at a corner of the desk.

Cragle was somewhere around five foot nine, and had an expansive chest. He was in his early fifties. His hair was silver, and there was a lot of it, rolling back in bunched waves from a broad forehead. He had a Romanesque nose, thick lips, and wore gold-framed eyeglasses with blue-tinted lenses. His suit was dark gray with chalk mark stripes and he had on a white shirt and a solid pearl-gray silk tie. There was a gold signet ring on the pinky finger of his right hand, a gold wedding band on the third finger of his left hand.

Cragle took out a cigar and lit it while Max Kauffman related to him virtually the same facts about Paul and Adrienne Driner that he had told Millicent Lauder. When he finished, Cragle asked, "Do I understand that you really believe this man the newspapers and television call 'the Christmas Bomber' is Paul Driner?"

"I said we have reason to believe they're the same man," Max Kauffman said, nodding.

Cragle thought for a moment and then said slowly, "I suppose it's possible. If it was actually Adrienne who was killed in the bus accident, I suppose it's possible. God knows, the man was—well, I don't think it's too strong a word to use—enthralled by her. You see, you have to understand what kind of man Paul Driner is to understand his relationship with Adrienne."

"And what kind of man is he?" Max Kauffman asked.

Cragle took a puff on his cigar. "I've known Paul for years. Back even before he started his own construction company. Since right after he came out of the army, in fact. You did know he was in the army?"

"Yes, a demolitionist, we've discovered."

Cragle nodded. "I had supposed you'd already uncovered that fact. He was a captain. Anyhow, after he got out of the service, he came to work for a construction company where I was employed as bookkeeper. He was a hard worker, obviously ambitious, and he quickly became a foreman."

He paused and swallowed uncomfortably. "He was something of an expert on explosives. The company did a lot of demolition work, as part of its construction business. Within a few years Paul was ready to branch out into his own company. He raised the necessary capital because of his good reputation in the construction field and started the Driner Construction Company. He asked me to go with him. I was his head bookkeeper and he also made me treasurer of the company."

"You were going to tell us what kind of man he was," the Inspector prodded gently.

"Uh huh." Cragle thought for a moment and then said: "For all his drive and all his success, and his company was quite successful, he remained an unsophisticated, even naive, man—especially where women were concerned. In fact, I don't think there ever was a woman in his life until Adrienne came along. Which explains why he fell for her so completely, I suppose. And especially since she was, uh, something out of the ordinary to look at."

Cragle paused again. He frowned and took a couple of puffs on his cigar before continuing. "You understand I would not say what I'm about to say about her, about Adrienne, except for the circumstances of what you've told me today. And I assume that what I say will be kept confidential."

"You can be sure of that," Max Kauffman said. "Unless of course there's a trial and your testimony is necessary."

"I accept that." Cragle nodded his head. "Now; Adrienne. She came to work at the Driner Construction Company approximately four years ago. She was a clerk in the office. She was a stunningly beautiful young woman. Tawny-haired, a gorgeous face and body. Uh, intellectually, I guess you could say she was a bit limited. And you could also say she was on the make. She liked men. And of course men liked her."

The Inspector interrupted. "Do you know anything about her before she married Driner?"

"She was born and raised in Pottsville, Pennsylvania. Came from a Lithuanian family. Her maiden name was Adrienne Kolawal. That's K-o-l-a-w-a-l. The men of the family worked in the coal mines near Pottsville. After she left there, she worked in Pittsburgh and Baltimore before she came to New York. She was twenty-four when she went to work at Driner Construction. Driner was forty-seven. When she found out he was not married, she set out to snare him, and she did. But she still liked men, and I don't think the poor bastard ever had another moment's peace. He was crazy about her and pathologically jealous—with reason. However, she could always twist him around her little finger." He shrugged.

The Inspector blew out a mouthful of smoke. "And there were men after she was married."

"Oh yes," Cragle said. "At least I think so. But I never knew for a fact."

"And were you, Mr. Cragle," Max Kauffman asked, "one of those men?"

Everett Cragle looked startled for a moment and then he laughed. "Ah, I understand. The estimable Millicent Lauder has, I imagine, suggested such was the case. Well, I'll be perfectly frank with you, Inspector. There was a one night's indiscretion on my part, but it occurred shortly after Adrienne came to work at the company. I believe Paul suspected it at the time. But it occurred only once, and never after she and Paul were married."

The Inspector nodded. "However, you did say there were other men after the marriage?"

"I said I thought there were, and I think Paul thought so, too. You understand, he wasn't easy to live with, either."

"Even if it's only a surmise," Max Kauffman said, "it might be helpful if you could supply us with the names of the men you suspected."

Cragle shifted uncomfortably in his chair. "Well, Paul had hired a couple of Vietnam vets to help him with the demolition work. Paul was a real nut about explosives, you see. And because of his own army background, I guess, he seemed to like to help young guys who had had similar experience in the service. Anyhow, both of these fellows were good-looking, young, footloose; and I noticed Adrienne had an eye for them. I always suspected there was something going on between her and one of them, or perhaps both. Or maybe she just liked to kid around with them because they were both closer to her own age. Their names were Shirer and Vogler, Burt Shirer and Lloyd Vogler. They had both done construction and demolition work in the army."

Max Kauffman jotted down the names. "Do you know where we could get in touch with them?"

"Oh, God, no," Cragle said. "Burt Shirer took a construction job out on the West Coast just before the company closed down. And the last I heard of Lloyd Vogler, he came to ask me to write a reference for him for a job in the Mideast. This was about a month or so after the company went out of business. Later he phoned me and said the job had come through and he was leaving at the end of the week for Saudi Arabia. That was summer before last; it was the last I heard of him."

"And after that, as far as you know, there were no other men."

"No." Cragle shook his head. "Not as far as I know. In fact, the last time I saw Paul, he led me to believe that he and Adrienne had never been happier. I assumed from that that he meant she had stopped playing around. He said it was the happiest time of his life—"

He hesitated as if he had just thought of something and then said: "Now that I recall the meeting, Paul didn't look right to me. I even said to him that he looked under the weather and asked him if he'd seen a doctor. His pallor was bad. He had a kind of unhealthy grayish look. He just shrugged it off. He didn't like doctors. It was another subject he was a nut on. If Paul is the man setting off these bombs, I wonder, looking back now, if at that time he wasn't beginning to have a mental breakdown."

"Exactly when was this meeting?" Max Kauffman asked.

"June of last year," Cragle answered. "He phoned me from his place in the country—hey!" Cragle sat bolt upright in his chair. "You did know he had a place in the country, didn't you?"

"In the country? No," the Inspector said. He couldn't keep the excitement out of his voice. "Where? What's the address?"

Cragle put a fist to his forehead. "Damn, that I don't know. I never knew it. But I'm sure you can find it. The place was up in Pound Ridge, I do know that. He converted an old mill into a house. Put a lot of work in on it the last year the company was in business. After he closed down the company, I think he and Adrienne spent most of their time there. Anyway, he phoned me from there and came into the city a day or so later and we talked. He told me then that he and Adrienne planned to take a year or so away in Europe. I assumed they had. I never saw him again." Cragle leaned forward and stubbed out his cigar in the ashtray on the desk.

"Tell me," the Inspector said, "did Driner drive an old Mercedes?"

"Yes," Cragle answered. "He drove it back and forth between Pound Ridge and the city."

Max Kauffman glanced at the notes he'd made and looked up. "Perhaps, Mr. Cragle, you could enlighten us on another matter connected with Paul Driner's affairs."

"Certainly, if I can."

"Tell me this: do you have any idea why Paul Driner would close out his personal bank account and put all the money in his wife's name?"

"He did that, huh?" Cragle said and nodded his head. "Yes, I think I can explain why he did it. You see, the last big construction job Paul undertook was for a large middle-class housing project over in New Jersey. The idea was to create a whole new suburb. It was ambitious. Paul and several other men formed a separate corporation for the project. The others were to put up money and Driner Construction was to supply the labor and the know-how. Even before the units were completed, they were sold. But what happened was, halfway through the construction, Paul's associates ran out of money—because of the recession. The project was never completed, the corporation was forced to declare bankruptcy, and there was a deluge of lawsuits."

Everett Cragle stopped talking and took a fresh cigar out of his coat pocket. He unwrapped it but then stuck it back in his pocket without lighting it. He cleared his throat and said, "It was because of the threat of lawsuits that Paul decided to liquidate Driner Construction. He did all right on that, too; walked away with nearly a million dollars. But even then he couldn't protect his money if the lawsuits went against him. The day he talked to me, that last day in June a year ago, he wanted my advice about putting the money in Adrienne's name."

"And you advised him to do it?" Max Kauffman asked.

Cragle shook his head. "Actually, I didn't. What I suggested was that he try to come up with an alternate solution. It wasn't that I didn't trust Adrienne. But, Anyhow, obviously, he didn't follow my advice." Cragle made a wave of dismissal with his hand. "Not that any of it matters now."

The Inspector leaned forward. "Do you have any idea at all why he wouldn't want to identify and claim his wife's body after the accident, or why he wouldn't try to get back the money he'd put in her name after she'd been killed?"

"No," Cragle said, "I don't have any ideas. Except that Paul was always a bit—a bit peculiar. Rigid, unpredictable; always had his own way of doing things. Maybe Adrienne's death brought out the worst of those traits in him. Or maybe he wanted to do—well, what you allege he's doing—and claim the money later. I don't know. I suppose it's more a matter for the psychiatrists to explain."

There was silence in the office and then Max Kauffman asked Cragle if he would be willing to help the police put together a composite photograph of Paul Driner. When Cragle agreed, Max Kauffman stood and Cragle got up and they shook hands. Cragle also shook hands with Tynan and both police officers thanked him for his time, the Inspector saying, "Certainly we have a much clearer understanding of the individual we're up against. We appreciate all your help."

Tynan showed Cragle out and came back. Max Kauffman motioned him to a chair and Tynan sat and lit a cigarette. The Inspector buzzed Officer MacKay on the intercom and said: "Check with the telephone company and see if you can find an address in Pound Ridge, New York, for a Paul Driner." Then he swung around in his chair and said to Tynan: "You'd better get in touch with one of the assistant D.A.s and get a warrant for Paul Driner, in case we need it. Hang around now for a minute, though, and let's see what we get on this Pound Ridge place."

Tynan nodded.

Max Kauffman tilted back in his chair. "What'd you think of Cragle and his story?"

"He's a smooth one, I'd say that," Tynan said.

"You're being kind, Jack, or imprecise. I'd say unctuous is more like it."

"Unctuous, then," Tynan said. "Still—"

"Still," Max Kauffman said, "everything he told us about Paul Driner hangs together as far as this case is concerned, correct?"

"Correct."

The Inspector rubbed his chin reflectively. "Remember when Doctor Myles gave us his 'psychological profile' on the kind of man the bomber would probably turn out to be? That he'd probably suffered a recent injury to his ego, felt frustrated, persecuted, was full of hostility, and was likely to be suffering from a serious sexual maladjustment? Fits our man to a T."

"Yeah," Tynan said.

The intercom buzzed and Officer MacKay said: "Sir, the telephone company says they have no listing for a Paul Driner in Pound Ridge, New York."

"All right," Max Kauffman said, "contact the State Police. You can call their Bureau of Criminal Investigation at the World Trade Center here in Manhattan. Find out which barracks has jurisdiction over Pound Ridge, New York, and the name of whoever's in charge up there. Then get him for me on the phone."

Tynan stood. "While you're doing that, I'd better get in touch with one of the assistant D.A.s on that warrant for Driner," he said. "I won't leave until after you've talked to the State Police."

"Yeah, good," Max Kauffman said. When he was alone, he got up and walked over to the window. It was dark outside, the time was close to 8 P.M. When he raised the window to air the room out from the clouds of cigar smoke, a strong, icy draught of wind blew in, scattering papers across his desk. He quickly lowered the window except for a crack at the bottom and went back and tidied up his desk. The phone rang. He expected it to be Officer MacKay with the State Police Commander; instead it was the precinct dispatcher. "Sir, we just received a report from Headquarters. Nine-one-one advises there's been another call from the bomber. The message was: 'It's the eighth day of Christmas.'"

Max Kauffman hung up the phone and the intercom buzzed. Florence MacKay said that the State Police barracks with jurisdiction over Pound Ridge, New York, was on Route 9, north of Tarrytown, and that she had the officer in charge, a Captain Walter Hedloe —she spelled the name for him—holding.

Max Kauffman got on the phone and told the State Police officer that he was trying to locate the residence of a Paul Driner in Pound Ridge, that there was no telephone listing, and that Driner was the prime sus-

204

pect in the city's bombing cases. Captain Hedloe said he had been following reports on the case and that he and his men would be glad to cooperate. "The only thing is," he said, "since you tell me he doesn't have a phone listing, we'll have to check the property deeds. They're in the Department of Land Records at the County Office Building in White Plains, and we won't be able to get in there until after nine tomorrow. Even though it's Saturday, the building'll be open then."

"All right," Max Kauffman said. "Why don't we meet up there in White Plains as close to nine as we can make it? And Captain, we'll have an arrest warrant for Paul Driner if he happens to be there. Also, I'd like you to get a search warrant for the premises from that end."

"It'll be done," Hedloe answered promptly. "You'd better take down the address of the County Office Building. It's One-four-eight Martine Avenue, White Plains. See you at nine."

The Inspector called Tynan and told him of the arrangements he'd made with the State Police. "We'll plan to meet here at the precinct at, why don't we say, eight. Let's take three or four of your men with us. You pick them, and we'll use two cars. Make the arrangements, will you?"

"I'll attend to it," Tynan said. "And one of the assistant D.A.s, Burchell, is processing the arrest warrant for Driner. We'll have it in the morning before we leave."

Max Kauffman cleared off his desk, put on his hat and coat, and called down for his car. Policewoman MacKay was still at her desk which surprised him since she'd completed all the work he'd given her. She said she was just getting ready to leave. He said good night and went downstairs. Two of the vice squad plain-clothesmen were standing at the booking desk with the hooker, Felice Morrissey. They'd just brought her in again.

"Fucking pig inspector!" she cursed at him as he went by. He just shook his head, amused.

He wasn't looking forward to the meeting with his father. He hated to have to tell him the news about

Marvin, even though it had to be done. On the way to his parents' apartment, on Park Avenue in the eighties, he had his driver detour over to First Avenue and Fifty-seventh Street and stop at a delicatessen called The Hole in the Wall to pick up one of the best cheesecakes in the city as a present for the old man.

Max Kauffman's first thought when he finished telling his father about the trouble Marvin Katz had gotten himself into was: *Jesus, the old man's going to have another heart attack!*

They were sitting in the dining room. Aaron Kauffman's face had first flushed as purple as one of the hexagon designs in the Turkish rug on the floor, and then all the blood seemed to drain from his face, and his body was wracked by a series of tremors.

"Papa! Papa! Are you all right?" the Inspector asked, half rising from his chair and reaching a hand toward his father.

The old man's head slowly nodded and he lifted a palsied hand motioning Max Kauffman back to his seat. His father took a couple of sips of his weak tea and set the cup back into the saucer with a rattle.

"A real *bulvon,* that son-in-law of mine is," Aaron Kauffman whispered; "an oaf, a dolt." He shook his head sadly.

"It'll be all right, Papa," Max Kauffman said reassuringly. "You mustn't let this upset you so. I had to tell you because you had to know, but everything will be all right now. Seymour can run the business, so don't worry about that. The only thing we have to work out is for Marvin to repay the money he owes, the twenty-two thousand, five hundred dollars. That *has* to be done, no matter how the trial turns out. If Marvin and Rachel don't have all of it, I can help—"

"No, no, no," his father said in a stronger voice. "The money, I will do. He will repay it with his sweat, if no other way."

"Then there's nothing more to worry about," Max Kauffman said soothingly. "Arrangements will be made to pass the money back to this gambler or to the men behind him."

His father nodded. "Monday I will cash a check." He put his hand down flat on the table which was a gesture he always used to signal that he wanted all further discussion on a subject ended.

Max Kauffman sat on at the dining room table with his father and they discussed other matters— Belle Kauffman, the Inspector's children, the garment business. After a while Max Kauffman's mother, Sara, came in from the living room where she'd been waiting while the two men talked in private. She was a tall and, the Inspector thought, still beautiful woman. Her hair was silver, and her face had been softened rather than made haggard by age. Her carriage, the way she held her body whether standing or sitting, was gracefully regal. The three of them discussed the Inspector's wife and children and the garment business. Finally Mrs. Hillsman, the housekeeper, appeared and began clearing the tea cups and cake plates from the table. The Inspector himself had eaten the largest portion of cheesecake. He kissed his mother and he and his father embraced. Then he left.

Downstairs again and out on Park Avenue, he lit a cigar. He had dismissed his driver for the night. Now he walked up the street for a couple of blocks until he found an empty phone booth. He called Catherine Devereaux. He could tell by the way she sounded that she was more like herself again. He was relieved. She said he sounded very tired and he told her he was but that he'd come to the apartment if she was expecting him.

"No, please, darling," she said. "I'd rather you'd go home and get a good night's sleep. I worry about you. I'll go to bed early myself. Tomorrow night we can do whatever you like."

"I love you," he said.

"I love you," she said.

He stepped out of the phone booth and caught a taxi. He felt as old as his father had looked.

As the cab sped south on Park Avenue, the Inspector could see the lights on the little Christmas trees in the center island dividing the street twinkling cheerfully in the cold, windy darkness down the length of the avenue. In the distance, as was traditional each Christmas season in the city, lights set in the north wall of the Grand Central Building at Forty-sixth Street formed the outline of a huge white cross high over the avenue.

"You know what the *Farmer's Almanac*'s predicting for next week?" the taxi driver said over his shoulder.

"Mmm," Max Kauffman grunted, trying to discourage conversation.

"We're going to have a white Chanukah."

Max Kauffman had to laugh.

CHAPTER TWENTY

The two N.Y.P.D. squad cars pulled into the curb in front of the County Office Building in White Plains at 9:19 the following morning. Max Kauffman rode in the lead car with Tynan and Detective Ernie Raucher. Raucher sat in the front seat next to the uniformed patrolman who drove. Detectives Braxley, Cohen, and Garibaldi were in the second squad car.

They had left the 16th Precinct in plenty of time to complete the trip by nine, but they'd been delayed by an accident ten miles south of White Plains. A truck loaded with Christmas trees and headed for Manhattan had skidded on a patch of ice on the Thruway, wound up in a ditch, and scattered Christmas trees across the road. Once past the accident scene, the patrol cars had used their sirens but had still been nineteen minutes late in arriving.

The day, December 21, was sunless. A low overhang of sullen, gray clouds covered the sky and the air was full of the kind of abrasive cold that bit deep through clothes and skin to nerves and bone.

Max Kauffman's car had parked behind three State Police cruisers at the curb. Before he could open his car door, one of the State Police troopers, dressed in a gray wool uniform and Stetson hat, walked back from the cruiser ahead. He was a man of medium height, slim, about forty-five years old. His dark complexion and high cheekbones gave his face a slightly Indian cast. Max Kauffman rolled down the car window. The trooper stepped in close and asked: "Inspector Kauffman?"

Max Kauffman nodded.

"I'm Captain Hedloe," the State Police trooper said. They shook hands through the open window.

"Did you get the address for Paul Driner?" the Inspector asked.

"Yep," Hedloe said. "The search warrant, too. We're ready to roll. The only thing is, since you were late getting here I radioed one of our cruisers that was in the vicinity of Driner's property to take a look up that way. Just a minute or so ago we got a frantic call from the cruiser asking for an ambulance. I don't know what the hell's going on up there; I haven't been able to raise the trooper who called in. The ambulance is on its way." Hedloe put a hand on the pistol hanging from his waist and shifted the holster higher on his hip.

"Let's go," Max Kauffman said.

Hedloe pointed to the cruiser parked just ahead. "That's my car. You and your other squad car follow us. My other two cruisers'll bring up the rear so you don't get lost." He swung around, walked to the waiting cruiser, and got in.

There was a scream of sirens and the State Police car shot out into the street. The car carrying Max Kauffman followed close behind and was trailed by the second squad car and the other two State Police cruisers.

As soon as the five cars were on the open road outside White Plains, they accelerated to seventy and then eighty. Max Kauffman bit down hard on an unlit cigar and hoped to Christ they didn't hit an icy patch on the road. Once he glanced at Tynan and noticed that the lieutenant, who was a notorious fast driver himself, was white-lipped.

It had been years since Max Kauffman had been in the area of Pound Ridge. Most of the houses were well back off the roads, in secluded woods, and little could be seen from the highway except for trees and brush. Pound Ridge was an affluent community populated mostly by wealthy commuters from Manhattan and those who kept summer houses there. But even though the scenery remained unchanged, what little he could see of it from the speeding car, he knew when
210

they were in the vicinity because of the rolling, curving roads. Soon, as they rounded yet another curve, the cruiser up ahead slowed its speed. Coming from the opposite direction was an ambulance. It turned off the highway onto a narrow road approximately the width of two cars, and the cruiser followed it, leading the two squad cars and the other two State Police cars in through a thicket of trees, standing leafless and stark as wooden poles on either side of the pavement. The road wound through the dark trees for two or three miles and then Max Kauffman saw they had emerged into a clearing.

The ambulance and police cars following it came to a stop in front of a high chain link fence. The State Police cruiser that had arrived earlier was also parked outside the fence, both front car doors swinging open. Behind the fence was what looked like a split-level house with a peaked roof, a lot of glass picture windows, and a wooden sundeck that encircled the house just below the windows. There was still some snow on the ground from the snowfall of a day or so earlier, lying in scattered spots in the yard. A trooper inside the fence was walking slowly toward the men climbing out of the ambulance and police cars, and another trooper lay stretched out on the ground, just outside the entrance to the house. Farther back in the yard Max Kauffman could see two small dark shapes lying in the snow but couldn't make out what they were.

The trooper in the yard and the men who had just arrived met at the fence. The trooper's face was dead white. There was a dazed look in his eyes, and he was carrying a .38 revolver in his hand, muzzle swinging downward.

"Jesus, Sergeant Otis, what happened?" Captain Hedloe asked.

The trooper shook his head. "See for yourself, Captain." He pushed the steel gate open and turned and walked ahead of the others, talking back over his shoulder.

"Northlin and I got here a little while ago, after we received your radio call. The place appeared to be deserted so we decided to take a look around. We shot the lock off the gate and approached the house. I was in the lead, Northlin covering me. I had just gotten up on the sundeck there and was approaching the front door when I heard this terrible scream from Northlin. I turned and these two animals—at first I thought they were wolves—had Northlin down on the ground and were tearing at him."

The trooper stopped talking and wiped the sweat from his face with the sleeve of his uniform. The group had reached the spot where Northlin lay.

Trooper Otis made a gesture with his hand. "Take a look."

As the group crowded around the body on the ground, Max Kauffman could see that the dead man's throat had been completely ripped away and there were jagged teeth marks in the flesh that covered his jawbone. The ground was saturated with blood.

Trooper Otis looked sick. "I shot at the animals and drove them back. I got between them and the body but they kept snarling and circling from back there." He pointed to the two dark shapes in the snow and started walking toward them. The others followed silently.

"Finally, I managed to kill them," he said. He was standing over the dark shapes. He lifted the tip of his booted foot and raised the head of one of the animals. Max Kauffman could see that it was a dog, a Doberman pinscher. Both of the Dobermans were wild-looking creatures, bodies emaciated so the rib cages were outlined under their hides, and the heads like skulls.

"Dobermans," Trooper Otis said. "Afterward, I figured out what they were. I figure their owner must have abandoned them, and they reverted, living off the land in the wilds around here. There's a dug-out space under the fence back there where they went in and out of the property. Maybe the people that own this place abandoned them." He jerked a thumb over his shoulder toward the house, shook his head, and whispered, "Oh, God, I don't feel so good."

Captain Hedloe stepped forward. "Sergeant Otis, you go on back to the barracks."

The captain then instructed the ambulance attendants to remove the dead trooper and take along the bodies of the two dogs, to be held as evidence for the inquest. He also ordered another of the troopers to drive Sergeant Otis back to the barracks.

Max Kauffman had walked away from the others and was looking at the house. It had a neglected, abandoned look about it, the dark windows dull mirrors, revealing nothing behind them. He noticed an empty swimming pool in the yard back of the house. Dead leaves and broken tree branches littered the bottom of the pool. The wind from the north whistling through the stand of trees at the edge of the clearing stirred the dead leaves in the pool. Max Kauffman stuck his gloved hands in his coat pocket and walked back to the front of the house.

The ambulance and one of the State Police cars had gone. Captain Hedloe beckoned to Max Kauffman. "Ready to try the house, Inspector?"

Detective Ray Braxley, with his ring of keys, opened the front door to the house, just as he had done at Driner's other house, on West Seventy-ninth Street, in Manhattan. Inspector Kauffman and Captain Hedloe entered the house first, followed by Tynan, the four bomb squad detectives, and the five State Police troopers.

The door opened directly into a large living room which was enclosed by glass windows on three sides. There were a couple of doors to the rear, which opened into two bedrooms. There was a waist-high countertop separation between the living room and kitchen, which was also in the rear of the house. Again, the living room was virtually empty. There were no rugs on the floor, no curtains or drapes at the windows. All that remained in the room was a built-in window-seat across the width of the living room and a large black steamer trunk standing against the kitchen divider. The house had the musty, unpleasant smell of mold and mildew.

Max Kauffman moved on into the living room after he had taken in the general interior of the house. When he looked around at the walls of the living room, he suddenly stood stock still at the sight: every

213

inch of wall space, around the picture windows, above them, and below them, was covered by large glossy photographs of the same woman, stark naked, in various poses. The photographs had been carelessly stuck to the walls by bits of Scotch tape, some of them hanging crooked or by one corner.

The other men came into the house and saw the photographs. No one spoke. They all simply looked at the reproductions of the nude woman, heads turning slowly as eyes moved from one photograph to another around the four walls.

The Inspector had stepped closer to study the series of pictures on the wall nearest him. As he looked carefully at the face of the woman, he was struck by the remarkable resemblance she had to both the girl, Caroline Harger, and the hooker, Felice Morrissey. This woman—he was sure that it was Adrienne Driner —had tawny blond hair framing a quite beautiful face and she was approximately the same height as the other two women. In each photograph he could see that most of her body was a darker shade, from the sun, than the two narrow spots of smooth creamy flesh across her shapely breasts and in the blond furred space where her legs met. In each photograph, too, she was wearing the same delicate gold chain and heart-shaped locket around her neck. In some of the photographs the poses were crudely pornographic, extreme close-up shots of the lower part of her anatomy, pelvis thrust up into the lens of the camera with the legs spread wide.

Max Kauffman cleared his throat and pointed to Detective Garibaldi. "Take those photographs down and put them together so we can take them with us. Be careful how you handle them in case there are any prints on them."

The police officers then began to move through the rest of the small house, inspecting the other rooms. Max Kauffman went into the two bedrooms, one after another, and found both almost as empty of furniture as was the living room. The exception was that both bedrooms still had beds in them, one had twin beds and the other a double bed. The twin beds had only

214

bare mattresses on them but there was a dirty, gray sheet on the double bed, and a wool blanket, rumpled up, lay at the foot of the bed. There were also a couple of empty beer cans lying on their sides under the bed. There was one chest of drawers in the bedroom with the double bed but the drawers were empty. There was nothing in either of the bathrooms connecting with each of the bedrooms, and a layer of grimy dust had collected on the basins, in the showers, and on the fixtures. The steamer trunk in the living room was also empty.

Max Kauffman was back in the small kitchen—there was nothing there of significance, either—when he heard John Tynan calling urgently to him. Tynan had gone down to the basement through a door in the kitchen. Max Kauffman went down the short flight of wooden stairs. It was freezing cold down there and the light was dingy although there were a couple of small windows high up on the concrete wall. They'd already discovered that the electricity in the house had been turned off. Tynan was in a partitioned space under the front of the house. When Max Kauffman walked into the small, separate area, Tynan whispered, "Jesus Christ, Inspector, look!"

Max Kauffman saw them then: wooden crates, about a dozen of them, stacked on the floor. A couple of them had been pried open and the Inspector could see the deadly sticks inside the crates looking, in their red casings, like oversized candles.

"Dynamite," Tynan whispered. "There must be close to a thousand sticks of it here. Driner's source of supply. And all of it's rotten, aged, unstable, sweating. It could go up at any time. This whole place is sitting on top of a giant mine. We've got to get everybody out of here. This stuff's got to be blown up before it blows on its own. And there's no way we can move it."

The Inspector nodded. He thought for a moment and said: "Get Captain Hedloe down here."

Tynan looked at Max Kauffman anxiously. "Sir, I don't think it's safe for you to stay here."

The Inspector waved him away, "A couple of more seconds won't matter. Get Hedloe."

As he waited, Max Kauffman could smell the almost overpowering stench of mold which, he'd always heard, was the odor dynamite gave off when it became unpredictable.

Tynan came back with Captain Hedloe.

"Tell him what's going on here," Max Kauffman said to Tynan.

Tynan quickly explained the situation while Hedloe glanced, white-faced, at the crates. The lieutenant very carefully pointed out that if he didn't blow up the explosives now, under controlled conditions, the danger was that sooner or later they would blow on their own and could create a devastating forest fire in the surrounding woods. When Tynan finished, Hedloe said quickly, "Come on, let's get upstairs. We can talk about this outdoors."

When they were upstairs again, Max Kauffman and Captain Hedloe rounded up the rest of the men and they all moved quickly out of the house. Detective Garibaldi had collected the photographs of the nude woman, which was the only other evidence the house contained, so the Inspector didn't really feel that they'd been forced to leave anything behind, although he would have liked to have had the lab technicians check the house for prints and whatever else they could turn up. That, he knew now, was out of the question.

Max Kauffman, Captain Hedloe, and Tynan walked some distance out from the house, well beyond the chain fence, to confer. The rest of the men were told to move the police cars back up the road from the house.

"All right now," Hedloe said, "you say that stuff's got to be blown up as soon as possible, in a controlled manner. So how do we go about it?"

"First, we've got to have a court order condemning the property as a danger to the community," Max Kauffman said quickly.

Hedloe waved a hand in the air. "I'll take care of that," he said, "don't worry. Then what?"

Tynan explained that he'd call Headquarters in

216

Manhattan and have the Police Academy bomb squad send up some plastic explosives, which were safer to handle. He'd lay charges against the basement, near where the dynamite was stored, and lace the charges, that is, wrap his detonating wire around the plastic to achieve the maximum amount of heat direct from the wire at the time of detonation and thus create a more powerful explosion. He would run the wire from the plastic charges to a detonator, which would set off the actual blast, and the detonator would be some distance back from the house. What he expected was a series of explosions and an intense fire. He cautioned the State Police captain that all the available firefighting equipment in the area should be brought in as soon as possible and that the trees and brush surrounding the house be wet down before the dynamite was set off.

"I'll start calling them in right now," Hedloe said briskly. "And I'll get that court order. You contact your people."

Tynan looked at Max Kauffman.

"Yes," the Inspector said, "do it."

It wasn't until 1:20 P.M. that the explosives Tynan had been waiting for arrived from the city. The New York Police had borrowed a special truck from a company in the city which was licensed by the Fire Department's Bureau of Combustibles to transport explosives. The truck was constructed to withstand a collision without its cargo exploding. The body of the vehicle was lined with a layer of hardwood, a second layer of metal, a third layer, yet again of hardwood. Fitted over all this was a steel apron. The truck carried extra heavy bumpers inside which was a lining of manila rope insulation to protect against friction. On the run from Manhattan the truck was accompanied by two squad cars from the 16th Precinct.

By the time the truck reached the house in Pound Ridge the grounds were swarming with men, firemen and volunteer firemen from surrounding communities, seven fire engines, and a half dozen State Police cruisers. The firemen had drenched the trees and brush and grounds around the house, and Captain Hedloe had obtained a court order condemning the property.

Max Kauffman and the other men had withdrawn from the grounds immediately adjacent to the house and stood watching from the end of the road while Tynan, Raucher, Braxley, Cohen, and Garibaldi laid the plastic charges against the foundation of the house. They inserted the detonating wire in the plastic, and spooled out the roll of electric wire, running it back across the ground before connecting it to the detonator set near the road where the other men stood.

Tynan crouched over the detonator. He raised his head and looked around him. "Everybody in the clear?" he asked in a loud voice.

"Everybody accounted for, Jack," Max Kauffman called back. "Go to it."

Tynan grasped the handle of the plunger atop the detonator and shoved it down.

Max Kauffman braced himself for the shock but he still wasn't prepared for the ear-shattering blast and the blinding white-hot inferno of flames which simultaneously erupted inside the chain link fence. He could feel the earth shake under his feet and had to turn his head away briefly from the fiery glare which exploded high into the air brighter than flashes of sheet lightning. The first heart-stopping blast was quickly followed by six to ten more explosions of less intensity. When Max Kauffman looked back the house was obliterated by fire. Exploding flames catapulted through the air, struck the drenched trees, and went out; flames hedgehopped across the ground and fizzled out.

The fire that engulfed the house burned first white-hot, then red, then blue, and finally with a steady orange flame. One of the firemen yelled, "Come on, let's put it out," and other firemen began moving in with hoses and chemicals, spraying the flames, circling around, feinting quickly in and out, almost as if fighting a duel, until finally, after a long time, the fire was put out. There was nothing left of the house. It had been leveled; all that remained was a black hole in the earth where the basement had been, and it was deep in sooty water. Scattered around were pieces of charred wooden beams and fragments of stone that had once been the foundation. The air was full of the stench of smoke. Firemen continued to spray water and chemicals over the ruins and the ground around the black hole.

Max Kauffman suddenly felt tired and depressed. He forced himself to walk over to Tynan, clasp him by the shoulder, and say, "Nice work, Jack."

Tynan, too, looked tired and unhappy and only nodded his head without answering.

The Inspector shook hands with Captain Hedloe. "We appreciate all your help, Captain."

"We appreciate yours, Inspector. If this damn thing had blown up with nobody around, it might have burned up half the county. I'll leave a car and a couple of men here for the next couple of days to keep watch. First of the week we'll drain all that water out and make sure there's no more unexploded dynamite down there. I'll give you a call and report when we've done that. Hey!" Hedloe exclaimed, looking skyward. "I just felt some snow. That's a good sign. It'll keep things wet."

The Inspector felt it, too—big, wet flakes splattering against his face. "We'll be getting back to town," he said and left the captain and walked over to one of the N.Y.P.D. squad cars. Tynan followed him into the car, and Raucher climbed into the front seat again. The other policemen from New York City returned to the remaining squad cars and the truck that had transported the explosives out from Manhattan. As the cars and the explosives truck turned around in front of the chain link fence, and headed back up the narrow road toward the highway, Max Kauffman could see the men still standing in a circle in the yard. As they stood there, heads bowed, peering into the hole in the earth, unmindful of the steadily falling snow, they reminded him of funereal figures paying their last respects at an open grave.

CHAPTER TWENTY-ONE

The snow had turned into a full-blown blizzard by the time the four squad cars got back to the 16th Precinct a few minutes before 4 P.M. On the drive back Max Kauffman had been in touch by radio with the precinct and had ordered that unmarked police cars be sent to pick up Millicent Lauder and Everett Cragle and bring them to the station house as soon as they could be located. Also, he and the other policemen had been advised by the precinct that there had been another bomb incident in the city that afternoon while the Inspector and his men had been out of contact in Pound Ridge. This time the explosion had taken place in a sidewalk phone booth on the south side of Forty-ninth Street just west of Fifth Avenue. The blast had demolished the phone booth which, fortunately, had been empty. The bomb had gone off at precisely 2 P.M. when the streets and sidewalks were congested with shoppers and cars. There had been two injuries. An elderly man had been struck on the shoulder by a piece of flying metal, and a young woman standing near the phone booth had been knocked down by the force of the blast. Both had been taken to Roosevelt Hospital and later released.

When the report came in to the squad car, Max Kauffman had remarked sourly, "Well, at least the bomber won't be calling nine-one-one from *that* phone booth." Now as he came into the station house, stomping the snow off his shoes, the desk sergeant handed him two envelopes and said that 911 had reported receiving a call from a man who identified himself as

The Christmas Bomber," and whose message was: "It's the ninth day of Christmas."

"It's like a fucking broken record," Tynan complained as he followed Max Kauffman to the elevator. "'The millionth day of Christmas,' 'the billionth day of Christmas,' 'the zillionth day of Christmas.'"

They had to wait for the elevator. The ancient radiators in the station house were hissing and knocking, the windows were glazed with steam, and there was a smell of damp wool throughout the building.

When they reached the third floor, Max Kauffman's office door was shut—Policewoman MacKay was off duty—and he had to use his key to get in. He turned the lights on and then stopped so suddenly in the doorway that Tynan bumped into him.

"I'll be a son of a bitch," the Inspector said, looking around the room with delight.

While he had been away, the painters and decorators had completed their work. The paneled oak walls of the room and the exposed oak beams across the ceiling gleamed richly brown in the soft, indirect lighting that came from fixtures recessed in the ceilings and the tops of the windows. New deep gold, thick pile carpeting covered the floor from wall to wall. Drawn across the windows were gold drapes that matched the carpeting. His collection of abstract oil paintings had been hung on the walls and his collection of sculpture placed again on low pedestals where they were illuminated by soft light. His mahogany desk was shined so the light reflected in its surface, his leather chairs had been cleaned and positioned around the room, and there were even fresh-cut chrysanthemums in the crystal vase on the mahogany coffee table. The stone fireplace had been cleaned out and fresh logs laid on the andirons. The whole room had a clean smell of rich leather and oil polish, the way he liked it.

There was a small envelope propped up against the vase of chrysanthemums on the coffee table. He wiped the soles of his shoes carefully outside the door and motioned for Tynan to do the same. He crossed the room and opened the envelope. The card inside read: "Hope you like it, sir. Happy Holidays—Officer Florence MacKay."

"That's very nice," he said and showed the card to Tynan. "She must have come in today on her own time and supervised all this so it would be a surprise. That's very nice. Very."

He looked around the room again with pleasure and took off his coat and hat and hung them in the closet and sat down at his desk. Tynan draped his coat over a chair and sat in another chair. He was carrying several envelopes containing the photographs they'd recovered from the house in Pound Ridge.

Max Kauffman tore open one of the envelopes he'd picked up from the desk sergeant. It had been sent from Headquarters and contained a composite photograph of the purported likeness of Paul Driner based on the descriptions supplied by Millicent Lauder and Everett Cragle. Tynan came around the desk and looked over the Inspector's shoulder.

The composite showed a man with a narrow, tapering face that ended in a small square chin. His hair was dark with some gray in it and he wore it in a stubby brush cut, almost a crew cut. His eyes were dark and close-set. His nose was thin and so were his lips, and he had a neat, dark moustache not much thicker than his eyebrows.

"Not a face that would exactly warm your heart," Tynan observed.

Max Kauffman stared intently at the photograph. The face seemed to match the facts they knew about Paul Driner, if the composite was an accurate representation of the way Driner looked. There was a definite off-putting quality about the face. The eyes were cold, the whole set of the face rigid, even self-righteous-looking. He turned the composite over and read the physical description typed on the back: HEIGHT: 5'10"—WEIGHT: 165 POUNDS—COMPLEXION: DARK—EYES: DARK GRAY—HAIR: BLACK WITH SOME GRAY—UNUSUAL PHYSICAL CHARACTERISTICS: NONE.

The Inspector laid the composite photograph on his desk and with Tynan still looking over his shoulder, opened the second envelope which had come from Dr. Wallstein, the assistant medical examiner at the morgue. There were five X-rays of the skull and skeleton of the woman's body which had been recovered from Potter's field. There was also a note from Wallstein. Max Kauffman said: "He says they've completed casts on the teeth and bones of the skeleton as well as these X-rays, and are holding the casts at the morgue." He glanced up at Tynan. "What I want you to do is pick a man and have him get to Pottsville, Pennsylvania, as soon as possible. He can take these X-rays along with him. Have him check on all the doctors and dentists there and see if he can find any matching records on—as she was called then—Adrienne Kolawal."

He handed Tynan the X-rays. The desk sergeant called and said that Millicent Lauder and Everett Cragle were on the way up. Max Kauffman hung up, saying: "Lauder and Cragle'll be here in a minute. Pick out a couple of the less explicit photographs of the naked woman and let's see if they can identify her."

Tynan leafed through the photographs hurriedly, laid two glossy ones on the desk, and stuffed the rest into the envelopes. He picked up one of the photographs of the seductive-looking nude woman and one of the X-rays of the bony skeleton, holding them up side by side. He started to say something, then just shook his head and put the X-rays back in the envelope when there was a knock at the door.

One of the plainclothesmen led Millicent Lauder and Everett Cragle into the room. Both the woman and Cragle looked angry and upset. Before either of them could say anything, Max Kauffman stood up.

"I appreciate the way both of you are cooperating," he said, but he kept his voice cold, and his words were clipped. "In a major case such as this we always have a problem trying to decide what to do about material witnesses like yourselves. Because of the inconvenience it would cause you we prefer not to have to take you into custody and hold you until there's a trial or the case is disposed of." He smiled easily. "By your cooperation, you make it so much easier for us and for yourselves, of course."

He had no more trouble with them. Both sat meekly in front of his desk while he recounted the results of the police visit to Driner's house in Pound Ridge. Then Tynan showed them the nude photographs. Millicent Lauder blushed furiously but neither she nor Cragle hesitated before identifying the woman as Adrienne Driner.

Max Kauffman next held up the composite photograph of Paul Driner. "Do you both agree this is a reasonable likeness of Driner?"

"Absolutely," Cragle said.

"Yes," Millicent Lauder said. "I'd know him from that photograph."

"The likeness is uncanny," Cragle added. "I don't know how they do it."

Millicent Lauder nodded her head.

"Good!" Max Kauffman said. "There's just one other matter I want to ask you about while you're here. Do either of you know where Driner got all that dynamite?"

"I can answer that," Cragle said slowly. "Paul frequently went out of state to get his explosives. I knew he did some experimenting with the stuff from time to time, but I never knew he had that much on hand."

"All right," the Inspector said. "Thank you again. We'll try not to bother you any more except when it's absolutely necessary. And I'm sure I don't have to remind you that if Driner should contact either of you, you're to let us know at once. Again, we appreciate your help. The officer will drive you home."

As soon as they'd gone, Max Kauffman said, "Jack, pick whoever you want to send to Pottsville and get him on the way, then come back, I want to talk to you."

Tynan took the envelope of X-rays and left.

The Inspector swung around in his chair and phoned Headquarters to try to locate the Commissioner. He had to wait and while he waited, holding

225

the phone cradled to his ear with his shoulder, he glanced idly through the collection of nude photographs of Adrienne Kolawal Driner. There was no prurience in his appraisal of her exposed body, although he was male enough to appreciate the sexuality of her body in some of the poses she had struck while the pictures were taken. It was, he thought, a body that might well have helped drive a man crazy if he were suddenly deprived of it, especially a man like Driner.

When the Commissioner finally came on the line, Max Kauffman put the photographs away, to be sent to the lab. He knew he'd never look at them again.

As he talked to the Commissioner, he could hear sounds of laughter and conversation in the background. The Commissioner apologized for the noise, explaining that he was entertaining at home.

"I wanted to bring you up to date," Max Kauffman said. He gave a full account of the day's events, concluding with: "Sir, at the last meeting we had, you told me if I needed additional help, I should ask. Now that we have a composite photograph of Driner and there's some chance we may be able to apprehend him on sight, I'd like to be assigned two hundred and sixteen officers to work on decoy in plainclothes, and to try to saturate the midtown area with them. Also, I would like a surveillance van assigned to me."

Surveillance vans were nondescript panel trucks which were used by the police in Times Square and in other high-crime areas of the city to keep the streets under observation. The vans, which were totally enclosed, had television cameras mounted unobtrusively on the outside to scan the streets and feed the pictures to monitors inside the vans. The vans were also equipped with field telephone switchboards.

Max Kauffman explained his plan for using the men, adding that he'd like to set the whole operation up the next morning.

"All right," Commissioner Hilliard said. "I'll pass the order. I'll have every precinct contacted and the appropriate personnel report to you at eight A.M. You'll have your surveillance van at the same time."

When Tynan returned to the office, Max Kauffman lit a cigar and leaned back in his chair.

"Check me out on this, Jack, will you, on what it appears to me happened with Driner, following his wife's death, based upon the information we've uncovered these last few days."

"Go ahead," Tynan said.

"When she was killed," Max Kauffman said, "all the money was in her name." He paused, then continued, "Come to think of it, she did make a withdrawal of twenty-five hundred dollars the day she was killed. She may have been carrying it with her at the time, which could account for her handbag being missing. Driner could have gotten that. Anyhow, apparently he lived at the place in Pound Ridge for a while and maybe the place here in the city, too. At some time or another, he also transported explosives in his old car, apparently from up there to the city. Evidence would indicate that at some point, probably because he was short of money, he started selling most of the furniture, from both places. Then for a while he must have stayed in the city until he was scared away from it, possibly after he took that girl, Caroline Harger, there. Since then he's been holed up somewhere here in the city, and he has a weakness for girls who remind him of Adrienne. As for the money in the bank he's never claimed, the only theory I can think of is that he must have wanted to wait and see if he got away with his bombing spree before he tried to get the money."

"It all hangs together," Tynan agreed.

"Yeah."

Max Kauffman leaned forward, cleared off his desk, and took from the drawer the map of the city he'd been using to keep track of the bombing incidents. He made another red X on the map, at the corner of Forty-ninth Street and Fifth Avenue, where the bomb had exploded in the phone booth.

"What's that?" Tynan asked curiously.

227

The Inspector shifted the map around so it faced Tynan. "I want to show you something." He pointed at the map with the red felt-tipped pen. "So far we've had nine bomb incidents. Five have taken place on Fifth Avenue between Forty-first and Fifty-ninth Streets, a sixth at Fiftieth Street and Sixth Avenue. I don't have to point out, of course, that that's the general area where the woman was killed by the bus."

"Yeah," Tynan said. "The pattern's there, all right."

"Presumably Driner plans three more incidents, and we now know what he looks like."

Tynan said "Yeah" again.

"I've asked the Commissioner to send us additional manpower. Plainclothesmen. They'll be here at eight in the morning." Max Kauffman hunched forward. "Here's my plan: we'll put a man in every block on both sides of Fifth Avenue, from Forty-first Street to Fifty-ninth Street. We'll also put an additional man on either side of the street in every block between Fifth and Sixth and Fifth and Madison from Forty-first to Fifty-ninth. That's a total of one hundred and eight men. We'll work two eight-hour shifts, from eight A.M. to four P.M. and four to midnight. That's a total of two hundred and sixteen men, which is what I've asked the Commissioner for."

Tynan whistled softly. "That's a big undertaking."

"Exactly," Max Kauffman said. "Each man will familiarize himself with the composite photograph of Driner. If Driner sets foot anywhere within the area—and he will—we'll nab him." He paused and pointed his cigar at Tynan. "I've also asked for a surveillance van to be put at our disposal. We'll move it back and forth in the area and use it as a command post. Either you or I will be in it at all times while the operation is in effect."

"I like the plan," Tynan said.

"Good." Max Kauffman folded up the map and handed it to Tynan along with the composite photograph of Paul Driner. "And Jack, get a blow-up made of the map and about three hundred copies of the composite of Driner."

Tynan nodded and said: "I sent Frank Pennell to Pottsville to check out the doctors and dentists there. See you at eight in the morning, sir. Good night."

"Good night." Max Kauffman waved his cigar and then glanced at his watch. It was quarter after six. He'd have to hurry. Catherine Devereaux didn't know it but he was taking her to the City Center's seasonal performance of the *Nutcracker Suite* and, afterward, to Luchow's for dinner. He'd phoned her that morning before he went to Pound Ridge and told her to be ready to go out at eight. Also that morning he'd ordered a chauffeured car from the Carey Limousine Service to pick them up at her apartment. He'd just have time to go by his apartment, shower, shave, and change into fresh clothes and still be at her place at 8 P.M. He planned to spend the night with her. Tomorrow his wife would be home from Cambridge.

After he'd put on his hat and coat, he opened the drapes at the windows. It was still snowing heavily. They were having a real old-fashioned blizzard. He turned away from the window and looked around the office for a moment before turning off the lights. He was absurdly pleased at the way the room looked. It was, he felt, a good omen. On his way to the elevator he noticed that one of the ornaments had fallen from the Christmas tree on Policewoman MacKay's desk. He picked up the ornament, a miniature Santa Claus made of plush, and hung it carefully back on the tree. It was a pretty little tree, he decided, after all. For a plastic tree, that was.

CHAPTER TWENTY-TWO

Sheila Yen left her apartment on Mott Street in lower Manhattan's Chinatown at 7:15 Sunday morning and caught the uptown BMT subway. Snow was piled almost a foot high on the streets from the night's blizzard and the temperature was five degrees above freezing. The only other person in the subway car was an old man reading the Sunday *News*. The front-page headline was: CHRISTMAS BOMBER STRIKES AGAIN.

Sheila Yen opened her pocketbook, took out her compact and put on fresh lipstick. She had a narrow face with high cheekbones. Her hair was coal black, fell to her shoulders, and was parted on the left side. She had dark brown eyes, slanted at the corners, long black lashes, curving eyebrows, and tiny, delicate ears. She was five feet six, twenty-seven years old, and the beauty of her face and figure had already given her dozens of chances for marriage, both inside and outside her race, all of which she had refused. She was wearing a cocoa wool dress, knee-high boots, and a dark muskrat coat. Before she put her compact away, she tied a silk scarf around her head. When she returned her compact to her pocketbook, she touched her wallet to make sure her detective's shield was pinned to it.

For the past five years she had worked the Chinatown beat out of the 5th Precinct, the last two years as a detective, second-grade. This morning she was excited about her trip uptown, and a bit mystified. All she knew was that the evening before, as she was going off duty, the desk sergeant had told her orders had come through from Headquarters assigning her to temporary duty at the 16th Precinct. Her instructions were to report to Inspector Max Kauffman at the 16th by 8 A.M.

At approximately the same time that Sheila Yen was heading uptown on the BMT, Detective First-grade Roberto Teresa was heading downtown on the west side IRT subway from his home in Hamilton Heights in upper Manhattan where he lived with his wife, Juanita, and their two-year-old daughter, Maria. Detective Teresa was slim, five feet ten inches tall, and was thirty-two years old. He was wearing a bulky car coat that came to below his waist, dark trousers, Tote boots which reached halfway up his legs, and was hatless. His hair was neatly parted and black and he had long sideburns. The olive shade of his skin, from his Hispanic origins, made his big, strong teeth look dazzling white. Detective Teresa worked out of the 25th Precinct on East 119th Street. Like Detective Yen, he had been notified of his temporary assignment to Inspector Max Kauffman at the 16th Precinct on the previous night. Unlike Detective Yen, however, he had figured out—when he was told the orders came from Headquarters—that his assignment was somehow connected with the case of "The Christmas Bomber." He checked his watch and saw that he would be at the 16th in plenty of time. The movement of his arm had caused the handcuffs attached to his belt to jangle. There were only four other persons sitting in the subway and none of them seemed to notice. *Gracias Dios*, he murmured to himself.

At six minutes past eight Detectives Yen and Teresa gathered, along with 214 other police officers from all over the city, in the lineup room in the basement of the 16th Precinct. In order to make space for the crowd, all the chairs had been removed and the police officers stood jammed in side by side in the room. Earlier, as each officer had entered the room he had had to produce his ID card which was entered on a record being kept by Detectives Braxley and Garibaldi of the 16th Precinct bomb squad. Each policeman was, in turn, handed a copy of the composite photograph of Paul Driner.

Inspector Max Kauffman, followed by Lieutenant John Tynan, came through the door at the end of the raised platform in the front of the room at 8:07. Tynan was carrying a large blowup of the section of the map of the midtown area. He thumbtacked the map to a giant bulletin board in the middle of the platform. Max Kauffman stood next to the map and faced the assembled police officers. He noticed that there was a large representation of women in the group, and blacks, some Hispanic, and even one Chinese woman officer. He was satisfied that it was an interestingly varied group to do decoy work.

"I'm Inspector Kauffman," he said. He paused and looked around the packed room. "I hope there are no pickpockets among us."

That got a nice laugh. Max Kauffman then went on in a more serious tone, explaining the assignment and the urgency of trying to apprehend the bomber before he struck again. He explained the markings on the map, indicating the various spots where previous bombs had exploded and describing his theory of why the bomber would attempt to set off one or more explosives in that area. He told them that lists were now being drawn up, assigning each of them to either the 8 A.M. to 4 P.M. shift or the 4 P.M. to midnight shift. As they left the room they would be told by the 16th Precinct detectives at the door which shift they would be assigned to. Each officer would also be given a walkie-talkie to carry while walking his post. The Inspector explained that the surveillance van would be a rolling command post and would be in the vicinity at all times. He introduced Lieutenant John Tynan and said that the lieutenant would be in charge of the operation under his, the Inspector's, command. One or both of them would be in the surveillance van at all times.

"In conclusion," Max Kauffman said, "I want to impress upon you the importance of studying the composite photograph which each of you holds of the man we believe to be the perpetrator. I want every

233

feature on his face burned into your brain so that you see him even when you're sleeping." He paused, looked around the room, and added: "If you apprehend this man, use caution. He's extremely dangerous, psychotically dangerous. Try to handcuff him as quickly as possible. This operation will remain in effect indefinitely. Good luck."

Max Kauffman turned and left the room as the rest of the officers filed out the other door, soberly quiet. He went upstairs to his office, put on his hat and coat, and came back down to meet John Tynan in the lobby of the station house.

The surveillance van they'd requested was parked outside the front entrance. There was a driver and a second man, in plainclothes, sitting in the front. The second man got out and came around and opened one of the back doors of the van and Max Kauffman and Tynan climbed into the interior, pulling the door closed behind them. The back of the van was fitted out with several small but comfortable chairs bolted to the floor. Arranged in front of the chairs were four television monitors; on the screen of one of them was the scene looking east up the street in front of the van, on another the scene to the west behind the van, and a view of the station house and of across the street on the remaining two screens. Two men worked in the back compartment. One was a TV technician who adjusted the direction and focus of the cameras mounted on the outside of the vehicle, while the second man, who wore earphones and an attached microphone, handled communications. He was in direct contact with Headquarters. In addition, he sat at the field switchboard, which was connected to six telephones inside the van. There was also an intercom connecting the driver and his partner in the front compartment with the rear of the van.

"Where to, Inspector?" the disembodied voice of the driver asked over the intercom.

"Fifth Avenue and Fiftieth Street," Max Kauffman ordered. "Try to find a parking space there until our personnel begin walking their posts."

"Roger," the driver said and as the van pulled

away, the communications officer whispered softly into the microphone: "S-V one-four to dispatcher. Proceeding eastward. Destination: Fifth and Fiftieth. K."

Max Kauffman and Tynan had taken seats in the chairs in front of the TV monitors and were trying to familiarize themselves with the workings of the van. On the TV monitors they had a four-angle view of each block as they rolled east and then north up Sixth Avenue. The snow was still piled high on the streets but the sanitation trucks and plows were out and at work. Because of the early hour and the snow, there weren't yet many pedestrians or private cars on the street. At Fiftieth Street the van pulled into the curb near the corner west of Fifth Avenue and parked.

"And now we sit and wait," Max Kauffman said to no one in particular.

At 10:27 P.M., over ten hours since they'd first entered the van that morning, Tynan said, "Jesus, I could use a good stiff brandy."

Max Kauffman nodded without really hearing him. His eyes were on the TV monitors as the van rolled east on Fifty-second Street in the block between Fifth Avenue and Madison. There were only two figures visible along the length of the entire block, one on either side of Fifty-second Street, trudging through the now hard-packed snow. In the hours that had passed since the operation went into effect, the Inspector—working from names on the record sheet which had been sent to him from the 16th Precinct—had gotten to know the identities of most of the plainclothes police working the beats they had been assigned, first on the day, 8 A.M. to 4 P.M. shift, and now on the 4 P.M. to midnight detail. For example, he knew that the man patrolling the north side of Fiftieth Street was a detective named Roberto Teresa from the 25th Precinct, and the detective on the south side of Fiftieth alongside St. Patrick's Cathedral was Sheila Yen, from the 5th Precinct Chinatown squad.

As the van rolled on its circuitous route through the icy midtown streets that were all but deserted except for the patiently patrolling 108 plainclothes policemen, Max Kauffman's own sense of depression was deepening. It wasn't that he'd been that confident they would trap Paul Driner on the first day they put the operation into effect; it was that less than two hours remained until midnight and so far there had been no reports of any bombings anywhere in the city. This was supposed to be "the tenth day of Christmas," which meant another bomb. As yet there had been no explosion. He didn't want bombings, but he did want the bomber.

During the past ten hours there had been several false alarms. Three times police had mistaken innocent passersby in the midtown area for Driner. But none of them was the man. Frustrating. On the other hand, there had been several other developments in the case: the vice squad had reported they'd hassled the hooker, Felice Morrissey, so frequently on Saturday and Saturday night, hauling her into the precinct every time she set foot out of her hotel, that she had taken to her room and remained there all day Sunday and so far this night. Max Kauffman hoped she might be about ready to cooperate. Also, Detective Pennell had phoned from Pottsville to say that he had two positive identifications, from a dentist and a dental lab technician there, who had X-rays of Adrienne Kolawal Driner's teeth. It looked like eleven of the teeth in those X-rays matched the teeth in the skull of the unidentified traffic victim. Pennell was coming back in the morning with the X-rays.

During the day and evening, Max Kauffman and Tynan had taken short, separate breaks from the van. In the afternoon Tynan had gone for a couple of hours to visit Barbara Costa at her apartment, and in the early evening the Inspector had left, from 6 P.M. to 8 P.M. His wife and two children had gotten back from Cambridge in the afternoon and he thought he'd have dinner with them. As it turned out, both Lawrence and Debbie had made plans to go out with their friends that evening, so Max Kauffman saw his

236

son and daughter for no more than fifteen minutes and then he and Belle had eaten dinner alone. Before he had returned to the surveillance van, he had stopped in a phone booth and called Catherine Devereaux. She said she was putting her Christmas tree up and decorating it. She sounded happy and busy, and he was glad.

For the next hour and a half that Max Kauffman and Tynan rode through the streets in the back of the van, they spotted nothing significant. The streets were dreary and ghostlike. At five minutes after midnight, Tynan looked over at the Inspector and said: "Damn! I guess that's it for the night."

"Yes," Max Kauffman agreed. The van was making its final sweep through the streets for the night. The special police they'd put out on patrol duty had now finished their shifts and were heading to the precinct to check out for the night. All their efforts for that day had been for nothing. The Inspector had had the communications officer radio for two squad cars to meet the van on Fifth Avenue and Fiftieth Street, one to take Tynan to wherever he wanted to go, the other to drive him to his apartment.

Now, as Max Kauffman, legs cramped from sitting so long, climbed out of the back of the van and prepared to go home, he muttered to himself, "What happened to the son of a bitch? Why did he change his pattern after all this time?"

It would not be until the following day that he would have his answer.

CHAPTER TWENTY-THREE

There were seventeen policemen, some in uniform, the others in plain clothes—detectives from the 16th Homicide Bureau, a police photographer, three lab technicians—crowded into the small hotel room by the time Max Kauffman arrived. He had to push his way into the room until they recognized him and moved aside to let him pass. There was a lot of activity in the room but almost no talking. Detectives were looking into the closet and searching through the drawers of the dresser that stood against the wall. The lab men were dusting likely surfaces for possible prints, other detectives and lab men were busy at work in the bathroom. Some of the detectives were just moving in small circles around the bed in the center of the room. It was 11 A.M., Monday, December 23.

Felice Morrissey, the prostitute, lay on her back in the bed, her head propped up by two pillows. A length of lamp cord was wound around her throat and twisted into a knot behind her neck. It had been wound so tight that in some places it couldn't be seen it was embedded so deep in the flesh. The small lamp the cord had been pulled from lay on the floor beside the bed. So far none of the policemen had touched it.

Max Kauffman stood by the bed and looked down at the dead girl dispassionately. She was naked except for a copy of the Sunday *News* which covered her breasts. The newspaper was lying with the front page face up. The headline read: CHRISTMAS BOMBER STRIKES AGAIN.

The murderer had used the girl's lipstick to scrawl across the top of the front-page photograph—which was a picture of the phone booth demolished by the bomb on Fiftieth Street on Saturday—the words:

THIS IS THE TENTH
DAY of CHRISTMas!
THE BOMBER

The lipstick tube lay on the sheet next to her bare right thigh.

Max Kauffman's eyes traveled down her body. He could feel his flesh crawl when he saw that she lay with her legs spread wide and rammed into her body was a long, cylindrical object in a familiar red casing, a stick of dynamite with an unlit tipped fuse at the head. Both of her feet lay flat on the bed. The blood-red polish on her toenails was chipped and flaked on every toe except the big one on her left foot.

An hour earlier Brodeman and Chavez, of the vice squad, who had taken over surveillance of the Sydney Hotel at 8 A.M. became uneasy when the girl, who hadn't been seen all day Sunday and Sunday night, still hadn't appeared by ten that Monday morning. They went up to her room and when she didn't answer their knocks, they got the manager to open the door and they found her. It was their theory that, despite the close watch police had kept on the girl and the hotel, she had somehow managed to contact Paul Driner and he had slipped into the hotel unobserved, through the basement or up a fire escape, and murdered her.

Max Kauffman turned away from the bed and said: "Jesus!" in a loud voice that startled the other men in the room. He twirled and took his anger and frustration out on the police photographer. "For

240

Christ's sakes, can't you shoot your pictures any faster? Cover her up and get her out of here!"

"Yes, sir," the photographer said quickly.

Max Kauffman pushed his way out of the room. There was nothing more for him to do there. As he went, he said to himself: "She *had* to try to play it cute, blackmail Driner instead of cooperating with us. And she got herself killed. Oh—hell."

He went down to the street where his limousine was waiting and rode back to the precinct in brooding silence. With the death of Felice Morrissey they'd lost their best lead to Paul Driner. Driner was still operating on his twelve-days-of-Christmas schedule. They'd just been late one day in discovering the latest death, and there were still two days to go. Now, more than ever, the apprehension of Paul Driner depended on the efforts of the plainclothes force who were out patrolling the midtown streets. They were out there right now, he knew, and so was Tynan in the surveillance van.

When the Inspector reached his office he found he had several phone messages, including one from his father and one from Milt Nevers at the lab. He buzzed Florence MacKay and thanked her for supervising the decoration of his office before he returned the phone calls. He called his father first, surprised that the number the old man had left was the office of Kauffman and Son. His father answered the phone and said he was sending the company guard, Abe Schechter, over with the money to be repaid to the gambler. Max Kauffman didn't think his father should be at the office, but Aaron Kauffman said, "No! No! It's all right. I feel fine," and hung up.

Next the Inspector talked to Milt Nevers at the lab. Nevers told him that the dental records they had received from Pottsville positively matched eleven teeth in the skull of the woman who had been buried in Potter's field. "It's the same woman," Nevers said. "The ID's positive."

At least that detail was out of the way, Max Kauffman thought, with a sigh of relief.

241

He made another call, this one on his private line, to Leo Morgen. Morgen said he'd see to it that the money Marvin Katz owed to Moe Blum was returned to the gambler, or someone in the Gallano family. He promised to send Detective Arnie Silverman to the 16th Precinct to pick it up sometime after lunch. Max Kauffman said there would be an envelope waiting with the desk sergeant with Silverman's name on it.

When he had completed that conversation, he phoned Commissioner Hilliard. The Commissioner was in conference. Max Kauffman left a message that he'd called.

Still holding the phone, Max Kauffman instructed the 16th Precinct switchboard operator to put him through to John Tynan at one of the phones in the police surveillance van. He told Tynan that the identification of Adrienne Driner was now positive and about the discovery of Felice Morrissey's body in the hotel room.

"That figures," Tynan said in response. "So we still have a chance to nail him."

Max Kauffman agreed and said, "Listen, Jack, I'll be leaving shortly to come over to the van and relieve you for a couple of hours."

He waited in his office for another quarter of an hour until Abe Schechter arrived with the money from his father. Max Kauffman put the money in a manila envelope and scribbled Arnie Silverman's name on it. On his way out of the office, he told Officer MacKay he could be reached at the surveillance van, dropped the envelope of money off with the desk sergeant, and had one of the squad cars drive him over to where the van was parked, on Fifty-third Street between Fifth and Sixth Avenues. There was still a lot of snow on the streets although most of the sidewalks in midtown were cleared off. The sky had been clouded over all morning and the temperature still hadn't risen above freezing. Whether it was because of the weather or the bombings, there appeared to be fewer people out on the streets, particularly since there were only two shopping days left until Christmas.

242

Tynan was sitting in the back compartment of the van, drinking coffee. There was another container on the floor between his legs in which a dozen cigarette butts floated in shallow dregs of coffee.

"So far, nothing," Tynan said, shaking his head when Max Kauffman sat down in one of the chairs. He motioned to the TV monitors with his hand. "And I can tell you our troops out there are keeping a sharp eye on the city. So far today, they managed to arrest three pickpockets, a molester, and a guy pushing drugs over on Sixth Avenue. Even if we don't catch the bomber, we might wind up cutting the crime rate in midtown." He thought for a moment and said, "Of course, come to think about it, today it looks like there are more cops on the street than civilians."

After Tynan went on his break, Max Kauffman stayed on in the van until midafternoon. While he was there he received a phone call from the Commissioner, who sounded tired and discouraged.

"I had another session all morning on your case with both of the mayors," Hilliard said. "I assured them the Department was doing everything it could and that I still had all the confidence in the world in you. But tell me frankly, Max, do you really think we're ever going to catch this bird?"

"Yes, I still think so," Max Kauffman answered carefully. "That is, *if* he continues with his plan of twelve bombings. In my guts, I feel that at least one of the two bombings he probably still plans, if not both, will occur in the area we're covering. If it does, if they do, there's no way we're not going to get him. We just have to hang in there."

"All right," the Commissioner said. "I'll take your word for it."

They discussed the death of the prostitute. The Inspector said a report on it would be sent to Headquarters later in the afternoon. And there was the positive identification of the body of Adrienne Driner. "Certainly we're making some progress," Max Kauffman pointed out.

"That's true," Hilliard said. "Well, keep me advised."

243

When Tynan returned at 2:30, Max Kauffman decided to pick up a couple of Christmas presents before he returned to the precinct. He'd placed the order for his gift for Catherine Devereaux with Van Cleef and Arpels some weeks earlier—*parure de diamants,* a matched set of diamonds set in a bracelet and ring. He strolled up Fifth Avenue to the store, picked up the package, and paid for it by check out of his private account. He caught a cab at Fifth Avenue and Fifty-sixth Street and went to the diamond district on West Forty-eighth Street between Fifth and Sixth where, in one of the small jewelry stores, he bought a thin solid gold necklace for Policewoman MacKay. He was pleased that all his Christmas shopping was done. He was giving his wife a new 25-inch color television set—it would be delivered to the apartment tomorrow—and a two-week-visit at Elizabeth Arden's Maine Chance resort in Arizona, both of which she'd announced she wanted as Christmas presents. And Belle had bought presents for Debbie and Lawrence.

When he returned to the precinct, he locked both of the presents he'd bought, for Catherine Devereaux and for Policewoman MacKay, in his office safe. Then he began dictating the report he'd promised to send to the Commissioner.

There was a thin sliver of new moon in the sky that night. Max Kauffman could see it clearly, high in the heavens to the east. He had gotten out of the police van, which was parked halfway between Fifth and Madison Avenues on Fifty-third Street, to smoke a cigar. It was so close inside the van that when he lit a cigar the air soon became unbearably stuffy. It was 7:46 P.M. and another freezing night, although for the moment he found the air bracing. In the distance, down at the corner of Madison Avenue, he could see a plainclothesman patrolling this block turn and start slowly back toward Fifth Avenue.

Tynan was still inside the van presumably, Max Kauffman thought wryly, watching him on one of the

TV monitors as he smoked his cigar. There were a good many people out on the main thoroughfares, Fifth and Madison, because the stores were open for Christmas shopping until nine that night, although the side streets like Fifty-third were deserted. Just up the block toward Fifth Avenue, on the opposite side of the street, was Paley Park, the little oasis of solitude where there were benches and, in the summer, a waterfall. It stood empty and forlorn-looking on this winter's night.

Max Kauffman took a last puff on his cigar and dropped it in the gutter. The plainclothesman who had been approaching from Madison Avenue had now reached the van. He was one of the black men assigned to the detail, a detective named Freeman Royce. The Inspector nodded to him.

"Everything all right, Royce?"

"Yes, sir. I'm glad I wore my thermal underwear, though." Royce moved on past.

"Take it easy now," Max Kauffman said.

"Yes—" Royce never finished his sentence. The sound of the explosion came at that precise moment. It was in the distance, but not too far away, and came from the direction of Fifth Avenue. Freeman Royce started running for the corner. Max Kauffman barely had time to yank open the rear doors of the van and pull himself inside before the van went streaking toward the corner, siren wailing. When it reached Fifth, Max Kauffman and Tynan could see on the TV monitors that people were running north on the avenue. Fifth Avenue was one-way, downtown, but the van swung around the corner on two wheels and sped up the one-way downtown street, moving oncoming traffic out of its path with screaming sirens and flashing red lights. Whatever had happened was near Fifty-seventh Street. They could see on the TV monitors that a crowd was already beginning to collect on the west side of Fifth Avenue between Fifty-six and Fifty-seventh.

As the van slowed a half block away from the congestion of cars and people, Max Kauffman and

Tynan shoved open the rear doors and dropped to the pavement. Tynan was in the lead. He jostled people out of his way as he ran forward, the Inspector directly behind him. Now they could see only black smoke rising in the air a few yards up the block. There were crowds of people and several cars and taxis blocking the street across the width of the avenue.

Tynan shouldered his way through the crowd and in and out between the cars and taxis, shouting in a loud voice: "Police! Clear the way! Police! Move aside! Police coming through!" The Inspector followed him through the crowd and then they were in the clear and for the first time Max Kauffman saw the scene of the explosion and his first thought was: *Of course. Of course. It had to be.*

The Number 4 bus had jumped the curb a few feet south of Fifty-seventh Street, its front end plowing up snow banked in the gutters and scattering it across the sidewalk, and now stood with its two front wheels up on the sidewalk. The rear of the bus had been blown completely away and metal lay strewn along the street pavement for several yards up Fifth Avenue. All the lights on the bus, the interior lights as well as the headlights, had gone out and a mass of oily black smoke poured out of the blown away back end of the vehicle so it was impossible to see inside.

Four of the plainclothesmen who had been patrolling that section of Fifth Avenue had already reached the bus and were trying to pry open the door at the front. There was already the sound of dozens of sirens coming from far away, the rising and falling wails echoing and re-echoing through the cold winter air.

By the time Max Kauffman and Tynan reached the front of the bus, the plainclothesmen who had preceded them had the door open and, holding handkerchiefs over their faces, were moving into the dense, impenetrable smoke in the interior of the bus. Max Kauffman pulled out his own handkerchief, covered his face, and tried to enter the bus only to be pushed out by two plainclothesmen who backed out

246

of the bus. The two men were lifting the bus driver out. He was unconscious.

The police officers were coughing spasmodically as they laid the bus driver down on the sidewalk. Max Kauffman tried to enter the bus again and one of the plainclothesmen grabbed him by the arm and held him. "Can't go in there," the man gasped. "You can't breathe, can't see."

By then the street was full of ambulances and fire engines. Several of the firemen had already jumped from the trucks which had not yet come to a stop and, pulling on their oxygen masks, pushed past Max Kauffman and disappeared into the black smoke inside the bus. More firemen had moved up and were spraying chemicals and water into the rear of the bus. Ambulance attendants from Roosevelt Hospital placed the bus driver on a stretcher and were administering oxygen to him. The unconscious man's chest was heaving.

Max Kauffman, Tynan, and the other policemen waited anxiously outside the smoke-filled bus and several more ambulance attendants stood by with stretchers to aid the other victims. It was several minutes before two of the firemen who had entered the bus stepped out again. One of them yanked off his oxygen mask and rubbed his sooty face.

"What's going on in there?" Max Kauffman asked, holding up his inspector's shield.

"There's nobody in there," the fireman said in a puzzled voice. "The whole damn bus is empty."

"Empty?" Max Kauffman said. He walked backward on the sidewalk and looked up at the sign on the front of the bus: 4. NO PASSENGERS.

He shivered. Dear God, he thought, they'd been lucky. Sometime after Paul Driner had planted the bomb and gotten off the bus, it must have emptied and been headed back to the garage when the explosion came. It had been sheer good luck. But he had no doubt that this had been Driner's handiwork; a Number 4 bus, the same number that had killed Adrienne.

He walked quickly over to where the attendants

247

were placing the bus driver into the ambulance from Roosevelt Hospital and identified himself. "How bad off is he?" he asked.

One of the attendants answered that it looked like the bus driver was just suffering from smoke inhalation. But they might find other injuries after they examined him at the hospital.

It was another three quarters of an hour before the firemen had finished spraying down the bus and a police tow truck came, hoisted the back end of the bus up into the air, and hauled the battered 4 away for the bomb squad and lab technicians to examine.

Max Kauffman crossed the street to the van parked at the curb. Tynan followed him. The Inspector used one of the field telephones to call Headquarters and file a report on the bombing of the bus.

Afterwards, Tynan said: "Look, sir, nothing else is going to happen tonight. Why don't you let me finish off the watch till midnight and you go on home? If anything happens, I'll contact you. You have your beeper."

"Yes, all right," Max Kauffman said. He was sure nothing else was going to happen that night.

"And you know," Tynan said, "your theory was right. The bombing did occur in the area you predicted. There was just no way we could have figured he'd plant it outside the area and the bus would bring it in. But we've still got another chance at him tomorrow."

"Yes." The Inspector's smile was tired. "'The twelfth day of Christmas.'"

As Max Kauffman started to leave, Tynan asked if he wanted a squad car called to take him home. The Inspector shook his head; he said he thought he'd walk for a few blocks and then catch a cab.

When the van pulled away, headed south on Fifth Avenue, Max Kauffman walked up the street past Fifty-seventh, and on to Fifty-eighth. The cold stung his face and made his ears burn. He kept his gloved hands stuffed deep into his overcoat pockets. When he reached the Pulitzer Fountain, he decided to step in at the bar of the Plaza Hotel and have a drink.

In the bar he got a table by the window, looking out at the snow-covered slopes of Central Park across the street, and ordered a double Chivas Regal on the rocks. He sat there a long time, smoking his cigar and sipping his scotch. Then he ordered a second Chivas Regal.

There were three couples sitting at the table next to him, close enough for him to overhear their conversation. Attractive people, well dressed. One of the women said: "These awful bombings. It's not safe to be out on the streets. And we had to pick this time to visit New York."

"I know," another of the women said. "You'd think the police would do something to stop them. No wonder nobody wants to live in this city any more."

"It's all right, honey," the man sitting next to her said; "we'll be back home this time tomorrow night."

Max Kauffman, listening, ruminated morosely that everybody was always ready to put the knock on New York City. He did it himself sometimes. But tonight the unfairness of the remarks irritated him. What would the tourists at the next table think, he wondered, if he leaned over and gently pointed out to them that despite Manhattan's problems—and, God knows, there were plenty—they were safer in this city, statistically speaking, than they'd be in twelve other cities in the United States, from Philadelphia to Portland and including, among others, Atlanta, Detroit, and Dallas. And that, despite the fact that it had become commonplace for crimes to be staged on the streets of every major city in the world, they were, again statistically speaking, safer from violence out on the streets than they were inside their own homes.

His eye was momentarily caught by a scene outside the window of the bar where a group of Con Edison workers had dug up a section of the street and were down underneath the pavement doing something to the power lines. He was reminded of a remark made to him once by another character of a cab driver when they were held up in traffic by other Con Edison workers who were tearing up and repairing a section of Park Avenue: that Manhattan was going to be a great place—if they ever finished building it. Maybe he should tell that to the tourists at the next table.

Of course, he didn't tell them anything; he paid his check, caught a cab in front of the Plaza, and went home.

CHAPTER TWENTY-FOUR

On Christmas Eve day Max Kauffman didn't reach his office at the 16th Precinct until midafternoon. Before he could leave his apartment that morning there'd been a phone call from the Police Commissioner ordering him down to Headquarters. There, he'd been trapped in an acrimonious meeting which had lasted all morning and into the afternoon.

Attending the meeting were the same people who had been present at the last meeting they'd held on the bombing cases at Headquarters: Commissioner Hilliard, the two mayors, Forester and Angleton, Harlow, the PR Deputy Commissioner, Eberhard of the FBI, Briggs of the Police Academy bomb squad, and Max Kauffman. The difference between the two meetings, as Max Kauffman was quick to grasp, was that today the Commissioner wanted to pull him, the Inspector, off the case, and turn the investigation over to Captain Joseph Briggs of the Academy bomb squad. Once Max Kauffman understood that fact, he soon perceived that the Commissioner's purpose in calling the meeting was to get approval for his action from the others who were present, and also to give Max Kauffman the chance, if he so chose, to remove himself from the case.

Commissioner Hilliard had put all his dissatisfaction into his opening remarks: "Gentlemen, we simply are not making sufficient, making any, progress in this investigation. To date, we've had a force of almost four hundred men working on the case, at one time or another. Not to mention the supporting technical efforts of the Department. And the truth is that we're no closer to apprehending the perpetrator than we were on Thanksgiving Day, when the first bomb exploded. Frankly, I'm disappointed. I've said it before, and I say it again—there must be *something* we can do that we haven't thought of yet." He swung his eyes to Max Kauffman. "Inspector, this is not to place blame anywhere, and I'm sure you have done your very best in pursuing the case. In fact, I can't see how you could help but be exhausted."

Hilliard paused to give Max Kauffman time to reply. The Inspector stared back at him unblinkingly, and said nothing. *You want me off the case, you prick*, he thought, *you've got to say it.*

After a few moments, Hilliard moved his eyes away and said: "Perhaps what we need is some fresh thinking. I welcome any suggestions, including yours, of course, Inspector Kauffman."

For the next several hours the discussion rambled on as, one after another, the participants in the meeting put forth suggestions of how to stop the bomber, each of which was inevitably dismissed by all the others in the room. Several times Max Kauffman could detect that the meeting was subtly going against him, for him, then against him, from hour to hour to hour. Throughout the meeting, unstated, was the knowledge which each of them shared, Max Kauffman perhaps most of all: that they were all frustrated and aware of their powerlessness. When it finally became apparent that there would be no consensus in the meeting as to which course of action to take in the case, Robert Harlow, Deputy Commissioner for Public Affairs, surprised Max Kauffman by saying: "Since we've each been asked to make a suggestion, I'd like to state that, after having listened carefully to everything that's been said here, it's my opinion, for what it's worth, that possibly no one in the Police Department could do a better job on the continuing investigation of this case than the man already in charge—Inspector Kauffman. Whether we eventually succeed or fail in capturing the bomber, I think the

Inspector must remain in charge, if only because of the knowledge and experience he's already gained of the case."

On that inconclusive note—which Max Kauffman was beginning to realize was the way all such meetings seemed to end—they left the Commissioner's office. Eberhard of the FBI walked with Max Kauffman out to the street.

Eberhard shook his head and said, "That Harlow, those PR guys sure know how to do some fancy footwork when the ground begins to shift under them."

Max Kauffman looked puzzled. "What do you mean, Martin?"

The FBI man put a hand on the Inspector's shoulder. "It's been common knowledge, Max, that ever since this case began, Hilliard and Harlow have been agitating to get you off it. Oh, it was nothing against you personally. They both saw it in PR terms, wanted to exploit it more flamboyantly than you've given them an opportunity to do, in hopes of remaining in office under the new His Honor."

"But then why did Harlow say what he did today?" Max Kauffman asked.

Eberhard laughed. "He must have smelled something in the wind; he couldn't have known it for a fact."

"Known what?"

"Hilliard's out," Eberhard said. "The new mayor, Angleton, is picking another man. He told me so himself this morning, just before the meeting. But Hilliard doesn't know and neither could Harlow. I also know for a fact that Angleton thinks you're doing a good job on the bomber case. Harlow was just putting some icing on the cake for you. Police politics—aw, hell, I'm not even going to dignify it by repeating the rest of that old quote. Take care, Max."

The weather forecast for Christmas Eve was for heavy snow during the day and evening. The sky had remained dark and foreboding ever since sunrise although so far there had been no snow. Driving back to the precinct, Max Kauffman examined the sky

253

anxiously. He didn't want another blizzard which might keep the bomber indoors.

It was 3:30 P.M. by the time he arrived at his office for the first time that day. Before he did anything else, he took from his safe the little gold necklace he'd bought for Policewoman MacKay. He buzzed her and asked her to come in. When she opened the present she was so happy with it that she kissed him full on the lips, a kiss which surprised him with its intensity, and flustered him.

"It's just beautiful," she said. "I love it. Oh, thank you very much. Thank you."

"Yes," he said, "and I hope you have a lovely Christmas."

He eased her out of the office and went to his desk where she had placed the telephone messages that had come in during his absence. His father had called, and so had his wife, and Leo Morgen and there had been several routine precinct calls. He disposed of the precinct calls first. The Homicide Bureau had made an arrest in a year-old case involving the murder of an old woman on welfare who'd been mugged and killed in her room in a shabby hotel over on Tenth Avenue. The suspect was a drug addict. There were a dozen new cases on the books that day: a hit-and-run fatality on Seventh Avenue, five purse snatchings in the Times Square area, two rape cases, four breaking-and-enterings.

While he had been at the Commissioner's office, the Headquarters Communications Center had advised him that there had been the inevitable phone call from the bomber during the night with the inevitable message: "This is the eleventh day of Christmas."

He'd talked to Tynan several times during the day and knew that the patrol of the Fifth Avenue midtown area was proceeding without incident, and after he'd completed the other police calls, he phoned his father. The old man was back in the office again and his voice sounded stronger than at any time since he'd had his heart attack. His father had only called to say that he hoped he'd see Max Kauffman the next

254

day when the whole family was coming to the Inspector's apartment for dinner.

"Yes, Papa, I'll be there." Max Kauffman said.

He phoned his wife. She wanted to know if he was coming home for dinner. When he told her he didn't think he'd be home before midnight, she said she thought she'd take Debbie to the City Center to see the *Nutcracker Suite*. He agreed that would be a nice idea.

He phoned Leo Morgen who said the Blum matter was taken care of.

He put a call through to John Tynan in the surveillance van. Tynan said everything was quiet.

"I thought I'd take a couple of hours away from the precinct," Max Kauffman said. "Then I'll come over and relieve you. Any problems with that?"

"No, sir," Tynan said. "I have nothing I want to do today or tonight except catch our man."

The Inspector hung up the phone, took his private phone out of the desk drawer and dialed Catherine Devereaux. They always celebrated Christmas on Christmas Eve.

"I can get away for a short while right now," he said. "Is it convenient for you?"

"Yes," she said. "I've been waiting."

He took her present from the safe, said good night to Officer MacKay, and, after dismissing his driver for the night, hailed a taxicab to take him to Beekman Place. All the street lights were on in the winter darkness although it was not yet 5 P.M.

Catherine Devereaux was wearing a burgundy dress of soft wool with long sleeves and a high neck when she met him at the apartment door. She took his hand and he followed her into the living room which was in darkness except for the lights on the ceiling-high Christmas tree standing in a corner by the front windows. She had decorated the tree with blue lights and silver icicles so that the effect was one of a cool, shimmering beauty and there was a pleasant fresh scent in the room.

"What kind of tree is it?" he asked.

"A balsam pine."

255

"I like it," he told her.

He opened the bottle of Dom Perignon she had ready in a bucket of ice.

"Happiness always," he said as they touched glasses.

"*Chabibi,*" she said softly, pleasing him with the Hebrew word for "My beloved."

He gave her the present and she loved the beautiful ring and bracelet of matched diamonds and there were tears in her eyes when she kissed him.

She moved away from him to a dark corner of the room and lit two candles which were standing side by side on a table next to a pedestal covered by a drop cloth.

"This is for you, darling," she said, lifting the cloth. On the pedestal was a small piece of sculpture, the figure of a woman by Rodin. He had wanted a Rodin sculpture for years and he knew she had known he wanted it and had finally been able to purchase it for him, probably from the Southeby-Parke Bernet Galleries.

He was almost speechless. He reached for her, taking her head between his two hands and kissing her gently on the lips.

"The words 'I love you' pass so easily between us," he said softly, "that sometimes I think we take them too much for granted and don't really hear them. I want you to hear them now: I love you. No matter what I'm doing, or thinking, or where I am, I love you."

She nodded.

He stayed on with her for another hour and then he told her he had to leave.

At the door she said, "You're working tonight, aren't you? You haven't caught—"

He put a finger over her lips.

"Shh!" he whispered.

"*Chabibi,*" she said softly again, and he was gone.

CHAPTER TWENTY-FIVE

The air in the back compartment of the surveillance van was foul. It smelled of stale cigarette and cigar smoke, of sweat, of bad breath, of rancid coffee. Tynan's eyes were bloodshot and bleary. His tie was pulled loose and his shirt collar was open. His coat and pants were stained with spilled coffee and there were spots from splattered coffee on the tops of his shoes. Max Kauffman was chewing on a dead cigar. They were sitting side by side in the chairs in front of the TV monitors. For the last hour neither had spoken. The time was 11:26 P.M. The communications officer manning the switchboard and the police TV technician hadn't spoken, either, for over an hour.

Max Kauffman's eyes were on the screens of the monitors. The van was parked on West Forty-ninth Street halfway down the block between Fifth and Sixth Avenues.

A taxicab came up the street from Fifth Avenue with its yellow "Empty" sign on the front lighted and appeared first on the screen of the monitor from the TV camera mounted on the rear of the van and then on the other two screens and it passed by the van and continued on to Sixth Avenue and turned the corner.

"And you can never get a cab when you want one," Tynan said.

A man and a woman, with their arms around each other, walked toward the van from the direction of Sixth Avenue. When they'd almost reached the van they stopped and embraced passionately. Then the woman started to walk on, but the man pulled her back and they embraced again. She pulled away again and started to walk away and then when the man didn't try to pull her back, she came back to him and they embraced once more.

"Hell," Tynan said disgustedly, "if they're that hot for each other, why the fuck aren't they somewhere in bed together fucking?"

"I've got something! I've got something!" the communications officer said excitedly. "Hang on!" Both Max Kauffman and Tynan half rose from their chairs. The communications officer had both hands pressed to the earphones fitted to his head as if he was straining to hear what was being said. It was clear from the expression on his face that he was listening intently.

"Jesus, oh Jesus!" he said to Max Kauffman and Tynan. "This is it!"

"What?" both men asked simultaneously.

The communications man quickly said: "K! K!" into his microphone. He looked at Max Kauffman and Tynan. His face was flushed and sweating and his voice shook with excitement: "The bomber just called nine-one-one. He's taken two hostages. He says they're a policeman and a policewoman. He's right here in the area in a phone booth. He's figured out the streets are crawling with police looking for him. He says he's got enough dynamite strapped to him to blow up a city block. He wants to talk to somebody in authority. He wants a deal or the dynamite goes, along with the hostages, and the block. Headquarters ran a trace on the phone booth. It's on the northwest corner of Madison and Fifty-first Street, across from the back of St. Patrick's."

"Tell Headquarters to keep him on the line," Max Kauffman ordered. "Tell them when we get into position where we can see him, we'll notify them and I'll want a line to the phone booth."

The Inspector touched Tynan on the shoulder. "You get out on the street, pull everybody back from anywhere around Fifty-first and Madison. I don't want him panicked. Then you catch up with us again.

We'll be parked somewhere on Madison between Fiftieth and Fifty-first."

Tynan moved quickly, dropping soundlessly out of the back door of the van.

Max Kauffman pressed the intercom button connecting the rear compartment with the front of the van. In short, terse words he explained to the driver and the officer with him what had happened. "I want you to circle around and take us up Madison to the block between Fiftieth and Fifty-first. Take it slow and don't try to get us in too close to the phone booth; just enough so we have it and him within camera range."

As the van got underway, Max Kauffman remembered Headquarters had said the bomber claimed he had two hostages, a policeman and a policewoman. He guessed it had to be Detectives Roberto Teresa and Sheila Yen who had been on duty in the block between Madison and Fifth on Fifty-first Street.

The three of them were jammed into the phone booth so tight that Detective Teresa felt like he couldn't breathe properly. He was still stunned by the suddenness of the events of the last quarter of an hour or so. He had been patrolling the south side of Fifty-first Street, and Detective Yen had been patrolling the opposite side of the street. There had been more people to watch because it was Christmas Eve and there was a midnight mass at St. Patrick's Cathedral. During the past hour he'd stopped several men who'd passed by on the block. None of them fit the description of Driner, the bomber. While he had been questioning one of the men he'd stopped, he saw another man enter the block down near the corner of Madison. His attention was on the man he was questioning, and then he noticed the other man had disappeared from view. He still hadn't been concerned. Maybe, he thought, the man was looking for a rear door to St. Patrick's. But he had gone to investigate. Out of the corner of his eye, he noted that Detective Yen, across the street, was questioning another suspect. He had gone down the block and was looking into the shadows near the rear of St. Patrick's. He thought he saw a figure and then it was gone. He walked in closer to the building. He had a hand on his gun but hadn't drawn it when an arm encircled his neck from the back. He was lifted from his feet and the pressure against his windpipe was unbearable. He began to lose consciousness, yet he heard the jangle of the handcuffs on his belt. The arm was still locked around his throat, but he could feel the man's other hand take the gun and the handcuffs. He was handcuffed to the other man and the muzzle of his own .38 was pressed against his temple by the time Detective Yen, who must have missed him, came to investigate. By then there was nothing she could do unless she wanted him killed. The man took her prisoner, too, also handcuffing her to himself on the other side, and dropping both Teresa's gun and hers to the ground. The man showed them the dynamite strapped to his chest, and that it was wired to a small, ticking clock, before he marched them across the street to the phone booth, forcing the two of them inside and crowding in himself before dialing 911.

"There he is," Max Kauffman said quietly, peering at the TV monitor which showed clearly the phone booth at the corner and the three people inside, the man in the middle talking into the phone. The surveillance van was parked on the east side of Madison Avenue only a few yards from Fifty-first Street.

"I think I can get you a better picture," the TV technican said. The screen of the TV monitor blurred for a moment. Then the Inspector could see the three figures in the phone booth surprisingly close up. Both detectives looked bewildered. The man between them wore a hat with the brim turned down, his coat collar turned up, and dark glasses over his eyes. Max Kauffman couldn't see that much of his face, but enough to see that he had shaved off his moustache.

"All right," the Inspector said to the communications officer, "tell Headquarters to inform Driner that

I have charge of the case and I'm ready to talk to him. Then I want a line to the phone booth."

It was a couple of seconds before one of the red buttons on a phone at the field switchboard began to blink. The communications officer said, "He's on the line."

Max Kauffman took a chair near the switchboard where he could still see the phone booth' on the screen of the TV monitor. He picked up the phone.

"This is Inspector Kauffman."

The voice that came back was surly and hostile: "I want to make a deal with you. You listen if you don't want a lot of people killed. I'm not kidding."

Max Kauffman took a deep breath and said in a calm voice: "It's no good, Driner. There's no way out for you. We know who you are, know everything about you. There's nowhere you can go now to get away. We know you've been under a strain. If you give yourself up—"

"Listen, you stupid cop, listen! I'm not giving myself up! I want a deal." The voice had risen hysterically. "I want a plane. I want a Seven-forty-seven, fueled up. I want safe passage to that plane. Once I'm aboard I'll release the hostages."

"Driner—" Max Kauffman tried to say, but he was cut off again by the man in the phone booth.

"You," the voice over the phone was shrill, "I want you to shut up. I've got enough dynamite strapped to me to blow up this whole block, maybe two blocks. The dynamite's set to a timer. Fifteen minutes from now it's going to explode. I can change the timer but I'm not changing it until you tell me I've got a deal. If you don't believe me, listen."

Max Kauffman, watching the TV monitor, could see Driner yank Detective Yen forward and hand her the telephone.

"Inspector?" she asked in a shaking voice.

"Yes, this is Inspector Kauffman."

"He means it, Inspector. He's really got all that dynamite set to a timer. He's got us handcuffed to him, one of us on either side of him."

"All right," Max Kauffman said. "Let me talk to him again."

The man said: "You've got fifteen minutes to call me back. I want a car, one man driving it, no funny business, safe passage to the airport, a gassed-up Seven-forty-seven. You tell me before fifteen minutes are up, and I set a new time for the explosives to go off."

The phone disconnected. Max Kauffman sat for a moment with a blank expression on his face. The back door to the van opened and Tynan climbed in. He started to say something but Max Kauffman silenced him with a motion of his hand. Then he spoke to the communications officer: "Call Headquarters. Tell them to seal off this area with unmarked cars, but to stay away from Fifty-first Street where Driner might spot them from the phone booth; seal up all the other streets around. And we need fire equipment and ambulances, standing by on Fifth and above and below on Madison. All of the vehicles are to come in with sirens and lights off. Also, tell Headquarters to send in a dozen sharpshooters with high-powered rifles. Tell them to take up positions in and around St. Patrick's—in case Driner changes his mind and tries to make a run for it, I want him shot down."

Max Kauffman's mind had been working busily while he had been issuing orders; he was trying to come up with a plan, using Driner's own demands, to try to stop him. The Inspector had seen dozens of visions in his mind almost simultaneously—of Driner and the two hostages coming out of the phone booth, of them in the car which would transport them to the airport, of the ride itself—and of how at any of these points Driner could be killed without the dynamite being set off.

He looked up now at Tynan who was watching him expectantly. Speaking rapidly, the Inspector told Tynan what Driner wanted.

"So what are you going to do?" Tynan asked.

"In a few minutes I'm going to call him back and tell him he's got his deal," Max Kauffman said. "We're going to use his own plan to nail him. Here's how—"

The Inspector told Tynan exactly what he planned to do, taking his time to lay it all out carefully. When he had finished, Tynan said: "God, it's going to be risky, Inspector. It scares the living hell out of me. It just might work, though. If the Commissioner'll approve it."

"He has no choice." Max Kauffman got up from the chair. "You get on the phone to Headquarters and tell them what we need and tell them we need it fast."

The Inspector nodded to the communications officer. "Put a call through to the phone booth again."

In a few seconds, the Inspector picked up one of the phones at the switchboard and said, "Driner?"

"Yeah."

"This is Inspector Kauffman. You've got your deal. We're going to fuel up a Seven-forty-seven for you at Newark Airport. We'll need some time to get a car here and work out the rest of the arrangements. I'll be driving the car myself. Give us another half hour."

"You're being smart. You've got another half hour, no longer, to take me out of here. Then I'll set a new time."

Max Kauffman hung up. His hand was shaking. He glanced at his watch. It was 12:30 A.M., Christmas morning.

CHAPTER TWENTY-SIX

The car was an unmarked Plymouth. It was equipped with a siren but no flasher light, not that Max Kauffman cared; he didn't need either. It also had a two-way police radio. The radio was on, the dispatcher's voice periodically cutting through the static. Max Kauffman pulled the car up to the curb alongside the phone booth on Fifty-first Street. He decided he shouldn't get out. He leaned over the seat and opened the rear door nearest the sidewalk. The three of them came out of the phone booth, hand-cuffed together. When they reached the car, Detective Yen crawled in first, followed by the bomber who pulled Detective Teresa in behind him and slammed the door.

Max Kauffman sat very still behind the steering wheel. He could see all three of the figures in the rearview mirror. Driner still had his dark glasses on, his coat collar turned up, hat pulled low.

"Before we start, I want to explain something to you, Driner," the Inspector said. "There are going to be other police cars leading us and following us, to keep traffic away from us. I'm telling you that because I don't want you to be alarmed. We're going across to Ninth Avenue and through the Lincoln Tunnel to Newark."

"Yeah, all right, let's go!"

Max Kauffman drove carefully up to Fifth Avenue. There were four squad cars waiting there. Two of the cars pulled in ahead of the unmarked Plymouth, and two lined up behind. Max Kauffman knew that those in the back seat didn't see the bomb wagon, with Tynan driving, which followed the two squad cars trailing the Plymouth.

The caravan of cars sped swiftly straight across Fifty-first Street westward. The lead squad cars had their flasher lights rotating but didn't use their sirens except when approaching intersections since the streets were mostly deserted. At Ninth Avenue the convoy swung south. Max Kauffman used the rear blinker lights to signal to the squad car following them.

The radio dispatcher's voice came in almost immediately, calling, "Dispatcher to Y-E-N. Dispatcher to Y-E-N. Do you read me? Do you read me?"

Max Kauffman was watching Detective Sheila Yen closely in the rearview mirror as she reacted in surprise then quickly suppressed her reaction.

Good girl, he thought and he again used the rear blinker lights to signal the squad car behind.

The dispatcher came back on the radio and this time he said:

燈熄,時,握住他的手臂

Max Kauffman was watching Driner now. The man seemed to notice nothing, and appeared to be more interested in watching the streets ahead and behind and the streets they were passing through, as if he was afraid there was going to be an attempt made on his life from outside the car. The Inspector relaxed again. Then the dispatcher was back again, calling: "Teresa . . . Teresa . . . this is the dispatcher. Do you read me? Teresa, come in."

The Inspector couldn't be sure this time whether Detective Teresa understood, but he signaled with the blinker lights anyway and the dispatcher was saying: *"Aguantale su braco cuando las luces se apaguen."*

The Inspector could only pray that both detectives had understood the messages directed to them. It was too late now; they were past Forty-second Street and approaching the entrance to the Lincoln

266

Tunnel. There was a line of cars backed up at the approach to the tunnel where all traffic had been stopped by the police. The policemen out on the street waved the squad cars and the unmarked Plymouth, and the bomb wagon, on into the tunnel.

Max Kauffman sucked his breath in as they rolled deeper into the tunnel. He braced himself for the shock he was sure he would experience even though he knew full well it was coming and coming at any moment. And then it happened: all the lights in the tunnel suddenly went out. The Inspector braked the car to a stop, cut off the ignition, switched off the lights. The squad cars in front and to the rear had cut off their lights. The darkness was total. It had taken the approval of the governors of two states, New York and New Jersey, to authorize the turning off of the tunnel lights. But the approval had been given, and the lights had been extinguished on signal, according to Max Kauffman's plan, from the Lincoln Tunnel's headquarters in Weehawken, New Jersey.

Max Kauffman could hear Driner screaming and cursing and thrashing around in the darkness in the back seat. It was obvious that Detectives Yen and Teresa had received the messages the radio dispatcher had directed at them which, translated, was: *Hold his arm when the lights go out.* Now, handcuffed to him as they were, each was obviously holding an arm so he couldn't reach the dynamite strapped to his chest and explode it. Max Kauffman knew the rest was up to him.

He swung around in the seat in the darkness, hoisted himself up and went over the back of the seat, spreading his legs so he straddled Driner's lap. He knew they were face to face in the darkness, although he could see nothing. Their bodies were pressed together with the bulky dynamite between them. Driner was still thrashing around. Max Kauffman reached out his left hand, swept Driner's hat off, and grabbed a fistful of hair. Even as Driner screamed in pain, the Inspector reached his right hand down and pulled out the knife from the sheath strapped to his ankle.

267

Max Kauffman raised the knife. Driner was twisting his head, trying to yank his head backward. The Inspector tightened his grip on the hair. He kept remembering the instructions he'd been given by the police sergeant who had been an army instructor in hand-to-hand combat. The sergeant had come to the surveillance van and talked to Max Kauffman when the Inspector had figured out this was the only way to kill Driner. The sergeant had explained to him that it was vitally important to pull Driner's head forward before he used the knife. *If he throws his head back, as he'll instinctively try to do, the trachea will come forward and the carotid arteries will recede behind the neck muscles. You've got to sever the carotid arteries.*

For a moment, with knife upraised and poised to strike, he didn't think he could do it. For no reason at all, he was reminded of another time of total darkness like this, when he had made love to Kit in her bedroom. His hands shook. Then he remembered other things; the death and destruction, the mutilation, of the old Bowery bum, of the hooker, Felice, of the others, that this man had caused. If he failed, the explosives would blow up the tunnel and the whole Hudson River would flood down on them, all of them in the tunnel.

The head beneath his left hand jerked backward again and Max Kauffman yanked the head forward and slashed upward with the knife. The head stopped twisting and Max Kauffman felt the warm, sticky liquid that drenched him, soaking his clothes and hands, nothing more.

He shoved himself upwards, blindly reached a hand for the door, opened it and, crawling past Detective Yen, staggered out of the car, shouting: "Turn on the lights! Turn on the lights! Turn on the lights!" Then they were all there around him, the other policemen and Tynan who had pulled the bomb wagon up alongside the Plymouth. Headlights on the squad cars were switched on and, quickly, after the word was radioed in, the tunnel lights came on again.

"Get him out of there! Hurry," Max Kauffman ordered. He knew they had to still remove Driner from the tunnel before the explosives went off but he couldn't look at the man again. He stood aside while Tynan and the other police unlocked the handcuffs chaining Detectives Yen and Teresa to Driner, and then removed the blood-soaked body and loaded it into the reinforced cage of the bomb wagon. It was too risky for them to try to remove the explosives from the dead man's body. They'd have to take him out and try to let it blow up outside the tunnel, in the clear.

"You did fine, you did fine," the Inspector managed to tell Detectives Yen and Teresa before they were led away to one of the waiting squad cars.

Max Kauffman himself had gotten into another of the squad cars. One of the other policemen got into the Plymouth. Tynan had just started to drive the bomb wagon away toward the Jersey end of the tunnel with Driner's body in back.

"Follow him," the Inspector ordered the driver of the squad car he'd entered.

A couple of other squad cars trailed behind as the bomb wagon sped through the tunnel. The trip seemed endless to Max Kauffman before they finally emerged from the tunnel, over in New Jersey, the bomb wagon up ahead. Outside the tunnel, all traffic had again been halted and trucks and cars lined both sides of the highway. Tynan drove the bomb wagon well on past them and then Max Kauffman, in the trailing squad car, saw Tynan turn off the highway and send the bomb wagon heading toward the swampy marshes beyond the roadway. The marshes were blanketed with snow.

"Put your headlights on him! Keep the lights on him!" Max Kauffman shouted and the driver swung the squad car sideways across the highway. They could see the bomb wagon in the beams of light as it skidded down into the swamps. Then, suddenly, the ugly beetle-shaped vehicle overturned and went rolling over and over into the darkness.

Max Kauffman had the door to the squad car open and was standing out on the highway, shouting hoarsely, "Get out, Jack! Get out!"

The blast came out of the darkness seconds later; a sound like no other Max Kauffman had ever heard, annihilating in its intensity, accompanied by a searing flash of flame that lit up the night and the sky.

The Inspector stood, totally deaf, for a minute, two minutes, watching the inferno of flames in the distance. Now other squad cars had pulled up on the highway and were directing their headlights toward the mass of flames, and a couple of trucks joined them. Max Kauffman kept shaking his head. He heard a shout from a couple of policemen standing on the highway and he couldn't understand what they were saying. He was looking, he kept looking, but it was like he couldn't bring his vision into focus. There was a figure staggering up out of the swamps, silhouetted by the flames behind him. And Max Kauffman couldn't believe, couldn't let himself believe, that it was John Tynan, that Tynan had managed to jump from the bomb wagon before it exploded. But it was.

The Inspector and several of the policemen ran forward and helped Tynan up the rest of the way and over to a squad car. Tynan was shaken up, suffering from shock, mud-splattered, but in one piece. He kept nodding at Max Kauffman, he couldn't speak, but he kept nodding. One of the squad cars took him back to the city.

It was all over now, except for the picking up of the pieces. The Inspector stayed on at the scene until the morgue wagon came from Manhattan and took away what remained of the body, and the 16th Precinct Bomb Investigative Unit arrived with a tow truck and began sorting through the debris and the truck towed away the wrecked bomb wagon.

Dawn was in the sky when Max Kauffman finally left in one of the squad cars and headed back through the Lincoln Tunnel toward the city. Before he reached his apartment the Commissioner had radioed to him in the squad car, with congratulations, and said that he'd already talked to the two mayors, and they wanted to have a press conference at the 16th Precinct at noon, even though it was Christmas Day, and they wanted Max Kauffman there. The Inspector agreed, but added that he wanted John Tynan present. Hilliard agreed. This time, Max Kauffman thought, they were entitled to their ritualistic bull-shit.

CHAPTER TWENTY-SEVEN

At 12 Noon on Christmas Day, Max Kauffman was sitting behind his desk at the 16th Precinct. He was dressed in a blue pinstripe suit. He knew his eyes looked puffy but otherwise he didn't feel too bad. Commissioner Hilliard was there, and Mayor Forester and Mayor-elect Angleton, and Deputy Commissioner Harlow. They were waiting for John Tynan to arrive. The news of the death of the bomber, Driner, was all over the city. Policewoman MacKay had come in and was at the desk outside the office where the newspaper reporters, photographers and TV men were milling around. Max Kauffman had been congratulated repeatedly since he'd arrived at his office.

Tynan came in a few minutes later. Max Kauffman decided he looked fine, if tired and drawn. While the Commissioner and the others were shaking hands with Tynan, the intercom on Max Kauffman's desk buzzed. He pressed the switch and Officer Mac-Kay said: "Sir, a Milt Nevers at the lab is calling. He says it's urgent. Terribly upset. On extension one."

Max Kauffman started to say have him call back, but he saw that Tynan and the others were still talking so he leaned over and picked up the phone.

"Inspector," the lab man said, "you better brace yourself for a shock."

"Yeah?" Max Kauffman said.

"Well, sir—" Nevers paused, there was silence for a second, and then: "—the body the morgue guys brought in this morning, you know, this bomber?"

"Yes? Yes?"

"As I understand, sir, it's supposed to be Paul

273

Driner, is that correct? Paul Driner, 'The Christmas Bomber'?"

"Yes, that's correct," Max Kauffman said.

"Well, it's not," Nevers said in a firm voice. "This is not Paul Driner's body. We have all the finger-prints on Driner and none of the prints on this body match Driner's."

Max Kauffman couldn't speak for a moment. When he managed to find his voice, he asked, "*Are you sure?*"

"Positive, sir. Absolutely positive. I don't know what else to tell you."

The Inspector hung up the phone. His thoughts were in a whirl.

Who was the dead man? Where was Paul Driner?

"Gentlemen," he said, looking around the room, his face baffled. "I have some news for you. The man we killed this morning, the man with the explosives strapped to him, is not Paul Driner."

Two hours later, Max Kauffman and John Tynan sat alone in the Inspector's office. The Commissioner, the two mayors, the newsmen had long since departed. There had been no press conference. There had been confusion. Nobody knew what to do or say, least of all Max Kauffman. He felt that somehow he'd been tricked, cheated, by Driner. The man they thought was "The Christmas Bomber" *had* to be Paul Driner. Everything fit. He now had to believe that perhaps there'd been two bombers on the loose in the city at the same time or, no, that didn't make sense. The pattern of the bombings made the coincidence too great. Or that perhaps the man they'd killed was an individual who'd just started on his own bombing spree. In any event, Paul Driner was still on the loose and there was no way of knowing whether or not there'd be more bombings.

They'd released the composite photograph of Paul Driner to the newspapers and television and asked anyone who had seen Paul Driner to contact the police.

After the others had left the office, the Inspector asked Tynan to go to the lab and bring back all the evidence the bomb squad had picked up after the bomb wagon had exploded outside the Lincoln Tunnel, so they could see if they could discover any clue to the identity of the dead man. Tynan had just returned to the Precinct, carrying a large carton which he began emptying onto the Inspector's desk.

There were pieces of torn clothing and bits of the man's shoes and—because the blast effects of explosions were always erratic—there was a single dollar bill and a white handkerchief which still remained whole.

"What a glob of crap," Tynan said. He was digging through the scraps of cloth, looking for a label. He stopped and looked up. "Hey, what's this?" He held up a small chain with a locket attached. Both had been blackened by the fire from the blast but were intact.

"Let me take a look," Max Kauffman said. "He must have been carrying them in his pocket." He reached out a hand and Tynan passed over locket and chain.

The Inspector scratched at the chain with a thumbnail and some of the black stain came off and he could see it was gold. Curious now, he began to scrape at the locket to see if there was an initial on it and suddenly it snapped open in his fingers. Inside, he saw, were two tiny portraits.

"Jesus, look at this!" he said excitedly, holding up the locket so Tynan could see the tiny pictures inside.

"The woman's Adrienne Driner!" Tynan said, equally excited.

"Yeah, I know." Max Kauffman was frowning. "But who's the guy? It's not Driner."

"No, it's not. At least not the Driner in our composite photograph."

The sudden realization of what they'd discovered struck the Inspector forcibly then. "This means there's a connection. Driner—Adrienne—the whole thing."

"Yeah," Tynan agreed. "But who's the guy? How're we going to find out?"

Max Kauffman snapped his fingers. "Millicent Lauder and Everett Cragle, they ought to know. We're going to get them in here. *Now!*" He reached for the phone to send out the order to pick up the two people.

It was 3:45 P.M. before Millicent Lauder and Everett Cragle were brought to the station house by patrolmen.

"I'm not going to make apologies for dragging you both down here even though this is Christmas Day," the Inspector said. "This is critically important." He leaned over the desk, the open locket lying in the palm of his hand. "Who is the man in the photograph?"

Both Everett Cragle and Millicent Lauder were peering at the pictures inside the locket. Cragle looked up first. He had a puzzled expression on his face. "That's Lloyd Vogler. Vogler, I told you he worked for the company. Worked with Paul on demolition. But where'd you get this? And why is Adrienne's picture in the same locket?"

"It's Lloyd Vogler, all right," Millicent Lauder agreed. "But—but what's this all about?"

"That's what we're trying to find out," Max Kauffman said. "We'll let you know if *we* find out."

He let them leave then, and rocked back in his chair, staring across at Tynan. "If Lloyd Vogler was in the army in Vietnam, his prints'll be on file in Washington. We'll get the lab to send the prints of the dead man down right away for comparison. Now, today."

"Right," Tynan said, "I'll get on it." He started from the room.

"Wait, Jack!" Max Kauffman called out. "Aren't you supposed to be getting married today?"

"We put it off temporarily. Barbara agreed, because I want to stick around until this case is concluded. She knows how much I've put into it. She wants it out of the way, too, before the wedding." He had another thought. "Inspector, suppose the prints do match, what's that going to tell us?"

"That the dead man is Lloyd Vogler," Max Kauffman answered. "What else?"

276

CHAPTER TWENTY-EIGHT

The following day, December 26, they had their information from the FBI Identification Center in Washington: The dead man was Lloyd Ambrose Vogler, Army Serial Number 556–752–5103. Active Duty: Vietnam, U.S. Corps of Engineers—Demolition. Discharged, October, 1970.

Max Kauffman and Tynan read the FBI report together in the Inspector's office.

"So now we know that the dead man is Vogler," Tynan said, "but where is *he*?" He pointed to the copy of the morning *Daily News* which had a front-page picture of the police composite photograph of Paul Driner with the caption: HAVE YOU SEEN THIS MAN?

"I don't know," Max Kauffman said. "Like you said once, Jack, this case gets curiouser and curiouser. All the evidence we had all along said Driner was our man. Now—"

The intercom buzzer sounded. Max Kauffman pressed the switch. He'd been expecting a phone call from the Commissioner, the Mayor, somebody at Headquarters, all morning long. He'd been worried by the ominous silence from official quarters. But now Policewoman MacKay said: "Captain Hedloe of the State Police calling on two."

Max Kauffman picked up the phone and the voice at the other end said: "Inspector Kauffman?"

"Yes, Captain Hedloe, how are you?"

"I told you I'd report to you when we pumped out the bombed-out hole over in Pound Ridge. We didn't get to it until today because of the weather and Christmas."

"Well? Did you find more explosives?" Max Kauffman said.

"Not exactly," Hedloe said. "What we found was a body, a skeleton. It must have been buried beneath the cellar of the house. The explosion uncovered it."

"What!" Max Kauffman demanded.

"I said—"

"I know, I know," the Inspector interrupted. "Look, we have to get that body down here to the city right away. I know there might be a jurisdictional problem—"

"No problem," Hedloe said. "I thought you'd want it in a hurry. It's already on its way to you, to the city morgue, right?"

"Captain, I thank you."

"It's okay."

Max Kauffman hung up. "They found a body in the bottom of where Driner's house was in Pound Ridge. The body's on its way to the morgue here."

"Paul Driner!" Tynan said. "He's been dead all this time while we were looking for him."

Max Kauffman took a cigar out of his pocket. "I think you could safely make book on it," he said. He pointed the cigar at Tynan. "They murdered him. Her, Adrienne, and Vogler. They murdered Driner. It had to be that. And maybe, if we're lucky, an autopsy on the skeleton will prove how, even now."

"Arsenic," Max Kauffman told Tynan. "The Medical Examiner found it in the bones and the hair. He estimated the total dosage—which was taken into the body over a long period of time—at perhaps six, maybe ten, centigrams; five or six is usually sufficient to do the job, he says. They overkilled him." They already knew the skeleton was Paul Driner's; dental records had, again, proved that fact.

The two men were sitting in the Inspector's office. It was another cold, bleak day outside, but the wood in the stone fireplace was crackling cheerfully.

"Imagine it." Max Kauffman shook his head. "She must have been spooning the stuff into him daily— Driner must have actually been dying that last time

Cragle saw him—after she'd sweet-talked him into transferring the money to her name. She and Vogler must have had a big passion going for them and planned out the whole thing. They had his money, they killed him, they buried him, they'd keep the house in Pound Ridge locked up, they'd go away together and nobody would know. The only thing they didn't count on was that she'd get killed by a bus. Then Vogler was left with nothing. *He* couldn't claim the money. All of it together flipped him out, just as we thought it had flipped Driner out. Vogler assumed Driner's identity and went on a revenge bombing spree."

Tynan nodded. "Everything we uncovered about Driner's background also fitted Lloyd Vogler. We weren't that far off base."

"No," Max Kauffman said.

"Another thing," Tynan pointed out. "We actually cracked two cases in one. That ought to call for some kind of congratulations."

"It already has," Max Kauffman said. "So far today the new commissioner's called, the new mayor, and—the Governor."

"And I congratulate you, too, Inspector." Tynan stood up to leave.

Max Kauffman raised a hand to detain him. "Wait a minute, Jack. I have a kind of wedding present for you. You've been promoted to captain." He shook Tynan's hand. "You go on leave tomorrow. Get married and have a happy honeymoon."

When Tynan had left the office, the Inspector got a phone call from Patrolman Ralph Yost, the mounted policeman who'd been injured in the Thanksgiving Day Parade bombing, the first bomb in the case. Yost said he was home and recovering. Max Kauffman wished him good luck and thanked him for calling. Then he took his private phone out to call Catherine Devereaux. Before he could make the call, Policewoman MacKay buzzed him and said Sergeant Martinelli of Homicide was calling.

Max Kauffman picked up the phone and Martinelli said: "Inspector, you remember the severed heads of the three young women we found in the trunk in the Hudson River last summer? You remember, my partner, Cruz, and I've been working on it unofficially since then?"

"Yes," the Inspector said. He knew the case had been inactive since summer.

"Well," Martinelli said, "I'm phoning you from a booth across from Central Park. We got a call and went up, some kids sledding in the Sheep Meadow in the Park uncovered two more heads, both young women, no bodies. That's a total of five heads. It's got to be the same case."

"Rope off the area," Max Kauffman said. "Call the lab boys. I'll be right up."

He hung up the phone and felt a thrill go through him, not a pleasurable sensation; but one of anticipation: it looked like the City had a mass murderer somewhere in its midst. He reached for the phone again to notify the Commissioner.

ABOUT THE AUTHOR

THOMAS CHASTAIN, born in Sydney, Nova Scotia, grew up in Florida and Georgia. His career as newspaper reporter and editor took him to New York, Baltimore and Hollywood. For the last six years he has devoted himself solely to free-lance writing. During this time, he has published several novels, including the bestselling *Judgement Day* and *Pandora's Box*. Mr. Chastain lives with his wife in New York City.

RELAX!
SIT DOWN
and Catch Up On Your Reading!